CLAY JOINED THE others at the rail and studied the flat gray water of Skagway harbor, and the steep slopes beyond. The tree-covered mountainside plunged nearly straight down to the sea. Past the green heights he could see the far snow-covered peaks, veiled in a mist of ragged clouds.

And beyond those peaks, thought Clay, was the great Yukon and the river that bears its name, nearly two thousand miles of wilderness and treacherous water, an alien land that eats the unwary traveler for breakfast. Clay had heard the stories over and over again—churning rapids, sandbars and deadly avalanches. A country where snow covered the desolate landscape seven months of the year, the mercury plunged to seventy below and the dismal days were only three hours long . . . A trek through hell, thought Clay, and all for the privilege of clawing the ground with a thousand other fools, hungry for the sight of Klondike gold . . .

ALASKAN GOLD

ROBERT REESE

BERKLEY BOOKS, NEW YORK

ALASKAN GOLD

A Berkley Book / published by arrangement with
the author

PRINTING HISTORY
Berkley edition / April 1998

The Penguin Putnam Inc. World Wide Web site address is
http://www.penguinputnam.com

ISBN: 0-425-16263-X

BERKLEY®
Berkley Books are published by The Berkley Publishing Group, a
member of Penguin Putnam Inc.,
200 Madison Avenue, New York, NY 10016.
BERKLEY and the "B" design
are trademarks belonging to Berkley Publishing Corporation.

PRINTED IN THE UNITED STATES OF AMERICA

10 9 8 7 6 5 4 3 2 1

ONE

He DIDN'T SEE the fight start.

One man bellowed in anger, a dark string of curses that burned the ears of anyone who knew some gutter French. Another voice rose above the first, a ragged cry of pain that ripped through the crisp Alaskan air.

Clay Macon turned from the crowded bow of the *Queen,* too late to see more than the fight's bloody end. Half a dozen passengers and several burly crewmen had brought the Frenchy down. He was as big and hairy as a bear. Spittle hung from the corner of his mouth and his eyes rolled back in his head. He howled and thrashed about until someone had the sense to kick him in his oversized gut.

The loser lay a few yards away, sprawled on his back, arms and legs wide. No one had even went near the poor devil. They stood in a wide half circle with plenty of room to spare. Clay pushed through the crowd and went down on his knees, pressing two fingers against the scrawny neck, an act that he did without thinking, though he knew the man was dead. The victim's face was chalk-white. A great deal of blood had already soaked his clothes and spilled out onto the deck. He was gutted like a salmon, a deep and killing cut that had slashed him from just above the bladder to his rib cage, and almost to the heart. Even if he could have gotten this fellow some of the finest surgery in the land, Clay knew he could not have saved his life.

He stood and brushed his knees. What had the killer sliced him with? he wondered. A cavalry saber couldn't have done a lot more damage to the man's insides. A Bowie knife would do it, or one of those homemade dirks the dockhands carried in New Orleans.

"This'n done or what?"

Clay turned to see one of the ship's officers at his back.

"Yes, he's quite dead," Clay said. "I guess you have a passenger list. Someone will know who he was . . ."

"What do you care, mister?" The officer frowned. He was fat and bald as an egg. All the hair he had sprouted from his brows and a drinker's red nose. "Feller *dead,* and that's that. Isn't none of your business who he used to be."

"I'm a doctor," Clay said. "If you need a certificate of death or anything—"

"Shoot, *Doctor.*" The man laughed in Clay's face. "You ain't in Boston or San Francisco, friend, you're in *Alaska,* now. Dyin' isn't no big affair up here. Folks do it all the time." He glanced at the corpse, wrinkled his nose in disapproval and turned away from Clay.

"Mackey, Ivan, Clute," he yelled out, "git over here and haul this stiff down below and swab this deck sparklin' clean. I ain't talkin' next Tuesday, neither!"

The officer stalked off, muttering to himself. In a moment, two young, long-haired deck boys scurried past Clay. One dragged along a bulky tarp, while the other carried a mop. A third boy, smaller than the rest, appeared with a bucket of dirty suds.

The crowd had lost interest and moved off to light cigars or stare at the barren coast. There was no sign at all of the Frenchman who looked like a bear, or the men who had wrestled him down. Only the white-faced corpse gave evidence that anything had happened on the deck of the *Queen*. And, from the cold look in his eyes, he didn't seem to care.

Clay joined the others at the rail and studied the flat gray water of Skagway harbor, and the steep slopes beyond. The tree-covered mountainside plunged nearly straight down to the sea. Past the green heights he could see the far snow-covered peaks, veiled in a mist of ragged clouds.

And beyond those peaks, thought Clay, was the great Yukon and the river that bears its name, nearly two thousand miles of wilderness and treacherous water, an alien land that eats the unwary traveler for breakfast. Clay had heard the stories over and over again—churning rapids, sandbars and deadly avalanches. A country where snow covered the desolate landscape seven months of the year, the mercury plunged to seventy below and the dismal days were only three hours long.

Then, if a man survived that, he faced a summer where the ground became an impossible, muddy morass of melted snow, while the earth remained permanently frozen inches below the surface. The temperature climbed to over ninety degrees, and swarms of gnats, no-see-ums, yellow-jackets and mosquitoes big as buzzards drove a fellow mad. Old sourdoughs swore a summer in the Yukon set a man to praying for the cold, starvation and misery of winter. A trek through hell, thought Clay, and all for the privilege of clawing the ground with a thousand other fools, hungry for the sight of Klondike gold. It didn't make sense that a sane man would give up everything he had, very possibly life itself, for a chance in a million to make his fortune in the goldfields of the North.

Yet, there he was, sane or maybe totally mad, he couldn't say—one of the hundreds who had crowded aboard the

Queen in Seattle for the six-day trek up the coastway to
Skagway harbor.

"Lord help me," Clay said aloud, squinting at the sunlit
peaks, "a king's ransom for cramped and smelly quarters,
rowdy companions and food not fit to eat!"

He could scarcely believe he had slapped down so much
money for his passage, and held himself lucky to have gotten aboard for all of that. The docks of Seattle were packed
with men who would gladly have taken his place, men from
a nation caught in the jaws of a great depression, men who
had nothing to look forward to except lives of desperation,
or wealth beyond their dreams. It was early May now, and
they had been lined up more than half a mile deep since
July the year before, when miners bearing the first fat
pouches from the Klondike gold rush had reached San
Francisco. Men like George Carmack, Skookum Jim Mason
and Tagish Charley. Eight hundred dollars' worth of the
shiny stuff, they said, just for dipping your pan in the creek
once! One hundred and forty thousand dollars or more per
man, for a single winter's work!

Clay tried to tell himself that it wasn't just the money,
that more than the search for wealth had brought him from
New Orleans. Now, though, standing by the railing in the
shadow of the great Alaskan peaks, he could not be sure
that this was so. Maybe he was fooling himself—maybe he
was really no better than the Frenchman and his victim, or
the other men who'd died on the trip to the North. Five
others, if he could remember right. One of them likely from
disease, he knew, but the others men who had come to
violent ends—men who had drunk themselves into a rage
and slit a fellow's throat for a dollar, or killed for the pure
hell of it, for lack of anything to do.

That isn't me, Clay Mason told himself again. *I'm not
one of them at all* . . .

Still, he wondered if anyone looking at the grim, bearded

faces lining the bow of the *Queen* could pick the saints from the killers, the gentlemen from the thieves. It would be no easy task, and harder still once they got the smell of gold.

"Dastardly thing," the man said, "but no great surprise, considering the rogues and scalawags who find their way to our shores these days. Dregs and sweepings is what they are, the dregs of a country that—" The man stopped, caught Clay's eye and shook his head in alarm. "Oh, present company excepted, of course, Doctor. I'm sure you understand the, uh . . . *type* I'm referring to here."

"Yes, certainly," Clay said.

"We seldom see men of bearing and birth in these parts. Mostly the kind you saw back there. Terrible. *Terrible* thing."

Clay didn't answer. He pretended to be absorbed in the progress of the barge that was moving them sluggishly toward the tidal flats of Skagway Bay. The water was so shallow here that ships like the *Queen* had to anchor a mile or more offshore. Barges carried people and supplies from the big steamers and back. A steady stream of wagons traveled back and forth from the shore to the town. Skagway had brand-new docks of rough yellow pine that made all this unnecessary now, but a drunken captain had put the docks out of commission the week before.

The stranger's name, as near as he could recall, was Fuller, or Fullerton something. Oh yes, Fullerton Ash. He lived in Skagway and said he owned several mercantile stores and a bank. He had picked Clay out of the crowd on the first day of the voyage, and introduced himself. Clay felt he was likely a decent sort, just too full of himself. A tall, cadaverous fellow with saggy cheeks and dark, sad eyes. Clay remembered a bird dog he'd kept at the home place when he was a boy. The dog could shake any coon alive out of a tree, but his eyes had the same sorrowful cast as the man by his side.

"The Frenchy and the little fellow were partners," Ash said. "Lifelong friends. Came from somewhere in Illinois. The Frenchy said his friend had stolen half a pound of his Turkish tobacco and smoked it on the sly. Least that's what he says it's about. They have him in chains below. He'll get a free trip back to Seattle—I expect they'll hang him there."

Clay frowned at the man. "He *murdered* his friend, over a little tobacco?"

Fullerton Ash grinned, showing Clay a mouthful of teeth clean and straight as new ivory. "That is *not* a little tobacco in Alaska, my good doctor. Inhaling another man's *smoke* is justifiable homicide in the Yukon, I fear." He nodded toward the north. "Leave Skagway and head up the Chilkoot or White Pass and leave the trappings of civilization behind. You'll see."

"I'm sure what you say is quite true," Clay said. "Just takes some getting used to, I suppose."

"Oh, I'm certain you'll adjust." Ash raised his chin and looked at Clay. "If, of course, it is your intention to join the search for gold, sir."

Clay offered a noncommittal shrug. What did the man *think* he was doing here? What else but gold would bring anyone to this icebox on the edge of the world? At any rate, what he was or wasn't doing here was none of Ash's concern.

Fullerton Ash seemed to get Clay's message. He tipped his bowler hat and went his own way. Moments later, Clay stepped ashore into a chaos of horses, wagons and ankle-deep mud. Burly teamsters and somber Chilkot Indians labored to unload the barges that brought supplies and baggage in from the *Queen,* and cursed the man who had splintered their brand-new docks. A group of wranglers were rounding up terrified horses that had been pitched off the ship to make their way to shore. One fell down in the mud and kicked at the air. A Swede the size of two men began yelling and beating the creature with a whip, as if that might get the animal back on its feet.

Clay shook his head and slogged his way toward the nearest barge, slapping at the mosquitoes hovering around his face. It was only May, but the enormous bloodsuckers were already out in force.

"I'm Dr. Clay Macon," he told a man who seemed to be in charge. "I have a load of supplies from Cooper and Levy in Seattle. I would like to arrange for—"

"You got anything that ain't sunk, mildewed or turned to salt," the man said, "you kin claim it when it gits where it's going in town. If a redskin don't steal it 'fore then, you'll find your goods at Flatts's Warehouse."

Clay had several more questions, but the man turned away and left him standing in the mud. Clay had brought his small camp trunk and his doctor's bag with him. He shouldered the trunk and started across the flats. Skagway was still a boom town but it was growing by fits. A railroad aimed at White Pass was already under way. There were plenty of haphazard structures of crudely hewn logs or canvas, saloons and shops with only a plank on two barrels, but there were also brand-new buildings of yellow pine, some half-finished and some with a fresh coat of paint.

Clay made his way toward a board sidewalk, drawing one boot and then the other from the sucking mud. Teams of weary horses and mules plodded by, their wagons axle-deep in gray muck. He wondered where his friend Jordan LeSec might be staying. Knowing Jordan as he did, he knew it wouldn't be some humble, out-of-the-way inn. The flamboyant LeSec would choose the fanciest, and costliest, accommodations Skagway had to offer.

Scraping the mud off his boots, Clay eased the trunk

from his shoulder and set it on the board sidewalk. A pair of stern-faced women passed by and looked the other way. A pale-eyed gambler in black stopped to flick his cheroot into the street. Clay had hefted the trunk to his shoulder again when an old man with a food-stained beard and shaggy hair stepped out of the saloon and blinked in the light. He was dressed in worn butternut and an ancient Montana hat. Clay decided he'd likely been in Skagway as long as there'd been a town here, and would be here when it was gone.

"Pardon me, old-timer," Clay said, stepping into the man's path, "I'm new here and I'd trouble you for directions to a—"

The man went rigid and the color drained from his face. He stared at Clay, his mouth working like a fish sucking air. The words were on his tongue but he was shaking too hard to get them out.

"What's wrong with you, you all right?" Clay took a step forward. The man shook his head, stumbling away.

"Th-th—it's the divil hisself," he stammered. "God preserve me, the d-divil's come to take me back to hell!"

The man turned and lumbered crazily down the boardwalk, bringing angry words from the crowd.

Clay watched him go, wondering if the man were deranged or simply rotgut-drunk. He caught sight of him again, crossing the muddy street as if all the demons of the underworld were on his heels.

"Now, what was all that about?" Clay said aloud. Some people didn't care for doctors, that was human nature and you couldn't fault a man for that. Still, he'd only been in Alaska half an hour and he hadn't treated anyone yet.

TWO

CLAY SAT DOWN on the bed and pulled off his boots, thankful that he'd had the good sense to wear his best pair. Made to fit his feet, and shaped from the best Texas leather, they had served him well on the long trip from New Orleans. He longed for a bath and fresh clothes, but that would have to wait. Finding Jordan LeSec came first. Clay never felt easy when his unpredictable friend was out of sight for more than an hour or two. This time, he had been ahead of Clay by a week and a half. The boom town was full of diversions for a man like LeSec, who took his pleasures as seriously as a banker takes his accounts. Jordan would have no trouble at all finding whiskey, games of chance—and, if Clay knew his pal, women of uncanny beauty and doubtful reputation.

This last category was a given. There might be ninety-nine females ugly as weeds in town, but the one after that would be lovely as a wild Virginia rose, and Jordan would somehow find her the minute he stepped off the boat.

Clay sighed and pulled himself up, resisting the temptation to stretch out on the bed and close his eyes. The trip had nearly done him in—the endless train ride from New Orleans to San Francisco, a steamer up the coast to Seattle, then the *Queen* to Skagway. It was enough to wear any man down.

Peering out the window of his second-story room, he could feel the cool afternoon breeze sweeping down from the snowy heights. The Boundary Range was just outside of town, and he could see a slice of the notorious White Pass, the route across the mountains to the distant gold fields of the North.

Jordan can wait until I get a fresh shirt and clean socks, Clay thought to himself. *If he hasn't got himself shot or hung or married by now, a minute or two more won't matter either way.*

Down in the lobby, the owner and proprietor of Mrs. Poldofsky's Boardinghouse for Gentlemen was sweeping the rough wooden floor. Clay had chosen the place because he liked the solid, sturdy structure of the house. He was equally impressed with Mrs. Poldofsky, an imposing Russian woman as solid as her scrubbed-clean establishment.

"Is no dinner here," Mrs. Poldofsky said without looking up. "In my house, is no meals except breakfast."

"That'll do just fine," Clay said.

Stepping out onto the sidewalk, he headed back toward the center of town. The boardinghouse was about as far as you could get from the center of activity in Skagway. There were only three or four main streets—if a man was foolish enough to get lost, he could stop and listen to the whoops and hollers from the numerous dance halls and saloons, and find his way by ear.

The streets were crowded with the same mixed bag Clay had encountered on the *Queen*: men from California who had heard of the fabled gold rush there some forty-odd years before; Scots who had burrs in their speech; and tall, muscular Scandinavians who had left their farms and fjords for the promise of Klondike gold.

Clay kept a wary eye open for the old man who'd confronted him on the way from the shore. He couldn't imagine what had sent the fellow into a fit, but the mentally unstable were not uncommon in Skagway, or anywhere else in the North. Gold fever did peculiar things to a man. It could fill your head full of aberrations and fears that would never occur to a clerk from New York or a farmer from Tennessee. He remembered the wild-eyed Frenchman on the *Queen,* the madness in his eyes as he murdered his friend. The man clearly had no idea what he was doing at the time. His mind had simply jumped the track for a second or two, all the time it took to send another man out of this world and into the next.

A miner carried his wife across the street, piggyback style, his boots knee-deep in mud. Two drunks hooted at the couple, but neither the miner nor his wife paid them any mind.

Not for the first time, Clay Macon wondered how his father had fared among people like this. It did not seem possible that the solemn, reserved and always immaculate Randal T. Macon, a man who changed his shirt twice a day, had ever breathed this air and talked to the ill-kempt types who flocked to the North. Skagway, of course, hadn't been here until '97, the year before. But Randal Macon had been in the Yukon fully eleven years before that, in 1886. He had searched for gold on the Fortymile, then down the Tanana and the Copper, nearly freezing to death and losing several fingers and half his right foot, eating dogs and raw fish and making his way back to the coast alive, while all his companions died.

Clay wondered if it wouldn't have been far better if his father had met his death here instead of coming back to New Orleans with nothing left inside. It seemed a heartless thing to say, but Clay had never known a stronger, more determined man than the one who had left for the North—

or one more hollow, beaten and wasted than the one who returned . . .

Clay pushed his thoughts aside. It was too painful to follow that trail. That was then and this was now. And he was not Randal Macon, he was Clay, Randal's son. Just as there had been two Randal Macons, so there were two Clays as well. Nothing could change what either of the two had been before, when tragedy tore their family apart.

I suppose I'm the lucky one, Father, Clay thought. *I've still got a chance to make things right.*

On the other hand, he told himself, his father was at peace with himself, and Clay wasn't sure at all he would reach that state until he, too, passed to the other side.

"Sorry, Squire . . ."

Clay felt a shoulder brush roughly against his arm, the action coming in the instant a hand snaked smoothly up the side of his jacket, past the lapel and inside.

Very well done, Clay thought, almost as good as the light-fingered pickpockets that bred thick as fleas in the Quarters back home.

Turning on his heels, Clay reached up without looking and grabbed a skinny wrist in his strong right hand. The wrist was attached to long and practiced fingers, and the fingers held Clay Macon's calfskin leather wallet.

"Hey, that hurts!" The thief looked startled and tried to break away.

Clay shook his head. "You're lucky I didn't break it off. You want to get better'n that if you figure on staying out of jail."

"I ain't a crook," the boy protested. Clay saw the fellow was no more than seventeen or eighteen years old, a freckle-faced youth with a pug nose, curly red hair and ill-fitting baggy overalls. "I'm not, an-and you got no right to call me that!"

With his free hand, Clay plucked the wallet from the

boy's fingers. "What were you doing with this, do you suppose? You thinking on getting a loan and telling me about it later on?"

"Yeah. Something like that." The boy blushed and gave Clay a surly look. "Reckon you can *afford* it. You look better off than most of the louts round here, haven't got nothin' in their pockets but lint."

Clay tried not to grin. The lad's speech had given him away the minute he opened his mouth. "Shoot, boy, I thought I'd left all the white trash back on the delta, and here's as good a specimen as you could ask, right on the fine streets of Skagway itself."

The boy blinked and stared open-mouthed at Clay. "Wha-what'd you call me?"

"White trash. Your ears froze or what?"

"I ain't any such thing."

"Uh-huh. I call 'em like I see 'em is all."

"Folks ain't always what you think," the boy said. "They might . . . They might seem something and be something else besides!"

"Oh, I see . . ."

"Well, they *might*. You haven't been right your whole life, have you?"

Clay looked at the boy. "No, now, I haven't. Not even close to it. Which doesn't have a whole lot to do with you stealing all my worldly goods and—"

The boy brightened, showing Clay clear blue eyes and good teeth.

"See, what I'm thinking, us both bein' *Southerners* and all, that makes us . . . sorta brothers in a strange land, you know? Why, we might even be cousins or something. Funnier things have happened."

Clay looked pained. "There isn't a chance in Hades you and me are remotely related in any fashion, boy. Now, what's this getting at—it's getting up to something, I just haven't figured what.''

The boy gave Clay a lopsided smile. ''I was thinking we could maybe forget this, uh, unfortunate incident, as it were, and start over fresh.''

''Like what?''

''Like, you maybe loaning me a dollar so's I could go straight and get a new start on life. If I had a chance like that, mister, I swear I'd never—''

''Hold it, just stop it right there.'' Clay raised a warning finger at the boy. ''I don't want to hear it. I can write the rest of this sorry tale myself.''

The boy tried to look hurt. ''Does that mean I don't get the dollar? How about a quarter or a dime? I *know* you got a dime . . .''

''Is there a lockup in this town?'' Clay said darkly. ''If there is, I'll bet you know the way by heart.''

''Mister, I can see right off you and me ain't ever going to be real close. It just isn't going to work out.'' The boy looked Clay Macon squarely in the eye, then kicked him soundly on the shin.

Clay gave a howl. An awesome surge of pain shot up his leg. It felt like lightning had struck him in the foot. He dropped the boy's wrist and hopped about the sidewalk, mouthing every foul epithet that came to mind, in English, Cajun and French. He leaned against the wall to get his breath. A scrawny yellow dog with his right ear chewed completely off came and sniffed at his boots, and gave Clay a painful look.

''Yeah, I know I haven't got good sense,'' Clay muttered. ''You don't have to rub it in . . .''

THREE

CLAY HAD TRAILED Jordan LeSec before, through the haunts of the French Quarter they both knew well, and into the less familiar, but equally disreputable alleys and side streets of St. Louis, Fort Worth and Denver. He knew where *not* to look. You could eliminate the temperance lectures and Bible study groups right off—if either of those existed in the raw mining town of Skagway, Alaska.

Saloons were the answer. Saloons where the whiskey wasn't watered too much and the poker stakes were high.

The first half dozen watering holes had names like the Nugget and Blue Caribou. Clay marked them off without even going in. They were little more than plank-and-barrel affairs—plain dirt floors and packing crates for chairs. The odor of sour beer and unwashed bodies nearly knocked Clay on his heels. He decided the grim-faced patrons were semiconscious or dead.

The Yukon Bear was more to Jordan's style, and he'd been there two or three hours before. The bartender knew him at once from Clay's description: a handsome scarecrow with a smile, straw-colored hair to his neck and a plum-colored coat.

"O'Toole's," the bartender told him. "Your friend was

looking for a place to lose his shirt, so I sent him over there.''

"That was mighty kind of you to do so," Clay said.

"All I do is pour whiskey," the man said shortly. "I ain't nobody's mother, friend.''

"I can see that," Clay said. He thanked the man for his trouble and made his way back to the street.

O'Toole's wasn't hard to find. It was two doors down, past the café and Flatts's Assay Office. Clay thought he'd heard the name Flatts before and remembered there was a warehouse sporting the name, the place where he was to pick up his goods that had come in on the *Queen*.

It was standing room only inside the bar. It might have been a weekday afternoon outside, but it was Saturday night in O'Toole's. The room had clapboard walls and real pine floors. A well-stocked bar stretched the length of one side, and there was room for a dozen tables or more. Fresh gilt lettering on the mirror behind the bar showed fish and potatoes were available for those who required solid food. Waiters in grease-stained shirtfronts circled through the room clutching foaming mugs of beer.

Clay caught a burst of throaty laughter, turned and got a glimpse of white flesh and red lips through the crowd. He was startled to see such a beauty in a place like O'Toole's. The woman had a wide and lovely mouth, a straight, regal nose and a touch of breeding about her that said she didn't truly belong here at all. Clay craned for a better look, but she quickly disappeared in the crowd.

"A bottle of your best," Clay told the man behind the bar. The fellow had more than he could handle, and he set Clay's order on the bar without ever looking up.

Clay let the bartender see a fat roll of bills, tossed a couple of them on the bar and waved the man away.

"Bless you, sir." The bartender's somber face split into a smile. "If there's anything you need . . .''

"There might be," Clay said. "I was thinking about a little recreational game of cards. Something to pass the time."

Clay watched as the bartender's practiced, buckshot eyes took him in at a glance: a broad-shouldered man with strong, chiseled features and clear blue eyes. A thick head of dark hair flecked with gray, a suntanned face and a hard, no-nonsense jaw. Clay's broadcloth jacket was somewhat soiled from travel, but the cut of his clothing and the clean white shirt said quality, same as the man himself. He clearly hadn't shaved in several days, but that, too, was the result of traveling far, and not the man's habits, which the bartender was certain were as refined as they could be.

"A gent like yourself might find some friendly sport upstairs," he told Clay. "Isn't anyone there but men of good taste like yourself, sir, I promise you that."

"That might suit me just fine," Clay said, peeling off another bill from his stack.

The bartender snapped it up quickly, like a lizard on a bug. "Jack-Boy," he called, "be gittin' your worthless self over here, 'fore I take a stick to your hide."

A skinny youth no more than ten hopped up out of nowhere from the back of the bar. His hair nearly covered his eyes, and his nose ran all the time.

"Jack-Boy here'll show you the way." The bartender grinned, patting the boy on the head like a favorite hound dog. "And good luck to you, sir. I have me a feelin' you'll do real well."

"Luck comes to those who least deserve it," Clay said, "and I nearly always win."

The man looked blank. "Yes, sir. That's what I always say, sir."

Six or eight rooms lined the narrow corridor upstairs. Clay heard deep guffaws and girlish laughter from behind the thin wooden doors. He stood to one side as a drunken prospector reeled out of a room, a puzzled look on his gap-toothed face.

"And don't be comin' back, neither," a girl shrieked from in the room. "Ruby Lee Wheeler can tell gold dust from gravel, you silly ol' coot!"

The lad named Jack-Boy paid no attention. Clay shook his head, certain the child had seen and heard enough in his few short years to make a seasoned whaler blush.

"Right in there," the boy said, pointing to the last door in the hall. "That'll be your gentleman's gaming room, sir."

"Many thanks," Clay said, and pressed a Morgan silver dollar in the lad's hand.

"Yes, sir!" Jack-Boy brightened. "God be with ye, sir!"

My wish as well, Clay said to himself. He pushed open the door, stepped inside and froze in his tracks.

A bright lantern hung low over the green baize table. Stale tobacco, whiskey, beer and sweat assailed his senses. Bright gold coins were scattered about the green. Someone had tossed a deck of Steamboat cards at the wall; overturned glasses stained the table, and a rivulet of whiskey dripped to the floor.

Five men sat around the table. Two more stood against the wall. Most of the faces were hidden in the lamp's harsh glare, but there was one that Clay knew. Jordan LeSec sat looking straight ahead. His hands lay flat on the table and he didn't move a hair. The sixth man in the room stood beside Jordan's chair. Half of his face was burned away, from his eyes to just below his chin. He had no mouth or ears, and he held a large pistol at Jordan LeSec's head.

Jordan looked up at Clay and tried to grin. "Glad to see you," he said. "I hope you had a pleasant trip."

"Not too bad," Clay said. "A little wearing is all."

The man with half a face turned his rage on Clay Macon.

"You know this fool? If you do, you better say your farewells, 'cause I intend to send him straight to hell!"

"I expect there's some mistake," Clay said, with no expression at all. "I have never seen this poor fellow in my life."

FOUR

LeSec gave his partner a sorrowful look. "You have a warped sense of humor, sir. I suppose one shouldn't expect too much from a Sewanee man. Tennessee makes fine whiskey, but I can't say much for the schoolin' over there."

One of the players laughed. Half-face gave LeSec a chilling look, then glanced at Clay again.

"What you want in here, mister? You know this weasel or not?"

"I have to say I do," Clay said and sighed. "I expect I've known him all my life."

Half-Face tried to grin, a ghastly sight in a man with no lips. "You got my sympathy, friend." He thumbed back the hammer of his revolver. "You want to stand back a little to your right. I expect he's a'going to splatter some."

"Wait a minute," Clay said. "What are you shooting him for? I'm sure you've got a reason—I'd just like to know."

Half-Face blinked. "He called me a name. He said I was a . . . a 'hair spick' or somethin'."

"A what?"

"Herr Speck," Jordan said. "I called him Herr Speck."

"That's what I said, dang it. *Hair* spick."

Clay forced himself to smile. "And you want to kill him for that?"

"Sure. Why not?"

"That's German. It means 'A man of great respect.' "

Half-face scratched his chest. "It does?" He looked at Clay. "You certain 'bout that?"

"Of course he is," Jordan broke in. "The man is a *licensed* physician. He went to the University of the South. They teach you things like that."

"You shut up." Half-Face frowned. "He want to say somethin' nice, a man oughter do it in plain English, he don't want to get hisself kilt."

"I quite agree with you, sir," Clay said.

"I do too," said LeSec. "It certainly won't happen again."

"Are we goin' to play cards or talk? Floyd, sit *down* over there and put that thing away 'fore I wrap it round your head. Faro, get me something to drink and a new cigar. Make sure it ain't older'n me or I'll shove it up your nose!"

The man who spoke leaned forward out of the shadows, blinking in the light. Clay almost took a step back. The man was enormous, three hundred pounds at a guess, and little of it fat. His fur-lined, sealskin coat scarcely covered his thick neck and barrel chest. His eyes were tiny ball bearings squeezed between heavy folds of flesh. A droopy mustache covered half of his mouth and his head was slick as glass. His skin had an unpleasant, greasy sheen, his face nearly covered with countless dark spots. At first, Clay thought the man had been shot close up, and his face was peppered with powder burns. A closer look revealed the awful truth: This slovenly giant had the biggest crop of blackheads Clay had ever seen.

"I'm bettin' I know who *you* are," the man said. He

pressed his bulk as close to the table as he could and pointed a stubby finger at Clay.

"*Dr.* Clay Macon of New Orleans, am I right?" His voice was like rocks in a can. Clay decided he might be well over sixty, but his strength belonged to a younger man. "Mr. Luh-*Sick* here's been jawin' on about his good friend. That is, when he ain't been teachin' us how to play cards."

Two of the other players laughed. The laughter seemed practiced to Clay, as if they knew their lines well. One of the men held back. He nodded silently at Clay, and Clay saw him clearly for the first time since he'd entered the room. Fullerton Ash, the talkative fellow from the *Queen,* and not nearly so talkative now. What was *he* doing here? Clay wondered. He wasn't any New York City Vanderbilt, for sure, but he seemed a head above this crowd.

The big man raised a curious brow at Ash. "You boys have met, huh?" He nodded at the others. "These two up-standin' citizens is Harper and Moran. The handsome feller wants to do your friend is Floyd Ray Johnson." He stuck out his hand. "I'm Scully Flatts. Welcome to Skagway, sir."

"Mr. Flatts." Clay Macon nodded, shook the man's hand and settled himself in a chair. He set his whiskey bottle on the table and looked straight at LeSec.

"How much, Jordan? How much are you down?"

"Well, I wouldn't put it that way, Clay. I wouldn't say *down . . .*" LeSec showed his friend a crooked grin. Seated next to Scully Flatts, he looked for all the world like a cast-off doll who had lost half his stuffing—all knees and elbows and a bony, angular face. Clay knew he was a mix of the old French court and the richer blood of the pirate Lafitte.

"You're winning, then, right?" Clay said. "Then I guess this gentleman's wrong."

"He is not *exactly* wrong," LeSec said. "He is merely

premature.'' He glanced at his poker hand. "I am fully confident I can not only recoup my meager losses, but win a considerable amount of these fellows' wealth before the day is done—''

"How *much,* Jordan?''

"Four thousand,'' said LeSec. "More or less.''

Scully Flatts laughed. "More, I'd say. Closer to *six* is what it is.''

Clay felt a chill at the back of his neck. He knew for a fact that five thousand dollars was very close to all his partner had. And, worse than that, half of that belonged to Clay himself. They had each put up an extra twenty-five hundred for expenses, over and above the cost of their passage and prospecting supplies—money that was not to be spent unless a dire emergency should arise.

Well, Clay thought grimly, *such a situation has arisen, there's little doubt of that . . .*

Getting out of this room with their money intact was about as grave an emergency as you could ask—short of not getting out at all. Clay prayed they could find some reasonable way out. He didn't want to die before he had a chance to beat his old friend half to death.

"You mind if I sit in awhile?'' Clay gave Scully Flatts his laziest, I-don't-give-a-hang smile. "I think I might be better at cards than my friend.''

Jordan stared at Clay. Scully's pig eyes nearly closed, then he showed his bad teeth. "I swear I don't see how you could be any worse, 'less you was a dead Eskimo. Where's that worthless Faro with my seegar? How am I supposed to play cards, I don't get a new seegar?''

Jordan LeSec had three fat aces, but Scully Flatts had four skinny twos. Jordan looked as if he might be sick. His face was the color of a catfish belly as Scully raked in the pot. He wouldn't even look at Clay.

Clay played cautiously the first half hour, betting light and dropping out at the first sign the stakes would run high, even when he had a fair hand. Now that Clay was in the game, Jordan did the same. He lost another hundred and won back half of that. Clay lost three hundred, and won back five.

He was two hundred ahead, and wiser than he'd been a few moments before. He was catching the flow of the game. The nondescript businessmen, Harper and Moran, played poker by the book. They didn't bluff or hold back. When they thought they had the odds, they bet. When anyone pushed them too hard, they backed down. Floyd, the man with the half-burned face, played like a man who was drunk or had totally lost his mind. You couldn't tell what he'd do next. Fullerton Ash played easy, a little bolder than Clay himself.

That left Scully Flatts. Everybody else had neat stacks of gold and silver coins beside his drink. Scully was the player who consistently won the big pots, the ones heavy with gold and big bills. No proper stacks for him—he liked his money in untidy sprawls; dunes of silver, gold and green that threatened to spill off the table to his oversized lap.

"The bet is fifty to you, sir," Fullerton Ash told Clay.

"Fifty it is," Clay said, tossing gold into the pot.

Floyd bet, for no real reason at all, and the businessmen passed.

"You in, LeSec?"

Jordan ran his long fingers through his yellow hair. "I am in," he said, his face betraying nothing at all. "I see your fifty, sir, and raise you another."

Scully made a noise in his throat. "You think you maybe got something, Luh-Sick? Huh? You got you some pretty bullets, couple of ladies, no?"

"Doesn't matter what I have, Mr. Flatts, as long as my

cards can beat yours." LeSec's voice was cool and de-
tached, as if he had all the time and money in the world,
and none of this mattered at all.

Clay glanced at his friend. He could usually read LeSec,
but not this time.

"Better have some real fine cards," Scully muttered under his breath.

"They're good enough to bring you down, my friend."

Scully didn't care for that at all. The Southerner's uppity
manner was getting on his nerves.

"You just gonna bark all day, little doggie?" he
growled, "or you goin' to show some *teeth*?"

"Teeth enough to bite your wallet clean in half," said
LeSec.

Scully bit his lips. The color rose to his shiny cheeks.

Clay let out a breath. *What are you doing, LeSec? If you
haven't got anything, get out of this now!*

The bet went around again and Scully raised it to a hundred. Clay saw LeSec fill his glass half full of whiskey.
His hand was steady, but Clay knew that didn't mean a
thing.

"A hundred it is," Clay said, and tossed his money in
the pot. He had three queens, and was almost certain they
weren't enough, but he didn't dare toss them in now. It
didn't make sense that staying in the game would help
LeSec, but it seemed like something he ought to do.

Just as he finished his bet, the door opened softly to his
right. Clay blinked in surprise as the redheaded boy who'd
tried to lift his wallet stepped in. The boy knew Clay at
once, took a step back, and then decided to hold his ground.
Scully Flatts didn't miss much. His little eyes shifted from
Clay to the boy.

"Looks like you two already met, am I right?"

"We're acquainted," Clay said.

Scully grinned. "You *acquainted* with Patsy, here, you're lucky you got a penny left to bet."

Patsy's face colored. Clay ignored the man's remark. "Anyone else playing this game?" he said. "You boys gone to sleep or what?"

Half a minute later, Scully Flatts grabbed a bunch of bills and tossed them on the table like so many wads of wastepaper. "I'm raising however much *that* is! Who's in an' who's out?"

LeSec blinked at Flatts. "You can't do that. You can't just . . . toss in anything you like."

Scully's eyes were shards of black glass. "You tellin' me what I can do, Luh-Sick? You saying what *Scully Flatts* can do?"

"My name is *LeSec*," Jordan said. A muscle twitched in his face. "You continually get it wrong, sir."

"Hah!" Scully made a fist and banged it sharply on the table. "I'll call any man whatever I damn well—"

Fullerton Ash swept his bottle off the table and filled Scully's glass. "Gents, I'm buying," he said. "Let's see some empty glasses there." He leaned across the table, splashing whiskey in Jordan's glass and then Clay's. "About time you boys had a taste of *good* liquor, instead of that mud you've been swilling down!"

Flatts gave Ash a curious look. It had been some time since he'd had cheap whiskey, and he wondered what Ash was talking about.

Clay was relieved. Ash's trick had worked; the moment of tension had passed. Scully and LeSec had cooled off, which didn't mean either man wouldn't blow his stack again. The businessmen had the sense to keep quiet. Floyd Johnson wasn't aware that anything had happened at all.

"I never seen you stand anyone to a glass of dirty water," Flatts said. "You sure I ain't drinking pizzen whiskey, friend?"

"If it is," one of the merchants said and grinned, "it's the way I want to die."

"Have another, gents," Ash said, pushing back his chair. "I have to go and relieve myself of what I got."

Someone made a crude remark, and just at the moment Fullerton Ash left the room, one of O'Toole's customers fell out of bed next door, or was pushed. He yelled like a wildcat and the lady with him joined in. If the incident hadn't occurred when it did, Clay wouldn't have quickly looked to his right, and he wouldn't have caught the blur of motion, the telltale flash of red, that passed between Scully Flatts and one of the henchmen who stood behind his chair.

Red—red *cards* they were, moving in the blink of an eye from hand to hand, slipping down the sleeve of Scully's man to Scully's hand—Scully Flatts trading his old cards in for a brand new set.

Lord, Clay thought, *why can't something go right?*

"Card sharpers!" he shouted. "Hit 'em low, LeSec!"

Clay gripped the neck of his bottle, sent his chair clattering to the wall and launched himself across the table at Scully Flatts . . .

FIVE

CLAY HAD BEEN in plenty of fights before. The whole thing was over before you could figure what happened—what you should have said and didn't; when you should've ducked; who you should've hit instead of who you did. By the time you knew that, you were sprawling on a sawdust floor with your nose bending every way but south, or picking the other fellow's teeth out of your fist and wishing you'd both gone to any saloon but the one you were stuck with now.

He knew a quarter of a second too late the table was half a foot wider than he'd thought. He swung the whiskey bottle at Scully's startled face, missed by a mile, and heard the table crack as his right knee went through the wood. Clay dropped into the chasm, bringing a shower of gold, silver, whiskey and wet cigars down on his back. He hit the floor hard, and took Scully's boot in the face. Shaking the pain aside, he came to his knees and drove his head into the man's ample belly. Scully Flatts cursed and went over on his back from the force of Clay's blow. Clay pounded the man with his fists. Scully's hands worked like pistons, fighting back.

From the corner of his eye, Clay saw Jordan LeSec spill one of Scully's henchmen with a solid right to the heart, then a punishing left to the head. The man tumbled over Clay's back, let out a breath and lay still. Clay glanced at Jordan and started to speak. The words froze in his throat. Scully's other man was flying at LeSec in a blur, a wicked-looking skinning knife flashing in his hand.

"*Jordan!*" Clay shouted. "Look ou—"

Clay didn't finish. Scully's stubby hands thrust through the hail of Clay's fists and clamped around his neck. Clay tried desperately to pull away. The big brute's hands were like a vise. Clay punished the man's face, but Flatts wouldn't let go.

Angry voices reached Clay from his left, and he turned his head to see the two local merchants and Half-face jammed in a knot across the room, fighting one another to get out the door. So much for the cavalry riding in to help.

Scully Flatts's grip was hard as steel. Clay struggled to break himself free. Everything began to look blurry and dark. He heard LeSec cry out and saw him go down, the knife blade humming toward him like a swarm of angry hornets in his face. The rage started churning in the pit of Clay's belly, then surged like a storm through his chest. Strength flowed into his shoulders and his arms and ex-ploded with a ragged cry as Clay broke Scully's grip and lashed his hands aside.

Filling his tortured lungs, Clay threw himself at the man who was about to slash at LeSec. The fellow roared in anger as Clay hit him hard at the knees. The knife clattered across the floor; the force of Clay's blow slammed LeSec's assailant against the wall. Clay heard bones break, and knew the man would be shopping for a brand new nose. Blood streaked the wall as he slid down to the floor.

"You . . . all right?" Clay turned to LeSec, who was staggering to his feet. Jordan looked beat and put away wet, but he was still in one piece.

"I'm fine," Jordan said. He showed Clay a weary grin,

wiped his mouth on his coat and spat on the floor. "Never did tell me about your trip, Clay. If it was anything at all like mine, it was a total crashin' bore. No one fit to talk to, and certainly no ladies you'd care even to speak to from half a mile away. There *is* one downstairs, incidentally. Hair black as a Mississippi night, and her eyes . . ."

"I saw her," Clay said, "and you're right." He shook his head at LeSec. "I don't suppose there's a chance in hell you'll ever grow up, is there, Jordan? I've never seen a sign of it yet. I suppose I ought to stop lookin' by now."

"Really, Clay . . ." Jordan ran his fingers through his hair. "That is not quite fair."

"It's fair, all right. It's *been* fair since we were seven, and you and Mary Lou Beecher talked me into stowing away on the *Delta Star*."

"Well, we had a grand time, as I recall, sir. You cannot deny that."

"We got our bottoms tanned," Clay reminded him. "Leastways *I* did. You likely wormed out of it some way, leaving me with the— *Hey, just hold it right there!*"

A little silver pistol had fallen from the folds of Scully's Eskimo furs in the scuffle. Clay hadn't spotted it before, but now Flatts was going for it, bellying across the wooden floor like an overweight roach. Clay stomped over to him, stepped on Scully's wrist and scooped the weapon off the floor.

"Blast you, Macon!" Scully's bad skin looked the worse for wear where Clay had pummeled it with his fists. "You don't know who you're messin' with, son!"

"Yeah, I guess I do," Clay said. He turned the derringer over in his hand. It was a silver-plated Remington over-and-under .41 with ivory grips. Scully's initials were engraved along the short barrel in gold—real gold, Clay imagined. He had seen plenty of the little pistols, but never one as fine as this.

"What I guess I'm messin' with is a fat card slick, and not a very good one at that." He studied the man on the floor. "Who you been playin' poker with, mister? They got a school for the blind around here? I don't see any normal-eyed man falling for that 'extra hand' trick."

Scully didn't answer. Jordan cleared his throat. "I, uh . . . suppose *I* did, Clay."

"You're an exception," Clay said. "There's the blind and the ignorant, and your eyesight's just fine as far as I know."

"You let me off this floor, I might not have you both skinned," said Scully Flatts. "You want to think about that."

"Shut up," Clay said. "I don't want to talk to you."

"Could I have a seegar?"

"What?"

"I said, could I—"

"You can *eat* all the stogies you can find down there," Jordan put in. "Now, do like Dr. Macon says and keep your mouth buttoned up tight."

Scully glared at Jordan and mumbled under his breath. Clay peered around the room and frowned. "This game got as popular as cholera all of a sudden. Where's Mr. Fullerton Ash, and that pickpocket, what's his name?"

"Ash went out on personal business, you'll recall. The thief's name is Patsy, and he retired along with those fellows in the bowler hats and the handsome Herr Speck."

"That was a real smart move," Clay said darkly. "What if that lunatic had known you were callin' him 'Mr. Bacon'? What you figure he'd've thought of that, LeSec?"

"I guess he would have shot me two or three minutes before you came in," Jordan said. "Anyway, he scarcely spoke English. He did not appear to me to be a man who'd be familiar with any foreign tongue."

"Lots of things don't appear to you. That doesn't mean they're not—"

A big fist hammered on the door. Clay jerked around, the derringer still in his hand. "Who is it?" he shouted. "Whoever you are, get away from that door!"

"It's the *law,* mister," said a deep-throated voice. "Drop whatever you might be holdin' 'cause we're a-coming in."

"How do I know you're the law?" Clay said.

"I got a Parker double-barrel twelve-gauge shotgun. What've you got?"

Clay looked at LeSec. LeSec looked at Clay's tiny weapon. It was almost lost in Clay's hand. "He has a point," Jordan said.

"Yeah, he does." Clay tossed the derringer in the corner. "Come on in," he called out. "We're unarmed in here."

The door opened quickly, and the dark twin barrels of a shotgun appeared. Behind the weapon was a tall, rawboned man with a walrus mustache, a worn black worsted suit and a mail-order hat from Sears.

"We are mighty pleased to see you, sir," Clay said. "I would like to press charges against this man on the floor. He's a scoundrel and a blatant card cheat. These other two rogues are in his employ. I am charging them with attempted murder and bodily assault."

The lawman didn't even look at Clay. His glance took in the ruined table, the money scattered on the floor, the two unconscious men against the wall. Finally, he took off his hat and leaned down to Scully Flatts.

"You all right, sir? You ain't hurt or anything?"

"I'm good enough, C. R. Much obliged for asking though," Scully said.

Clay stared at the two. "What . . . what are you asking *him* for? Did you hear what I said? This fellow's running a crooked card game!"

Jordan laid a restraining hand on Clay's arm. "You just

got in town, Clay. There's a couple of things you ought to know. Like the Flatts Warehouse, the Scully Flatts Hotel . . ."

"I know that." Clay jerked his arm away. "I saw the signs. The Flatts Assay Office, all right?" He pointed a finger at Scully. "That *does* not give this man a license to cheat at cards."

Jordan moaned. "I thought I was supposed to be the ignorant one around here."

"You forgot the Scully Flatts General Store, and O'Toole's Saloon, where you're standing right now." The lawman gave Clay a solemn look. "What you want me to do with 'em, Mr. Flatts?"

"What?" Clay clenched his fists and took a step toward the man. "What are you talkin' about?"

Scully grabbed the Parker shotgun, waddled up to Clay and jammed both barrels under Macon's nose.

"There's two things I can't abide," Scully said. "One is an educated man. I won't put up with a snot-nosed fool that's read a book. An' if there's anything I hate more'n that, it's an educated dude from the *South*."

"Now look here," Jordan said, "you can't talk to my friend like that. I am calling you out on a point of honor, sir! I expect you to—"

Clay saw it coming, but there was nothing he could do. The man with pig eyes and a million blackheads whipped the shotgun around and slammed the butt hard against the side of his head . . .

SIX

HE WOKE WITH his skull splitting open, rising to the surface with a dream of Adele Garnette fading quickly away. Her green eyes peered into his, dark hair blowing in a spidery veil across her cheeks. She tried to speak to him, that exquisite little mouth forming words he couldn't hear. The roaring in his head swept her sweet voice away, leaving him with nothing but a hollow image and a terrible pounding that wouldn't go away...

Clay Macon moaned and tried to sit up.

"Don't do it," Jordan said, from somewhere far away. "You won't like it in here."

Clay opened his eyes, sniffed the air and nearly gagged on the smell. The odor was a nauseous mix of vomit and urine, and strong enough to fell an ox. Looking into the gloomy half-light, he could see why these two odors were the dominant scents of the day. The shaggy-haired apparition teetering against the far wall was performing both acts responsible for making such smells.

"You ask me how I'm feeling, I'll throttle you, LeSec. You understand that?"

"I don't guess I have to," Jordan sighed. "I can see perfectly clear. You look like somethin's been run over twice. I tore up my shirt and made a bandage for your head.

It was my best linen shirt, by the way. The blood stopped flowing pretty quick. You were always one to clot up real good. I remember that, Clay.''

"That's a blessing," Clay said. He looked at his long-time friend. Jordan LeSec could maintain his fashionable appearance during difficult times, but at the moment he looked the worse for wear. His plum-colored jacket was gone, and his white suit vest was stained with dirt and a generous spattering of Clay's precious blood. LeSec didn't look much like the dashing Confederate cavalryman he surely would have been if he hadn't been born the year that terrible war began.

"I'm sorry," Clay said. "I got you into this. I swear I'll do what I can to get you out."

Jordan showed him a crooked grin. "I believe that's my line, Clay. I am almost certain that it is."

"Not this time it isn't. I'm the one that had to come lookin' for gold." Clay blew out a breath. "Go north and make your fortune. Pick up nuggets big as peach pits. You'll be a millionaire before noon."

"No one tied me up and made me come with you, Clay."

"No, but it was my idea. I take responsibility for that."

Clay pulled himself up farther against the wall. The throbbing in his head had eased a little, but the hurt was still there. His medical—and personal—experience told him he'd be lucky if he didn't have a concussion, or a hairline fracture of the skull. At any rate, it wouldn't do much good to worry about it now. He couldn't see any medical facilities from where he sat.

The cell was bare, cold ground, with pools of standing water and filth. There was one barred window in the crude stone wall, too high up to see out. The cell was maybe ten by twelve. No bunks, no place to sit except the floor. A slop jar in the corner that no one seemed to use. There were two other prisoners, the old vagrant who still leaned against the far wall, and another who was sleeping, sick or dead. The door was rusty iron. Clay had no idea what lay beyond that. He asked LeSec, and Jordan said there was nothing much to see, that the jail was half a block down from O'Toole's, close to the Scully Flatts Hotel.

"Owns the whole town, does he?" Clay said. "Everything in Skagway's his?"

"All of it, near as I can tell," Jordan said. "Leastways, whatever's worth having. I expect he doesn't want the rest."

"No, no, I guess not."

Clay leaned against the damp stone wall. Even though it was spring outside and the Alaskan daylight lingered on forever, it would surely get cold in this cesspool when the so-called night rolled in. Then what? he wondered. Would kindly jailers appear with blankets and soup? Possibly a steaming dish of Oysters Rockefeller, or a crayfish étouffée? Clay's hollow belly nearly cried out at the thought. He'd forced down a dish of greasy potatoes and stale black bread aboard the *Queen* that morning, and nothing but a little whiskey since.

Of all the lousy luck, picking a fight with the man who owned the gateway to the Yukon and all that Klondike gold! He'd have been better off if he'd attacked a polar bear. At least he'd have died in an honorable manner in God's clean wilderness and not in this foul-smelling pit where he'd likely perish now.

Clay Macon was not a man to give up and quit. He wouldn't do that. But at the moment he could see no reason why Scully Flatts should ever let him go. He and Jordan couldn't be the first men who'd crossed the ugly tyrant of Skagway Bay. Those poor devils in the corner, the one that was eternally sick and the one who might be dead. How long had *they* been here? Did Scully Flatts and his pet law-man remember they were there?

"I guess everyone in the saloon saw them hauling me out," Clay said.

"Most everyone," Jordan told him. "They took us down the stairs and out the front door."

"Quite a few people were there."

"A fair number, Clay."

"That, uh . . . dark-haired lady with the kind of Cajun tilt to the mouth, sorta grayish eyes."

"Silver," Jordan said.

"You think so?"

"Oh, yes. Silver for a fact. You wouldn't say gray."

"You know the lady, then?"

"I made her acquaintance. Briefly, that is. I cannot honestly say I know her. In the knowing sense of the word."

"I see." Clay thought about that.

"She reminded me a great deal of Adele," Clay said. "In some respects, I mean."

Jordan grinned. "Every lovely woman reminds you of Adele."

"No, now, that's not so. Not all of them, LeSec."

"Adele is much prettier than this saloon girl. There is no comparison I can see."

"There's some," Clay said. "The mouth in particular. You can't forget the mouth."

"I suppose that's true. The mouth, and possibly that rather queenly nose."

"Not the nose."

"You think not?"

"Adele Garnette's nose . . . There is no nose quite as exceptional in all of Louisiana. Or possibly anywhere else in the South."

"I would go further than that," Jordan put in. "I would say there's a quality to all aspects of Adele that rivals those of any woman in the nation. Certainly the ladies of the Northern states could not hold a candle to *any* beauty from the South . . .''

"Well, certainly. Goes without saying."

Clay Macon had been to cities like New York and Boston and knew this wasn't so. Jordan knew it, too, but voicing such a heresy was something else. There were things a man might dwell upon in his very secret thoughts that would not be proper to speak of out loud. Not even to a lifelong friend.

Clay stood and stretched his legs. He felt a little dizzy, and there seemed to be aches in parts of his body that he hadn't noticed sitting down. Thinking of himself as a patient, he was not a bit surprised. Scully Flatts had gotten in some very telling blows, and splitting a solid pine table hadn't helped.

"I wish I had a good cigar," Clay said. "That would surely be a blessing right now."

"It surely would," Jordan agreed.

Clay squinted at the dim half-light that filtered from the narrow window above, a straw-colored beam in the dusty air of the cell. He still had his watch, but it was too dark to clearly read the dial.

"A cheap cigar wouldn't be half-bad," Jordan said, cutting into Clay's thoughts. "I believe I'd settle for the cheapest, most foul-smelling cigar to be found in Terrebone Parish right now."

"There are some pretty bad cigars down there," Clay said.

"I stand by what I said."

"While you're dreaming, you might include a dry match. You'll surely need it for that cheap cigar."

"Well, there's that," Jordan said. "Thank you kindly for remembering, Clay."

SEVEN

CLAY DECIDED HE didn't feel guilty at all, thinking of the black-haired beauty at O'Toole's. That was plain foolish, and likely due to lack of sleep, an empty stomach and confinement in a totally disgusting environment. From a medical point of view, any of those conditions alone could bring on a bout of depression in an otherwise mentally and physically healthy man.

After all, it was Adele Garnette who'd walked out on him, not the other way around. She was the one who had turned her back on everything they had, all they had meant to each other as long as either could recall.

Maybe she had good reason, he told himself. *Maybe, in her place, I would have done the same thing.* Who could really blame her, after the tragedy they'd shared that last, awful evening together . . .

No! No, damn it all, he would *not*! He would not have done the same! He would have stood by her. He would not have let anything come between them.

The memory brought a mix of sorrow, anger and regret. The depth of that anger surprised him. It had been there, smoldering, since that early morning hour when he'd crossed the dew-covered lawn of Wind Tree, the Garnette family mansion, walking away from that house for the very last time. It did not feel like grass beneath his feet at the time. It felt like a bed of hot coals.

He could never have imagined he was capable of feeling such emotions toward Adele. Yet, there it was. A love he felt could never die had turned to bitterness. He knew things like that happened to men and women, but he'd been certain such couples were never as deeply committed as he and Adele. Their love, he was sure, was a love on a higher plane.

Now he knew that was wrong. It seemed that the well-bred Garnettes and Macons shared the same emotions and misunderstandings of people from that other side of town.

He wondered why he hadn't been wise enough to see this all along. He had seen countless people die of yellow fever, typhoid, cholera and dread venereal disease. Some had no names at all, and some had pedigrees leading back to kings. Money and privilege could shield you from a number of things, but life had a way of evening things out. *Look at us now,* Clay thought. Two men of family in New Orleans, but nobody cared about that up here. Now they were two poor fools in a stinking jail—and the man with all the power was an uncouth lout, a bully named Scully Flatts who was likely descended from people with no more breeding than a pack of wild dogs.

Clay squeezed his eyes shut a moment and tried to ease the throbbing in his head. The light had faded slightly outside, enough to plunge the cell into near total darkness. He envied Jordan LeSec. Jordan could sleep in a lumber mill with a buzz saw screeching in his ears. The creak of wagons passing by, the curse of the teamsters, a bottle smashed against the wall—nothing bothered LeSec.

Though he tried to dismiss it from his thoughts, Clay couldn't help but wonder how long they'd have to squat in the black and filthy hole the town of Skagway called a jail. If the town was truly lawless, the situation was truly hope-

less. Flatts could keep them here as long as he liked. A
man like that didn't need the formality of a trial, a judge,
and certainly not a jury. Two idiots from New Orleans had
come to the North to get rich and simply disappeared. So
what? Men vanished in the Yukon all the time.

Clay let out a breath. How could a man like his father,
the honorable, fastidious Randal T. Macon, have managed
to stomach the company of the crude, ignorant and oftimes
brutish men who traveled to this forsaken corner of the
earth in search of gold?

He knew the answer all too well: Pride, and utter desperation, had driven his father into a venture neither birth
nor experience had prepared him for at all. Pride in the
Macon name, and the desperation of learning his company
was hopelessly in debt, every red cent gone, every asset
pledged to the hilt and beyond. One day Macon & Benhurst
was the largest and most respected shipping broker in New
Orleans, in the whole of the South—the next, there was
only Randal Macon. His friend and partner, Forrest Benhurst, was on his way to South America with the company's
fortune, and a green-eyed Creole beauty scarcely sixteen.

Clay's father was left with his partner's debts and dishonor. Anna Lee Benhurst, Forrest's wife, was left with a
mortgaged house and grounds, a washtub full of bills and
three daughters older than her husband's new paramour.
Randal Macon had a large personal fortune, and it took
every dime of it to straighten out the chaos Forrest had left
behind. When it was over and done, Randal put all he had
left in trust for his family, enough to get by for several
years, then gathered his wife and son in the nearly empty
library of his home and said his farewells.

Clay's mother, Amelia, collapsed. Clay, for the first and
only time in his life, talked back to his father. He accused
him of deserting his family, and called him every kind of
fool. He regretted his words at once. He had never seen

such pain in his father's eyes. Clay Macon had wished, a thousand times since, that he could take that moment back, but the chance for that had passed.

Within the week, his father had left New Orleans for Alaska. The day was indelibly etched in Clay's mind: April 19, 1886—eleven years before, almost to the month. The day was wet and unseasonably cold. Randal Macon had not allowed any members of the family to accompany him to the train. Clay watched him hurry from the house in the early dawn hours, holding his hat down on his head, the pelting rain soaking him through before he reached the end of the walk. Adam Carlyle, Amelia's second cousin, was waiting there for him in a carriage. Carlyle had never accomplished much of anything except for raising good hunting dogs. It was Carlyle who had talked Randal Macon into going to Alaska for gold. He filled the desperate man with tales of gold strikes on the Stewart River, just the year before, in '85. There was a new trading post, Fort Nelson. Fortymile, on the river of the same name, had become the Yukon's first mining town. Prospectors were swarming to the Tanana, the Copper River, places no one outside of the North had ever heard of before.

Adam downplayed the reports that not a great deal of gold was being taken out of these strikes. It was enough, he said, and where there was the smell of gold, it stood to reason there was plenty more of the precious stuff nearby.

"All the more for us to bring home," Adam said. "Those ol' boys freezing their tails off wouldn't know gold if it bit 'em. I *do*. And I know how to find it!"

Clay's mother rolled her eyes at such talk. Amelia knew that Adam had gone to college two years, a school in Pennsylvania no one *she* knew had ever heard of. He had studied minerals there, though he had no profession or degree of any kind—and didn't want one either, it appeared. He was always spouting off about open-cut and sluice-box mining, and the hydraulic method of taking ores—things he'd learned out of a book, and a Yankee book at that.

Clay wanted to do what his mother was likely thinking about, which was knock cousin Adam senseless, but he knew it wouldn't do any good. His father's eyes had told him that. The man could already see himself returning wealthy, his pride, his family, his honor, fully restored. *Harper's* magazine was already calling it "Klondike Fever." Once a man caught it, there wasn't any cure.

There were two terrible moments in Clay Macon's life that would haunt him to the end of his days. One would occur much later, when Adele Garnette announced they could never be together, that she did not intend to see him again. But the first moment was that rain-swept morning when his mother said good-bye to his father. The parting itself was bad enough, but something else happened that marked itself forever in his mind. As Randal held Amelia in his arms, a bolt of lightning struck a great oak tree in the yard, splitting it in half. Everything in the darkened hallway was etched in painful light that burned all color away. Clay looked directly into his mother's eyes, and in that instant, he felt as if the lightning had ripped into his heart. Somehow his mother knew. How, Clay couldn't say and didn't want to know. She *knew,* though—there was no mistaking that. For a moment, she had looked into her to-morrows, and she knew she would never see Randal Macon in this life again . . .

Clay jerked up, startled for a second, and realized he'd dozed off. His stomach growled and his head still hurt. The light looked the same outside, and he knew he hadn't slept long.

"You all right?" Jordan asked. "I'm pleased you got some rest."

Clay saw his partner's concern. "Yes, I'm fine. Fine as can be expected, I suppose."

"You were dreaming some. It did not appear to be an overly pleasant affair. I do not believe you were running barefoot through flowered fields."

Clay laughed. "I don't recall exactly where I was, but I doubt there were any flowered fields." Clay patted his vest pocket. His watch was still there, but he remembered it would do him little good.

"It is an irritation to me that I cannot tell the time. I like to know the time, even though I apparently have nowhere to go."

Clay's words vanished as a metal door was opened nearby, then loudly slammed shut. The sound of heavy footsteps echoed down the hall outside the cell.

Jordan looked at Clay. The footsteps stopped. A key clicked in the door. Someone poked a lantern into the cell. Clay and Jordan blinked in the unfamiliar light.

"Come on, you two, git out of there. I ain't got all day."

Clay couldn't see beyond the light, but he recognized the voice as the rawboned lawman who owed his star to Scully Flatts.

Everything hurt, but he forced himself to stand. Jordan had the good taste to pretend he didn't need any help. As he stumbled weakly into the hall, Clay saw that the lawman wasn't alone. A short, surly Sitka Chilkot was with him. The Indian held the lantern. He looked as if he had no interest at all in what was taking place.

"Thataway," said the lawman, motioning with his shotgun to the right. "Down the hall, the way you come in."

Clay had no memory of coming in, but it apparently made no difference, since there was only one direction to go.

EIGHT

THE LAWMAN WOULDN'T speak to them again. He growled at his deputies and the men led Clay and LeSec through the office and back onto the street. If they slowed down or didn't walk straight, the barrel of a .44–.40 hurried them along.

Some people paused to give them a curious glance. Most of the citizens of Skagway didn't bother to waste a second look.

"Where are you taking us?" Clay asked the short deputy at his back. "I want to know, and I want to know now!"

"Clay . . . Just hold it a minute, all right? Don't get your dander up."

Clay shot his friend a dark look. "I am flat weary of bein' poked and herded about like a steer on a string, LeSec. I will not tolerate such treatment anymore."

"You'll shut yer trap or I'll blow a hole in your backside," the short lawman said.

Clay turned and faced him. Both the deputies backed off a step and kept their weapons high.

"I don't think so," Clay told them. "I don't think you've been told to blow a hole in anyone, mister, and I'm guessin' you don't either one of you relieve yourselves until you hear from Scully Flatts."

The tall deputy blinked. The short one turned red. "I'd
. . . I'd watch my mouth if I was you, mister."

"It's *doctor,* boy." Clay showed him a nasty grin. "And
I'm not moving an inch until you tell me where I'm going."

The two men looked at each other. The tall deputy
scratched his nose. "Won't hurt to tell you, bein' as how
you're there." He nodded over his shoulder. "You're going
to the *ho*tel."

Clay followed the man's motion. The sign on the build-
ing said, "The Scully Flatts Hotel."

"I'm not staying there. I've got a room outside of
town."

"You're stayin' here now," the deputy said. He screwed
up his face and studied Clay, nearly closing both eyes.
"You're right about us doin' what we're paid for, *Doctor,*
but there's a difference between me an' Artie, here. I got
a nervous tic in one finger and I ain't ever sure just when
the thing's going to start. You want to guess which finger
it is?"

"I will take your word for it, sir." Clay didn't hesitate
an instant. He knew when to bluff and when to drop out.
"You look to be an honest man to me . . ."

Jordan LeSec's room was on the second floor, facing the
street below. There was a small entry parlor with a table,
a hat tree and a lamp. An English hunt print hung on the
wall in an elaborate frame. Clay stepped through the hallway to the parlor. A marble-top table with fancy legs was
set before a pair of plush sofas. A rocker with a velvet-
cushioned back was nearby. Overhead was an embossed tin
ceiling. The walls were covered with scarlet-flocked wall-
paper, and a thick red carpet spread the entire length of the
floor.

Clay reached in his vest pocket and made a show of

checking his watch. "I expect the Queen of England herself'll be droppin' by for tea before long. It's nearly a quarter to two."

Jordan let out a breath. "You intend to keep it up, don't you? I'm not ever going to hear the end of this."

"Why, Jordan, I'd do no such thing." Clay brought a hurt expression to his face. "You wouldn't be living in such fine quarters if you couldn't afford it, I'm certain of that. 'Specially since your fortune and most of mine got left behind on the floor at O'Toole's. A man like yourself—"

"Clay, shut up and come in here. Right now."

The tone of Jordan's voice brought Clay up short. He stepped through the parlor and into the sleeping quarters of the suite. He stopped there and stared at the sight. All of his belongings had been brought from Mrs. Poldofsky's boardinghouse. Both his clothes and Jordan's were cleaned and pressed. Shirts, suits and heavy coats were hung in the big mahogany armoire. On a heavy oak table, two places were set. Clay breathed in the intoxicating aroma of hot coffee, prime roast beef, fresh bread, baked potatoes and a bowl of country butter. A bottle of Louis Jadot Beaujolais was set among the china and gleaming silverware. Across the room, next to the large four-poster bed, was the finest sight Clay had ever seen: two metal tubs full of steaming hot water, several extra bucketfuls on the floor, thick white towels and good soap.

Jordan LeSec finally broke the silence between them. "Clay, I know you don't know the answer, but I'm askin' anyway. What in blazes do you make of this?"

"I don't care for it," Clay said. "Not one bit I don't." He looked at Jordan, then turned and walked through the parlor to the small entry hall. In a moment he was back.

"The door's locked," he said. "I guess we could've figured that." He moved to the table and poured himself a generous glass of wine.

"Scully Flatts keeping us alive is one thing; I'm right grateful for that. But the rest of this business scares me out of ten years. Food and bathwater and good French wine . . . That's about three too many good deeds for me . . ."

NINE

CLAY WAS TIRED clear to the bone, but he was still sitting up by the darkened window when his watch read a quarter till ten. The hot bath, clean clothes and decent food had been heaven after his long trip on the *Queen,* and those harrowing hours they'd spent in Scully Flatts's jail. Jordan even discovered some cigars and a very fine brandy to top off the meal.

Clay wanted to stay up and talk, but Jordan didn't last long after a brandy or two. As ever, once a crisis had passed, he was ready for a good night's sleep. There might be an avalanche in the morning, or a dogfight in the parlor, but LeSec would face those problems as they came.

One of us might as well get some rest, Clay thought to himself. *Just like always, it's going to be him.*

He had stretched his imagination to the limit, but he still couldn't guess what the morning might bring. What did that oversized lout have in mind? Whatever it was, it couldn't be anything that would further the health and well-being of Dr. Clay Macon or Jordan LeSec. Tossed in a filthy pit, then pampered like honored guests. What was Scully Flatts fattening them up *for*?

Most of all, Clay hated the helplessness of their situation. There were men outside the door, and if you peered out the window to the street it was easy to spot the watchers Flatts had posted there. *It's my town, and I can do whatever I like,* he was telling them. That didn't go down easy with Clay Macon. That was the cause of the anger that smoldered within him, and kept him wakeful into the quiet hours just before the dawn.

Clay felt as if he'd scarcely closed his eyes when Scully's men pounded on the door. Jordan was awake and nearly dressed. One man opened the door and brought in coffee, bacon, half a roast chicken, scrambled eggs, hot biscuits and gravy. The other two guards stood back, weapons at the ready.

When they were gone, Jordan sat down and began devouring everything in sight. Clay walked around and studied the table, scowling at the lavish spread, then finally gave in and joined his friend.

"I'm beginning to think we've totally misjudged the man," Jordan said, talking around a mouthful of biscuits and bacon. "I believe Mr. Flatts has seen the error of his ways, and is doing all he can to get back in our favor."

"I believe Tahiti is due north of here," Clay said, "complete with coconuts and brown-skinned girls." He blew on his coffee. "The more fine meals come through that door, the less I like it." He looked straight at Jordan LeSec. "We're not playing this game anymore, old friend. No pig-eyed walrus is keeping Macon and LeSec locked up in a fancy hotel. We are puttin' an end to this *today*."

"I'm with you," Jordan said. He considered preserves for his biscuit and settled on peach. "One thing comes to mind, and I hesitate to bring it up, because I'm sure you have a perfectly sound and reasonable plan."

"What's that?"

"All our clothing and personal goods are here. They didn't even steal my new California shirt. What seems to be missing are weapons of any sort. I'd feel foolish tossing china at them, Clay."

Clay glared at his friend. "You eat that biscuit. I'm going to shave."

"Good idea," Jordan said. "In times like these, a gentleman needs to look his best."

Clay felt better after he'd removed a week's beard from his face. He changed into a cotton Pemberton shirt and heavy-duty trousers from Levi Strauss. He was struggling with his Texas boots when someone knocked discreetly on the door. It didn't sound like the heavy pounding of their guards. Clay went to the door, and found Fullerton Ash standing there.

Ash caught Clay's expression and smiled. "I know you were not expecting me, Dr. Macon, but I do hope you'll allow me in. I would very much like to speak with you and Mr. LeSec."

"Certainly," Clay said, standing aside. "Any news from the world outside is most welcome to us shut-ins, Mr. Ash."

Ash beamed. "You have a sense of humor, Doctor. I count that an asset in a man. I most assuredly do."

Ash took a seat, perching on the edge and carefully straightening the razor-sharp pleats on his pants. He was dressed in a blue plaid English worsted suit, a white shirt, a celluloid collar and gray silk tie. He looked the part of a merchant and banker, Clay thought, except for the dollar-sized crater in the sole of his left shoe.

"I hope you both will not mistake my words as my own," he said. "I must tell you that I have been asked by Mr. Scully Flatts to serve as a messenger on this occasi~ He feels that, uh . . . personal contact between the ~ concerned would be distasteful to you both."

"Speakin' for myself—" Clay began.

4

"Please, hear me out, sir." Ash held up a restraining hand. "Mr. Flatts feels that since you and I have met, Doctor, and there is no animosity between us, you might be open to what I have to say on his behalf."

Fullerton Ash cleared his throat and folded his hands together in his lap. "Mr. Flatts is not a particularly . . . pleasant man. I need not dwell on that. He is, however, a man of resource in Skagway. He does not like to be crossed. More than that, he will not *abide* such actions. When he is angry, he strikes out at those who have stirred that anger. He *punishes* his enemies, gentlemen, and he often punishes them severely."

Ash paused, and looked from Clay Macon to Jordan LeSec. His features showed no emotion at all. "I am aware of your shameful incarceration in that cesspool of a jail. That was *not* severe treatment. Believe me, it was not. I could tell you shocking things that I have witnessed in this town—"

"Damn it all, man, if this kinda thing goes on, why don't you worthy citizens of Skagway do something about it! Why do you allow this tyrant to run your lives, to treat you like dogs!"

Fullerton Ash was taken aback by Clay's sudden rage. One moment he seemed perfectly calm, the next he had lost control of himself.

"Because, Dr. Macon, we do not wish to catch a stray bullet from a drunken prospector," Ash said, "or burn up in a fire that *accidentally* starts beneath our beds."

Ash looked down at his hands. "Someday, we *worthy citizens* as you call us will no doubt take back our town. But not this year, I'm afraid, or the next. The West was lawless not too many years ago. That frontier is gone. The frontier of the Yukon is just beginning. People who come here are hungry for wealth, gentlemen. They will put up with men like Scully Flatts, because many of them would like nothing better than to *become* a Scully Flatts."

He stood and smoothed his lapels. "But that is not what I came to tell you, sirs, though it is, indeed, something you need to know. Here is how things are, my friends. Scully Flatts wants you out of his hair, so to speak. He wants you out *now*. He would have me tell you this is a burst of generosity on his part. I happen to know better. Mr. Flatts is engaged in a, uh . . . business ploy. That is to say, he plans to separate several wealthy men from Chicago from their money. These men arrive in Skagway tomorrow. Mr. Flatts does not feel it would be prudent to have you simply *disappear* at this time. This is why he is sending you on your way, out of his town, out of his sight."

Ash crossed to the window and motioned to Jordan and Clay. The two partners joined him and Ash pulled a curtain aside.

"Those two burros down there are loaded with the prospecting supplies you purchased from the Cooper & Levy outfitters in Seattle, Doctor. There are also adequate food staples, various other goods, and your weapons as well."

Ash drew a gold railroad watch from his pocket. "It is . . . eight-twenty-seven if I am correct. Men will be in here to pack your belongings in three minutes. Mr. Scully would like you to be out of Skagway proper by nine-twenty at the latest."

Clay stared at the man. He looked down at the neatly laden burros, then back to Ash.

"Please," Ash said, "forgive me if I anticipate your question, sir. No, you do not have a choice, and yes, he will make good his threat, I assure you, even if it is inconvenient to do so at this time. In Mr. Scully Flatts's words, 'Those Dixie *cheechakos* are out of my town on time or they're dead.' "

"What's a *cheechako*?" Jordan said.

"Please don't ask," said Ash.

TEN

BEFORE HE LEFT New Orleans, Clay had read all he could find about the gold routes to the North. There was plenty to read, too—it seemed as if everyone who'd ever *heard* of Alaska had something to say. Much of it was pure fantasy, gleaned from the public library or a rum-soaked imagination.

Still, those writers who clearly had knowledge of the place seemed to agree on one point: It was the devil's choice whichever path you took out of Skagway. The Chilkoot Pass might be the shortest route, but it could also prove to be the deadliest. Before you got there, you had to cross obstacles like the rocky gorge at Sheep Camp, a spot where prospectors usually abandoned their horses and wagons and trudged ahead on foot.

In winter, men scaled a sheer wall of ice and snow up the Chilkoot way. Besides the chilling wind that howled down the mountains and cut through flesh and bone, there were other hazards to face. If a man could reach the pass without freezing to death, he faced the danger of avalanches, or dropping into a glacial fissure that sealed him forever in a tomb of blue ice.

"They'll have a railroad all the way up here before

long," Jordan said. "I don't suppose you'd care to wait for that."

"I don't think so," Clay said. "And the way they're laying those tracks, I'm not real sure I want to ride it when it's done."

Clay looked past Jordan to the awesome mountains above. The pair stood near the end of the Skagway Trail. Rising steeply ahead was the ridge of White Pass. It cut through the Boundary Range a few miles south of the Chilkoot route. The White Pass had its drawbacks, but Clay felt they'd made the right choice. Men who'd crossed here and back said the trails were made for mountain goats, but that sounded better than the Chilkoot. Prospectors had hacked a way up that slope and dubbed it with a name that would appeal to the hearty adventurer: The Golden Stairs. But Clay had heard a more realistic description of that climb. Even in May, he didn't care for a path that most men called "the icy path to hell." A place like that had more than likely earned its name.

Clay glanced at Jordan LeSec and grinned. Jordan was posed by the pack mules in the shadow of the Boundary Range. The great mountains seemed etched with pen and ink against a startling blue sky. LeSec looked like a poster for luring men to the North, the picture of the hearty gold seeker who would conquer whatever stood in his way. Even though the temperature was somewhere close to seventy-five degrees, LeSec had insisted on wearing the magnificent black bearskin coat he'd purchased in St. Louis the month before.

"I paid out thirty-seven dollars for this coat," Jordan told him. "I assure you it is going to see some wear."

LeSec was sweating profusely under the heavy furs, and Clay figured the coat wouldn't last through the day. Especially after he got behind the sledge again and helped the mule pull it up the next hill.

The sledge had been a lucky accident. They had found it, perfectly intact, halfway up the Skagway Trail. It helped ease the burros' loads, and freed them to do more pulling. Horses, mules and burros often had short lives on the trail, and Clay and LeSec hoped the sledge might help their animals last.

There was plenty of equipment to be found on the way— broken-down wagons, food tins, heavy tarps—anything a man could imagine had been abandoned by weary prospectors sick of hauling themselves uphill, much less the equipment they'd brought along.

More than once, Clay and LeSec passed discouraged travelers turning back before they even reached the pass through the mountains. Probably a good idea, Clay decided. If a man couldn't handle the forty-five miles up the Skagway Trail and the pass to Lake Bennet, he sure as sin wouldn't survive the harrowing, five-hundred odd miles up the Yukon River to Klondike country. There were more drowned bodies and unmarked graves along the way than a man would care to count.

Clay helped Jordan push the sledge, slipping on the icy gravel. LeSec left him to it and went forward to urge the burros another step up the rocky trail. Behind the pair and ahead, a dark line of men and animals struggled upward toward White Pass. Some, like Clay and LeSec, had one or two burros, while others carried bulky packs on their backs. It was clear simply watching men struggle that many of them had never experienced anything remotely physical in their lives. A clerk in a hardware store thought he might be magically transformed into a seasoned mountain man if he bought the right gear and took off on the trail. He soon found that reading novels about the wilderness was not the same as being there.

Clay and LeSec often passed a team whose animals had

given out—or men whose bodies and hearts weren't up to the challenge.

Thinking about the long haul to Dawson City and the Klondike River, Clay was glad that their own path would take them another way. He and LeSec would follow the well-traveled route past Bennet Lake, to the Taglish River feeder creeks past Whitehorse and Lake Laberge. Just north of that they'd head west. And beyond that—paydirt.

The route itself was not written down, and never had been. It was in Clay Macon's head, passed along from his father before his death. The truth was—and Clay had shared this secret only with LeSec—Randal Macon had *not* come this way in 1886. He and Adam Carlyle had landed at Yakutat Bay on the Gulf of Alaska, some hundred and fifty miles west of where Clay and LeSec stood now—a hundred and fifty miles if you were an eagle. Considerably more for a burro or a man. Randal Macon and Adam had crossed glacier country and the St. Elias Mountains and through the Dawson Range. They had tried their hands at the Stewart River and then the Fortymile, finding very little gold.

Then the two had struck out west toward the tributaries of the Tanana River, followed the tangled waterways, and then turned south.

Why? Clay had asked himself this question a thousand times. *Why did you go that way, Father, away from any of the major gold fields?*

It was a question that had plagued him from the start, one he had tried to put aside. He did not want to test his loyalty to his father. Still, Randal Macon had never been the same after he returned from Alaska. He was sick in mind and body. A man who had never been afraid in his life now woke up screaming out of nightmares of hunger and cold. Sometimes he talked to Adam in his sleep— Adam, who was dead, left on the banks of some unnamed river because it was impossible to dig a grave through the snow and permafrost. There were other names, too—men who had died during that last terrible winter.

Yet Randal Macon swore to his son that he had indeed found gold—gold beyond his dreams. It was there for the taking, a vein like the spine of some long-dead dragon, its golden scales often breaking the surface to glitter in the light.

It was there, his father said, but he didn't have a nugget of it to carry home. Everything he'd owned was gone—everything, including a chamois bag of gold. He had barely made it out of that frozen hell with his life.

And if this great fortune was there, as Randal Macon said, it did not belong to him, for he had never had a chance to file his claim. For now, his great golden dragon belonged to any man who stumbled upon it. This was the fear that preyed upon Randal Macon until the day he died. He had succeeded—and he had failed. He had come upon a treasure that would let him restore his fortune and his pride, and he had nothing to show for it all.

And there was more, something else. Something had happened in the North that Randal Macon would never talk about, not even to his son. Clay had seen that haunted look in his father's eyes, a look that barely hid the pain, sorrow and terrible fear that was eating away his insides.

Again, the thought came to Clay that it would have been far better if his father had died in Alaska and never come home. A second failure in life was enough to break any man, but Randal Macon had endured more than that.

Clay could never forget that moment when his mother, Amelia, had held her husband before he left home. The lightning had struck outside, and Amelia's look had told her son that she would never see his father again.

Her prophecy had been fulfilled, maybe not in the way she had imagined. Or possibly it had. When Randal Clay returned from the North, his wife had been dead and buried two years . . .

A cold afternoon was setting in, and Clay and Jordan decided to ascend White Pass in the morning when they were fresh. They joined a circle of campfires where other men were waiting as well. More than a few of the men holding tin cups of coffee to their hands had already been across the pass and were coming back the other way—some for more supplies, some who'd found the hardships too great to bear.

As usual when prospectors met, there were harrowing stories of death on the infamous Yukon River, tragedy in the rapids above Miles Canyon. And that stretch of water was just the beginning of the trek to the North, thought Clay. A man could lose his life a few days from Skagway Bay, where he began.

There were stories of the stink of the carcasses of dead burros, horses and mules that blocked the narrow mountain pathways ahead. They had been loaded down with too much gear or died of starvation. Some old sourdoughs swore a horse got one look at the trail he'd have to cross and took his own life, jumping into the nearest ravine. Prospectors said a lot of things, and maybe it was true.

After supper, Clay and Jordan made their night camp a little away from the others. The supplies were stacked within reach, and the burros were staked close enough to deter all but the boldest thief.

"It bothers me some," Jordan said, peering up through the thick pines at the cold night stars, "there's so many of 'em, and there can't be gold enough in the earth to satisfy them all."

The same thought had occurred to Clay Macon when he saw the great crowds on the docks at Seattle. "There isn't," he said, "but I doubt there's a man goes up to the Yukon thinks he'll be the one to fail. How could you go through something like this, and imagine you'd walk back home with your pockets turned out?''

Jordan was silent a long moment. "I guess that kind of depends on what you were doin' before you came. Close to hopeless doesn't look bad to some men, when you figure where they've been . . .''

Clay didn't answer. Jordan was talking about the men in camp, many of whom had fled the poverty of America's great depression. In another sense, however, he might have been talking about himself. Jordan came from a fine Louisiana family, but time and reckless spending had eroded the fortunes the LeSecs had gleaned from shipping, cotton and—before Jordan's time—the importation of slaves. Jordan's father was an aristocrat of the old school. His time was past, but he was still alive. He had set himself the task of drinking himself to death and was well on the way to success.

Jordan had inherited his father's weaknesses and strengths: a love for women, cards and good whiskey, and no great affinity for work of any sort. On the other side of the coin, he could not be equaled for his courage, loyalty and unfailing good cheer.

And what about you, Dr. Macon? Where do you come in?

Right along with the rest of them, Clay decided. Family gone, no money, a medical practice he'd let go to seed . . . that, and the most hackneyed and pitiful excuse a man could have for running off and leaving everything behind— a tragic love affair.

Clay had to laugh at himself. Lying on the slope of the Boundary Range below the heights of White Pass, the lost passions of Adele Garnette and Clay Macon seemed less like one of those Dostoyevsky books Jordan was always trying to get him to read, and more like the comical parts of Mr. Twain's *Huckleberry Finn*. Adele had managed to break his heart, but the whole business didn't seem overly important in the shadow of mountains that pierced the night sky.

Before he turned over and drifted into sleep, Clay's thoughts returned to Scully Flatts. The man had never been far from his mind since he and LeSec had left Skagway.

No, he said to himself, *that isn't the way it was. Tell it the way it happened . . .* The truth brought bile rising up in Clay's throat. We *didn't* leave. *That ugly lout drove us out of town.* And that Clay could not abide. He could neither forgive nor forget. There would come a time when he would face the man again. That there *would* be such a time, he had no doubt at all . . .

ELEVEN

EVEN THOUGH HE was bone-tired from the day's trek, sleep eluded Clay most of the night. Many of the prospectors didn't seem to care that they faced a grueling climb the next day. Either that or none of them had good sense. Likely a little of both, Clay decided. There was a great deal of hurrahing and drinking, and once Clay was certain he caught a burst of feminine laughter.

Wouldn't surprise me, he thought. *Commerce and trade follows right on the heels of great adventure.*

Morning was more than welcome. He was glad to shed his blankets and splash cold water in his face. Jordan had coffee on and was doing something awful to the precious eggs they'd paid dearly for in Skagway. A sort of send-off breakfast, LeSec had announced. They wouldn't be seeing any Rhode Island Reds running wild in the frozen north.

Clay Macon made a mental note to take over cooking chores himself. LeSec thought meal preparation meant lifting a menu at a four-star Denver restaurant.

"I'm going to fry you up some toast," Jordan said, passing a scalding cup of coffee across the morning fire. "You want yours dark or light?"

"I'd like it plain uncooked, if it's all the same to you," Clay said.

Jordan shrugged. "Suit yourself. I'll tell you, I slept like a baby last night. I think it's that fine, invigoratin' mountain air."

"I think it's because you don't care where it is you sleep."

"Well now, there's that. You don't want your egg?"

"You take it."

"Something wrong with it?"

"Not a thing. It's a fine-looking egg. I'm just not in an egg frame of mind."

"Shoot," Jordan said. "I fixed it just like you like it, too." He scooped up the mess in the frying pan and scraped it on his tin plate. "No sense lettin' a good egg go to waste." He shook his head at Clay. "We are in the great wilderness now, friend. You've got to start remembering things like this . . ."

Clay paused to train his spyglass on the top of White Pass. The worst of the trip, he knew, awaited them up there. Many a man had lost pack animals and crucial supplies over the edge of the narrow, rocky path near the top. A great many had also lost their lives.

He and LeSec had climbed in silence for several hours, working together, but keeping to themselves. The task took its toll on a man and left him with little energy for talk. The cold near the heights began to bite, a warning of the winter that was never far away in this country. Soon, the almost nonexistent spring would disappear. Next would come a short, insufferable summer, and then the terrible cold. All but a few weeks of the year were miserable seasons here.

"Go on, get movin' there, I don't like this any more than you do!" Jordan kicked out at the slowest and meanest of the two burros. The burro snorted and kicked back. Jordan leaped away, startled. He looked as if he'd been betrayed.

Clay laughed. "What did you expect him to do, blow you a kiss?"

"He ought to know his place," Jordan growled.

"I'd say he does. Give me a hand with this sledge. It's like moving a wagon out of the mud."

The sledge worked fine over easy ground, but was a burden on rocky terrain. And that, Clay noted, was the only terrain they had on White Pass.

Jordan tugged at the lead mule and Clay put his back to the sledge. In spite of the cold, sweat was running down his brow to sting his eyes. The sledge moved a sluggish foot, then stuck again. LeSec pulled and cursed the burros, and Clay pushed. His boot slipped on the slick gravel and the sledge slid back an inch.

"I could use a little help," Clay yelled. "You think you could talk that animal into doin' a day's work up there?"

"You're the one's got a way with the critters," Jordan said, "not me."

Clay had an answer for that, but held his tongue. He bent to his work while Jordan tried to frighten the burros, and finally the sledge moved off center and onto better ground.

Clay sank back against the cold granite wall and wiped his face. "I'd like to have the crook who wrote that pamphlet about 'the wonders of the North' up here. I'd throttle the rogue within an inch of his life!"

"I read that pamphlet," Jordan said. "I'd hook him up to the burros and feed him grass."

"There isn't any grass."

"Then he'd have to do without. Far as I'm concerned, he deserves to do without."

It was no great revelation that most of the men who had grand ideas about the Yukon had never been north of San Francisco. Or possibly Dallas or Birmingham. Clay vividly recalled the man on the docks at Seattle who had tried to sell him a genuine Klondike Ice Bicycle—a contraption with skis attached to the wheel rims "For Easy Traction & Speed." Clay had been raised in the bayou country and was certain this machine would be about as useful in the Klondike as it would be in traversing the Louisiana swamps.

Near the top of the pass, they began to pass the slower groups of prospectors. Most of the men had paired off by now. It was one of the truths among the mass of fiction about the North: A one-man outfit was no good. It was insanity to scratch at the Klondike ground by yourself. Even the worst greenhorn could see you needed someone to count on in this desolate land. Going it alone was next to suicide.

Of course, that didn't hold true if a pair of miners struck it rich and one partner decided it might be best *not* to divide the find by two. It had happened more than once, Clay knew. He thought about the crazed Frenchman who'd murdered his friend as they pulled into Skagway Bay. That partnership hadn't lasted long enough to get ashore and hunt for gold.

"Look out there, watch yourself!" Jordan shouted at a pair of broad-shouldered Scandinavians in too big a hurry to reach the top. They squeezed past Clay and then the burros, forcing LeSec precariously close to the edge. One of the two muttered an apology and lumbered on.

"I could do without that." Jordan scowled at the retreating backs as they disappeared around a switchback ahead. "There ought to be some kind of rule. You can't be bigger than a certain size or you don't go up the pass. Then again . . ." LeSec considered his thoughts and closed one eye. "The fellows who *enforce* this rule would have to be bigger than those two louts, right? There might be a problem there."

"I think you need a little more time on this," Clay said.

"I do now, for a fact."

The way kept narrowing ahead. Every time Clay placed one foot before the other, he loosed a few stones on the path. It was nerve-wracking to listen to the shower of rocks down the sheer slopes of the pass. He tried not to watch them disappear into the granite valley below. Still, it was hard not to think about what would happen if you plunged down into that abyss. Death held a dark fascination for a man—especially when it was a few scant inches away.

The snowcapped peaks of the Boundary Range were awesome. He imagined this great spine of the North stretching down to the American Rockies, and even beyond, to the high Andean range of the southern continent.

His father and mother had taken him on a trip to the West when he was a boy, and Clay had marveled at the sights he'd seen. Back in New Orleans, he had run at once to Adele Garnette, a heartbreaker even then, a fiery little imp with black pigtails, tilted dark eyes and an enchanting mouth always on the verge of laughter. He had spilled out the details of his trip in a burst of excitement, regaling her with tales of Indians and buffalo, Pike's Peak and Denver, the legendary Rio Grande, the Pecos, Santa Fe and the wilds of New Mexico Territory.

"And what did you do while I was away?" the young Clay Macon had asked, and Adele had held him with those mischievous eyes and said, "Well, I didn't think of *you* all the time, if that's what you mean." Then, seeing the sudden misery in his features, she blushed and looked away and added, "I did *some*, though. I thought about you some, Clay Macon."

And, as ever, as it had always been, and would continue to be in later years, one shy look, one affectionate word, was all it took to please him, to turn his world from despair into joy, to bring Clay Macon happiness and—

The edge of the path gave way as a runner of the sledge tilted over empty space. Clay reached out desperately to bring it back, and knew in an instant that he'd leaned too far, that the sledge was going over and he was going with it.

He bellowed Jordan's name and clawed for a hold. His gloved hand slid along the cold granite—two fingers found a small crevice and Clay held on with all the strength he could bring to bear. The loaded sledge came after him. An iron runner smashed painfully near his hand, almost breaking his tenuous grip. He cried out again, caught a glimpse of LeSec's pale and startled face, one hand stretched out but too far away, much too far away.

He felt his hands slip. His hold gave way and his chest slid down the ragged granite face. When his legs ran out of rock and kicked freely in the air, he nearly threw up right there.

Time seemed to slow, the seconds dragging by, and he was very much aware of every precious inch of rock that passed before his eyes. He could almost feel the razor-sharp boulders waiting down below. The stone bit into his flesh and he slapped out blindly for the slightest indentation, for anything at all. The fingers of his left hand dug into a crack and held. An instant later, his whole body swung from the sheer rock wall beneath the dizzy heights of White Pass.

Clay's throat choked with granite dust. He cursed himself for a fool—dreaming, instead of concentrating all of his senses on the pathway ahead. Now he was paying the price, hanging by one hand over the abyss of eternity, with a feeble grip on life. He guessed he might last a good ten seconds before the tendons in his hand gave way.

"Clay? *Clay!*"

Clay looked up as the dark coil whipped past his face, slapped at his shoulder and dangled at his side. He reached out with his free hand, pawing at the rope and missing, his clumsy effort pushing it farther away.

A ragged cry escaped his lungs and he grabbed at the

rope with the tips of his fingers, feeling his left hand tremble as his grip gave way.

He hung free, swinging dizzily in the cold mountain air, forcing the numbed fingers of his left hand to close, to add whatever strength was left to the line.

"Hold on," Jordan called out, "I've got you, Clay, I'll get you up, I swear I will!"

We'll see if you do, Clay said to himself. He glanced up the rock face and saw LeSec's boot jammed against the stone ledge. His mouth was stretched across his teeth, and the tendons in his neck stood out like cords of wire. Then suddenly there were other faces there—two, then three, and others looking on, some loosing ropes of their own, shouting out advice, urging Clay to hang on.

He felt himself moving now, inching up the cliff, saw the bearded features of strangers he'd never forget. Strong hands stretched out to grip his arms and shoulders, and then men were cheering, slapping him roughly on the back, drawing bottles and flasks from beneath their heavy coats.

Clay took the first drink anyone offered, gripping the bottle with a shaky hand. Someone steadied him and Clay took a healthy swig. Whatever it was, it surged through his veins, flowed through his body like molten fire.

A grizzled miner caught his look, drew the bottle away and gave him a toothless grin. "That's the thing fer you, boy. If it don't kill you right off, it'll bring a dead man back to life!"

"I believe it," Clay said. "I'm grateful for the help."

"Don't mention it at all," the man said, "I might have a drop myself, just to sorta celebrate."

Clay knew the man was talking, but his words fell on deaf ears. Clay was looking past the miner's shoulder, staring at a face with a pug nose, freckles and a mop of red hair. For a moment he couldn't speak, unable to believe his eyes.

"*Patsy!*" he blurted out finally. "Wh-what in *blazes* are you doing here!"

"Huh!" The young thief raised his chin in defiance. "Now, that's a fine way to greet an old friend, Doctor. 'Specially since I'm going out of my way to save yourself from Scully Flatts . . .''

TWELVE

"GET THAT—GET that *felon* out of my sight! Get him away from here!"

Clay staggered to his feet, then sat down flat as his legs gave way. Showing a weakness in front of the others angered him further still. He grabbed the granite wall and forced himself erect.

"Take it easy, Clay," Jordan said. "You've had a bad time."

"You're right about that," Clay muttered. He glared at the redheaded boy, and Patsy backed off.

"That's all I need," Clay said. "Saved from the jaws of death and the first thing I see is *you*. And with a brand new lie on your tongue at that."

Patsy's eyes went wide. "I tol' you the Lord's truth, I did. On my mother's heart, sir!"

"Huh! Does your mother know you filch wallets for a living? I'll bet that'd do her heart good."

Most of the miners who'd gathered around drifted off. Those who were left nudged one another and laughed. Any interesting event—accident, fistfight, convulsion, drunken fit—was something to watch. Better than trudging up the mountain with a load on your back.

"You boys want a little amusement," Jordan said, "I'd

appreciate some help haulin' this sledge back up before my four-footed friend gets tired of waiting.

The mule was obviously weary of taking the strain of the sledge rope and let LeSec know it. Three of the miners edged up the narrow pathway past Clay and went to Jordan's aid.

Clay tried to avoid Patsy, but there was no place else to look.

"I don't know what you followed us up here for, but I want you to know I'm not swallowing that yarn of yours for one minute."

"It's the solemn truth," Patsy said. "Just because I used to be of the criminal persuasion doesn't make me a liar, too."

"*Used* to be?" Clay raised a curious brow. "And when did this miraculous change occur?"

"Why, when I met you, Doctor, sir. There on the street when you caught me at my shady craft. Right then I says to myself—"

"Stop it, boy, before lightning strikes you." Clay shook his head, amazed that this young thief could come up with such nonsense with a straight face.

"You ought to know it's a bad idea to lie when you're standin' in a high place, exposed like you are to the sight of God, and me standin' close enough to go with you, at that. Now, suppose you tell me the *truth* about what brought you here? It's got to come out, you know. You're fairly skilled at the falsehood game, but I think you've stretched it as far as it'll go."

Patsy looked down at his hands and rubbed them on his trouser legs. *Why can't the lad get clothes that aren't four sizes too big for his frame?* Clay wanted to know. *He always looks like he's walkin' in a sack.*

"It were nearly true, what I said," Patsy told him, still not meeting his eyes.

"Nearly true. How near would that be?"

"Scully . . . Scully Flatts told me to follow you and put a sad story on you. Say I'd been beat and the like, and would you be savin' me from the man. I told him I'd do no such thing."

"You did."

"Yes, sir, I did. You can believe that or not, it's the truth is what it is."

Patsy stuck out his chin, and Clay got ready. He had learned by now that Patsy did this right before another tall tale.

"I looked him in his dirty eyes, I did, an' said, 'No, sir, Mr. Flatts, I won't be the low-down sneak for you, sir. You've got no right to harass honest gentlemen that haven't done nothing at all to you but beat you senseless in a right fair fight!' "

"You told him that."

"I surely did, sir."

"And what did he say?"

"He said he'd flail me within an inch of my miserable life if I didn't follow you and the honorable Mr. LeSec. So I said in that case I surely would."

Clay was watching the boy closely, and he decided this was at least a part of the truth. Possibly as close as Patsy could get, considering he had no schooling in the honest and straightforward arts.

"Why did he want to do that, Patsy? What possible reason could he have for keeping track of us? What you're telling me doesn't make sense, boy. If Scully Flatts had cared to do us further harm, he surely could have done so anytime."

"He said he wanted to know where you *were,* is all. See, he had these men from Chicago comin' in—"

"Unh-uh, no." Clay drew a bandanna from his pocket and wiped the rock dust from his face. LeSec and his helpers had the sledge back on the path, and Jordan was patting the overworked burro on the back, as if the two were old friends. "No, I'm sure that's what he told you, and Mr. Fullerton Ash as well, and this is what Ash told Jordan and myself. But that was a flimsy story from the start, you ask me. All that fancy food and *helpin'* us out of town as nice as you please? That is *not* Mr. Scully Flatts."

"I don't know that, sir. Truly I don't." Again, Patsy's manner and voice were nearly convincing, but that innocent, boyish expression had fooled Clay before.

"Maybe you don't then," Clay said. "And I have to say I don't have the answer myself." He looked Patsy straight in the eye, certain he had his full attention. "But I will, you understand that? *I most certainly will . . .*"

From the top of White Pass, the way was downhill—a relief to the climbers in one respect, but in another just as treacherous as going up the other side. Everyone was anxious to get off the heights, and haste spelled disaster for any fool who thought his task was done. Clay heard that at least two men had been lost that day in sight of their goal.

The sprawling campsite at the foot of the pass was nearly a small town in itself. Here, prospectors readied themselves for the trek to Lake Bennet and beyond. For miles about, the forest echoed with the sounds of axe and saw, as men turned green timber into rough planking, and put together crude rafts and boats for the assault on the Yukon River. Many of them, Clay knew, would disappear in the rapids, or simply sink and drown in a relatively calm stretch of the river when their poorly built crafts fell apart.

As they settled in for the night, Clay was aware of the presence of a number of men from the Canadian Northwest Mounted Police. None of the prospectors seemed to care, but the so-called "Alaska Gold Rush" was taking place well away from Alaska itself. Since they'd come down from White Pass, Clay, Jordan and Patsy had been in British Columbia. And before they gained another ten miles or so, they would be in the Canadian Yukon.

Patsy thought the Canadians looked splendid in their uniforms, sitting tall in the saddle on sprited mounts. Clay had to wonder why Patsy would want to have anything to do with an authentic lawman, but the boy was clearly impressed.

Everyone in camp knew why the police were there. Because of the big starvation scare the winter before, they were doing all they could to see that it didn't happen again. The terrible cold of the 1897–98 season had forced the Canadians to put strict regulations on the prospectors. In March, just three months before the *Queen* had pulled into Skagway Bay, the authorities had declared that each man must take a thousand pounds of supplies with him into the Yukon. This meant *ten to twenty trips* over the pass, and most of the Americans broke the rule when they could.

''In Skagway, they said a lot of miners have tried to cross the Valdez Glacier to the Copper River,'' LeSec told Clay. ''And not many of 'em made it.''

Clay shook his head, thinking of the thousands of men dying in the cold, thinking of his father, who had come to the Yukon over another glacier, from Yakutat Bay, to the south of the Valdez. That any man had come through the forbidding ice fields alive was a miracle in itself.

Clay made no objection to Patsy sharing their camp. Better to have the boy in sight than wonder where he was and what he might be up to. Patsy inherited the jobs of gathering wood, cooking, burying garbage and scrubbing the pots and pans and eating utensils after supper.

Now that he knew Scully Flatts had not lost interest in their whereabouts, Clay made certain their weapons were in good condition and at the ready. As usual, LeSec carried his heavy Colt, a gun that had been in the family since the

War Between the States. It was an 1857 model, and one of Jordan's uncles had carried it during Pickett's charge at Gettysburg. The weapon had since been retooled, trimmed and fitted for rimfire use.

Clay also loaned Jordan his own Winchester .44 repeater, because he didn't think a man should be foolish enough to count on a pistol to save his life—no matter how good a shot he might be. Clay kept the small scattergun, which was handy for bringing down birds and small game. For his personal weapon, he kept his all-time favorite, the Sharps .50-caliber Professional Sportsman's model. It was an awesome gun, one only a big-bodied man could handle. It threw a slug big enough to fell small trees, and a man could sit and fire it all day out of range of anyone else.

"You figure we're going to be havin' us a war of some kind?" Jordan asked. He watched his friend sight down the long barrel of the Big Fifty, wetting his finger to remove a spot of dust.

"I figure I want to be ready if we do," Clay said. He glanced at Patsy across the fire, half-asleep and well out of hearing. "I don't know what to think of *him,* Jordan. And I sure don't know what to make of Scully Flatts."

Clay scowled into the embers. "Devil take the man!" He slapped the heavy stock of his weapon. "If he'd wanted to take our scalps, why didn't he simply do it? What'd he want to follow us around for? He doesn't know where we're going . . ." Clay tapped the side of his head. "Only you and I know that; it can't have anything to do with gold. If we had a *claim,* now . . ." He let out a breath.

"I have no brilliant ideas or advice except to keep our eyes open. And especially around *him.*" Jordan grinned. "I think you like the boy, Clay. That's how it looks to me."

"You *what*?" Clay frowned at his friend. "Why, I can't stand the sight of him. What in blazes made you say that!"

Jordan lay back on his blanket and folded his hands behind his neck. "I've never seen you give anybody fits unless you had a likin' for them, Clay. Shoot, I guess I ought to know."

"You ought to know *better*. In the first place, I put *up* with you, 'cause I'm used to it. That's a sight different than liking. And in the second place—"

"What? What's the second place?"

"I don't remember what it is," Clay said. "You got me all confused talkin' nonsense. You're always doing that, LeSec."

"Get some sleep," Jordan said, turning over in his blanket.

"That's not real likely," Clay said. "I doubt I'll close my eyes with that . . . that miscreant over there, resting up to steal us blind in the night . . ."

In spite of a dozen sore spots from his fall the day before, Clay Macon felt refreshed and good as new. He had slept all night without waking up once. From the look of things, Patsy hadn't walked away with their supplies. Both the boy and Jordan were buried under their blankets asleep.

The air was chill as he walked down through the trees to the creek. The smell of woodsmoke and coffee mingled with the heady scent of pine needles and the breeze off the Boundary Range. Clay felt his face and wondered if he should have brought his razor along to the creek. A cold shave wasn't the best way to start the long day, but he wasn't sure he had the patience for hanging around the camp. It didn't feel right, with so many people around. Safety in numbers might be true in some cases, but Clay was certain he'd feel more at ease when they were out on the trail with a little space around them.

A man shouted somewhere to Clay's right. He paused and looked out across the smoky woods. An early morning drunk was stumbling through the camp, rousing men out of sleep and bringing curses down on his head. Someone threw a skillet at the intruder, and another man kicked out with his boot.

Real good way to get shot, Clay thought, and turned back toward the creek. It didn't seem like the smart thing to do, messing around in a camp like this one. Every man there was dog-tired, and there was scarcely a one of them who didn't have one or two firearms under his blankets, and a skinning knife besides.

The water felt good. He gasped as it stung his face and ran down the collar of his shirt. It was just past the middle of May, but the night had chilled the water enough to make your fingers numb. He peered through the clear running water at the river-worn stones, the thin strands of moss trailing in the current. The creek where he'd fished as a boy looked just like this one, so many miles from the South. The water there would be cold this time of day, but nothing so cold as this.

There were likely fish upstream, where the water ran deep. Trout, or salmon, maybe. He'd have to ask someone. It would be a thrill to find a deep blue pond and drop a dry fly near the bank where an old tree trunk cast a shadow on the water . . .

Clay glanced up, his pleasant thought broken by a sound that didn't belong to the whisper of wind in the trees, the chatter of the stream. It sounded as if some animal were stomping through the brush, snapping small branches off the trees. A big animal at that, Clay decided, something like a—

The crack of a weapon sang through the trees and Clay instinctively ducked as lead whined above his head. A man screamed—a high-pitched cry of pain. Clay caught a blur of motion through the trees and his blood went cold as the creature burst out of the woods, splashing through the creek and coming right at him. Spittle flecked his mouth and his eyes were bright as fire. A .45 Colt blazed away in each hand and the bullets were kicking up mud and spraying Clay with gravel, thunking into trees behind his head.

Clay went flat, rolled and snaked one hand to his belt. His throat clamped tight and he knew he hadn't brought Jordan's pistol or a knife or anything else, and he felt like a fool forgetting the advice he'd drummed into LeSec. The man was right on him then, screaming hoarse babble that didn't mean a thing, and Clay knew he'd have to throw himself at the man's strong legs, and he knew it was too late for that, it was over and he didn't have a chance in hell . . .

The shots came in a rapid staccato, one on top of the rest. The man jerked back as if half a dozen hammers had struck him in the chest. He went down on his back, bobbed there a moment, then turned like a leaf and floated downstream.

Clay was scarcely aware of the Canadian lawman sliding off his horse and stepping quickly into the stream. He dropped his revolver in the holster at his belt, stopped the body with his foot and looked at Clay.

"You all right, mister? You hit or anything?"

"No, no, I'm fine," Clay said, "I'm just fine."

"Don't look it," the Canadian said and grinned. "You know this feller? Man was sure intent on having your hide."

"No, I don't know him. Never saw him before in my life."

"You sure?"

"Absolutely sure," Clay said.

Clay Macon had recognized the man the instant he exploded through the trees. They had met on the streets of Skagway when the old man had stared at him with ungodly fear and told him he was the devil himself come back to life. Clay knew he would never forget the expression on his face. He was dead now, and his blood was staining the creek, but the look of cold, unreasoning terror was still there . . .

THIRTEEN

EVERYONE GOT THERE at once.

A moment before there had been only Clay, the Canadian lawman and a corpse. Now the whole camp was crowded along the bank, pushing and shoving to get a better look at a dead man floating in the creek. A few of the prospectors were fully dressed. Most of them stomped around with blankets about their shoulders, or shivered in extra-heavy underwear from Sears.

"How many shots did it take?"

"Was he armed or you git him in the back?"

The Canadian calmly told everyone to go about his business, there was nothing more to see. No one paid him any mind until three more mounted policemen arrived and began moving their horses through the crowd. Most of the miners were Americans, and they didn't care for that. Just because they might be standing on Canadian soil didn't mean a bunch of fancy-dressed foreigners could tell them what to do.

Clay Macon watched as the lawman who'd done the shooting grabbed the dead man by the collar and dragged him up on the shore.

"You never seen him before. You're sure about that."

"I'm sure," Clay said. "If I did, I don't recall."

"Why you figure he was trying to gun you down?"

"I don't know. Why do you think he was running through the camp like a maniac waking everybody up? He acted drunk to me. You smell his breath?"

The Canadian looked at Clay as if he'd lost his mind. "Now, why in blazes would I want to smell a dead man's breath?"

Clay shrugged. "Might help tell you what kind of condition he was in."

"He was in a shootin' condition," the lawman said. "That's close enough for me."

Clay started to speak; he caught LeSec making his way through the crowd, Patsy at his heels. Jordan's face mirrored Clay's alarm. He saw Clay standing upright and decided that was a fairly good sign.

"Clay, you all right? What's going—"

The lawman took a step toward LeSec. Clay nodded, and the man stepped back and let Jordan through.

Jordan saw the body and blinked. "Well I'll be—who's that?"

"I don't know," Clay said. "I never saw him before."

"He try to kill you? Why'd he do that?"

"I don't know why. I don't have any idea."

"You mean he just did?"

"Yes, Jordan, he just did. All right?"

Clay tried to hide his irritation. He wanted his partner to know he did *not* care to pursue this at all. That the Northwest Mounted Policeman was watching all this like a hawk, that *he* wanted some answers, too.

"Oh, well then . . ." LeSec finally seemed to catch on. "Must've been mentally disturbed. Something like that."

"I think he was drunk," Clay said.

"Yes. That too."

"How about you?" The lawman looked at Patsy. "You know who this fellow was? You ever see him anywhere?"

Patsy shook his head. He stood well away from the bank, backed up against a tree as if the corpse might bite.

"N-no, sir, I never did. I never seen him, I swear."

Clay thought Patsy had turned a little white. He had an idea the boy had never seen anyone quite as dead before.

"Uh-huh." The lawman took a notebook and the stub of a pencil from his pocket and gave everyone a sour look. "I'll bet if I talked to every blessed man in this camp, there's not a one of 'em ever seen this old codger before. It's an unwritten law. Someone gets to be dead they don't come from anywhere, they don't have a name, they never had any friends. All right, least you can tell me who *you* folks are. I expect I'll have to settle for that."

Clay stopped on the trail and squinted into the mid-morning sun. The trees gave way to a broad, open meadow around the bend. Plants that looked a lot like the daisies back home turned the field into a sea of yellow gold. Jordan and the boy were just coming out of the woods, thirty yards behind. Clay looked at Patsy and tried to hold a good thought. The boy's sourdough biscuits felt like rocks in his belly. They were churning around down there with the slightly burned coffee, and Clay wasn't sure he wanted to keep it all down or go ahead and bring it up.

He had kept to himself after breakfast, and his companions had had the good sense to leave him completely alone. The thing that had happened back there kept working at his head and wouldn't let go. A crazy old coot in Skagway was one thing—that same man tailing you over White Pass to gun you down was something else. Not that a man who'd lost his wits was *supposed* to make sense. Still, it didn't feel right, and he couldn't get it out of his thoughts.

Watching the land ahead, he mapped out the path in his mind, seeing himself where he'd be when the sun was overhead. You didn't have to be a Daniel Boone to get to Lake

Bennet from the pass. The trail was worn smooth as paving stones from the countless men who'd already come this way. There were always men ahead of you, and on the path behind.

Fine enough, Clay thought, if there wasn't Scully Flatts to worry about. How much of what Patsy had told them was the truth? There wasn't any way to know, but it would be plain foolish to imagine that *whatever* Flatts had told the boy, there was plenty he didn't say. Maybe Patsy was just a chigger sent to get under Clay Macon's skin. *Maybe I'll be scratching,* Clay thought, *and I won't see the scorpion Scully drops down my neck . . .*

Getting off the trail might be a good idea, he decided. They'd have to sooner or later anyway. Why make it easy for Flatt's men to pick him off?

Reason said that didn't make sense. Scully Flatts didn't *want* to kill them, he wanted something else. Clay couldn't say what the overweight tyrant was after, but running off into the wilderness wouldn't help.

And when we do leave the trail, maybe I'll just hang around and play fox for a while, see if I can catch me some hounds . . .

The thought brought a smile to his face. When it came to fighting back or standing still, Clay Macon never had to think about it twice.

The afternoon was warmer and brighter than Clay had expected. Even in the North, May offered fair skies and sunlight bright enough to spread shafts of yellow through the trees.

The land leading up to the Yukon seemed like a place newly made. Between the Boundary Range and the next far ridge of ragged peaks there were broad stretches of grassland peppered with patches of color—wheat-brown, daisy-white and the melted gold of Scottish broom. Now and then, a creek shimmered across the plains. Clay saw a herd of caribou at a grassy curve of the stream. They scattered quickly when men approached, then wandered back to feed on tender shoots.

He didn't consider the docile creatures fair game, though it was clear from the rotting, half-wasted carcasses on the trail that many of the prospectors felt the Canadians had placed the animals here for their convenience.

Late in the afternoon, Clay announced that they would camp a quarter mile or so off the main trail. He had walked through the area and found a sheltering outcropping of granite and a branch of the creek nearby.

"Game shouldn't be hard to find, that far from the trail," he said. "Worst we can do, I figure, is a couple of squirrels for a stew."

"Fine," Jordan said, "I'd just as soon leave that to you. It isn't that I'm not a dead shot, you understand, but you're much better at targets that move around."

Once they reached the site, LeSec hobbled the mule, while Patsy struggled with a canvas sack of stores. Clay watched as the boy made a neat stack of supplies, and he didn't have the heart to say that was the very spot he'd saved for the fire.

"You watch yourself out there," Jordan said. "Take a care."

"I don't expect I'll get attacked by a squirrel," Clay told him. "If I do, I'll fire off a round."

"Not what I mean and you know it, partner."

"I know what you mean." He clapped Jordan on the shoulder. "And I *will* take a care."

"Patsy and I'll make you a lovely home, while you track down the evening meal."

"Patsy's coming with me," Clay said. "It'll do the boy good."

Patsy was close enough to hear. "Who, me, Dr. Macon? You surely don't mean me."

Clay grinned at the boy's expression of alarm. "It's you I mean indeed, Patsy. Let's get moving. I don't hunt in the dark."

Clay picked up his scattergun and an old game bag and started off.

"I don't know a thing about hunting, sir. I swear I don't," Patsy said.

"Grab a couple of canteens," Clay said without turning around. "I have a feeling you'll learn real fast."

Patsy gave Jordan a pleading look, then stumbled along behind, still protesting under his breath.

"And try to hold it down," Clay said. "You can near talk a person to death, I've seen you do it a dozen times. But it doesn't work with game, boy. They like their peace and quiet."

Patsy didn't answer. He walked behind Clay, staying well back. Clay guessed the reason for that. If anything happened—if lightning struck a tree or a tremor shook the earth—Patsy didn't intend to take the blame.

Have I been that hard on the boy? he wondered. He decided he probably had, but he could see no way he could have done anything else, considering Patsy's behavior. Saints alive, the boy had come right out and admitted he was supposed to be spying for Scully Flatts—and had the gall to swear he wasn't doing that at all!

Clay stopped and listened to the sounds of the forest. He walked a few steps to a spot where the ground was soft and moist, squatted down and rubbed his boots with mulch, then smeared the dirt on his face as well.

"Get some of the forest on yourself," he said quietly. "Game'll pick up on anything that doesn't smell like it belongs."

Patsy made a face. "You want me to . . . rub this stuff on me? That's what you're saying, sir?"

"That's right." Clay sniffed the air and shook his head. "I don't even know if it'll do any good as far as you're concerned. You mind me asking, you ever thought about applying a little soap and a stiff brush to yourself?"

Patsy colored under his coating of mud. "I stay as . . . as clean as I can *afford* to, Dr. Macon. Poor folks can't go fritterin' their hard-earned pennies on fancy French bubbles and the like!"

"I was thinking more in the line of lye soap," Clay told him. "And don't try handin' me any nonsense how the poor are dirty and the rich are clean. I'm a doctor, you'll recall, and I've seen them both ways."

"Yeah, right . . ." Patsy looked down and dug at the ground with his heel. "You'd know all about bein' hungry and down on your luck. I bet you haven't missed a lot of meals in your day."

"And you have."

Patsy rolled his eyes. "More'n I'd care to tell you, least I break your heart, sir."

Clay laughed. "I think you're a fraud, Patsy, that's what I think."

"What?" Patsy stared at Clay. "How could you say that, sir? How can you even think such a thing?"

The boy looked almost numb with disbelief. He was so good at his craft, Clay was almost taken in.

"Maybe fraud's too mild a word. Maybe *rascal* or *rogue* would suit you better. I might add deceit and fakery to that, to say nothing of—"

Patsy's eyes flashed and he swung his fist at Clay. The boy was unskilled at the game, and Clay had plenty of time. Besides, he'd been soundly kicked in the shins at their first meeting, and didn't intend to be caught asleep again.

Grabbing Patsy's small fist in his open palm, he turned

on one heel and let the boy's motion take him to the ground. Patsy went sprawling, rolled head over heels down the slope of the forest and came up hard against the trunk of a yellow pine.

Clay ran down the hill and stopped. "Just *stay* there," he said, stabbing a finger at the air. "It's easier to talk with you sitting on the ground."

Patsy glared and rubbed his knee. "You want to b-beat me, go ahead. I can't stop you, you're a lot bigger'n I am!"

"I didn't say anything about beating you, boy."

"Yeah? Well, what you call this?"

"I'd say you took a fool swing at someone and fell down a hill. You want to hit people *bigger* than you, you'd better get a big stick."

Clay took a breath. "Now. You and me are going to talk. Mostly it's going to be you."

"I got nothing to say to you!" Patsy yelled.

"I think you do. I think you have a lot to say, Patsy, and this time I'd like to hear it without any Irish fairy tales or lies. I don't care if you sit there clear into next week, *you are going to talk to me!*"

"Fine," Patsy said, "what do you want to talk about, Dr. *Macon,* or whatever your name is. Why don't we talk about your *father,* how'd you like that? I bet you'd *love* to talk about *him!*"

"What?" Clay shook his head in disbelief. "What are you *talking* about? You didn't know my father, you don't know anything about him. You don't know *any*thing about my family!"

"Hell I don't! I guess I know *a lot!*" A tic at the corner of Patsy's mouth was out of control and he was shaking all over. "Isn't anybody north of Juneau don't know all about Black Jack Foster. There's widows an' orphans a'plenty cryin' out that butcher's name!"

FOURTEEN

CLAY MACON FELT the sudden surge of anger, the terrible burst of pain inside his head. He fought against the blind, unreasoning rage that threatened to overwhelm him. It had seldom been this bad before—not since that time in the Halyard on the docks of Mobile, when the sailor from Maine had made unmanly remarks about the men of the South.

He was disappointed in himself, but he was furious at the boy. Patsy had clearly been so angry he had simply spewed out whatever nonsense came into his head. Very much like a child would do—though Patsy was clearly no child anymore. Even with his slight frame and boyish features, he had to be twenty, twenty-one. Old enough to act like a man, Clay told himself. Old enough to have more sense than to spout off foolishness about a man's family. No man should do that, unless he was ready for a fight. And Patsy needed a lot more muscle and bone for that.

Patsy was nowhere in sight. Sometime in the seconds Clay had let his temper flare, the boy had disappeared. Fine. If the little liar couldn't find his way back to camp, he could get himself lost. Likely do him good. The shadows were stretching along the forest floor, and he'd learn a little woodcraft fast enough if he didn't want to sleep outdoors by himself.

A tree had fallen over the narrow ravine years before, and now thick vines choked the trunk and draped a tangled veil of green to the ground. It was a distinctive landmark, and Clay started up the hill where a granite outcropping formed a natural set of stairs.

"Clay . . ."

Clay froze in his tracks. Without moving his head, he let his gaze dart across the darkening woods. A face took shape among the drapery of vines beneath the tree. Clay nodded, and LeSec stepped out into the half-light. He was carrying his revolver in his belt, and he was listening to the wind sweep down the hill.

"Riders," LeSec said softly. "Two of them, maybe three. They edged around the camp, never getting real close."

Clay studied his partner. "Could've been anyone, don't you think? We're not that far off the trail. There's bound to be other campers close by."

Jordan shook his head. "This was something else."

"All right."

"They didn't think about coming in and showing themselves. They just wanted to know we were snugged in for the night."

"That's a comfort," Clay said.

LeSec raised a curious brow. "Where's the boy?"

"I don't know where he is."

"You don't know?"

"I think that's what I said, Jordan. I believe I said I didn't know."

Jordan caught the edge in Clay's voice. "I don't think that's a good idea, him out there by himself. Especially with snoopers poking about. Patsy doesn't look a lot like Bill Cody to me.''

"He's just put out with me. I expect he'll be all right."

"That what you think?"

"No."

"Neither do I," Jordan said.

Clay let out a breath. He cocked his head and tried to listen to whatever there was to hear. "You start off west," he told LeSec. "I'm running back to camp to get somethin' besides this scattergun. Whoever's out there's likely bigger than a quail."

"I'm way ahead of you, partner." LeSec stepped back into the hanging vines and brought out Clay's Big Fifty. "I know you don't like to be without your artillery piece. Never can tell when you'll run into a Yankee cavalry charge."

"It does the job proper," Clay said. He ran his hand along the cold steel barrel. "I could stop a bull elephant with this weapon. Stop him right in his tracks."

LeSec made a noise in his throat. He'd heard all this before, and saw no reason to mention the odds of running into such an animal in the Yukon, any more than they had in Louisiana or Texas or Colorado.

Clay didn't like to admit it, but he was more than a little concerned about the boy. A good half hour of circling through the forest slopes had turned up nothing at all. Not even a track besides their own. On the edge of his circle, Clay had found the hoofprints of horses, and that bothered him even more. If Patsy stumbled into the riders that were dogging their trail . . .

He caught himself then and shook his head in irritation. Well, what if such a thing happened? Maybe Patsy was still lying, and really was working for Scully Flatts. Maybe that was the whole idea of the riders—they tail along, and Patsy sneaks off now and then to report whatever it is he knows.

Clay muttered to himself and started back down the draw, through the thick stand of pine toward the fallen tree where he and LeSec had agreed to meet. Maybe Jordan had found a footprint, something. If he hadn't, they'd have to quarter the area in a wider circle still.

Pushing the brush aside, he stepped into the clearing and stared. LeSec was sitting on a stone, smoking the stump of a cigar. Patsy was cross-legged on the ground, hands folded in his lap. He looked miserable and tired, and a little bit scared. That gave Clay some satisfaction, now that he knew the boy was safe.

"Where was he?" Clay asked LeSec. "I'd surely like to know."

Patsy looked up and saw Clay, and quickly looked away.

"Right where neither of us figured on looking," Jordan said. "It finally crossed my mind that he couldn't be anywhere else. He was up a tree not ten feet from where you left him. That's why we couldn't find him—he didn't *go* anywhere."

Clay felt the heat rise to his face. "Huh! Likely too ignorant to do anything else."

Without looking at the boy, he turned and stomped off up the hill. That had to be it, he decided. Plain dumb luck. Only an Indian—or a trail-wise woodsman like himself— would think to pull a stunt like that. Just perched in a tree like a bird, and worrying the daylights out of him and LeSec, wondering if he was hurt out there or maybe—

Clay shook off the thought. He was disgusted with himself for giving the little thief more worry than he deserved. The boy was a pure aggravation, Clay thought, nothing more than that. And that's what happened when you let someone get under your skin, started caring what happened to them. Pretty soon you were wasting your time on that,

when you should be figuring how to keep *yourself* alive.
The way things stood, there was plenty of need for that . . .

He didn't even try to approach the boy. He couldn't see
any use in that. And Patsy made no effort to come to him.
LeSec said that showed the boy clearly had some sense—
anyone who'd seen Clay Macon lose his temper likely
didn't care to see him do it again.

Jordan was outside of camp, taking a look around. Clay
heated the last cup of coffee in the pot. From the corner of
his eye, he saw Patsy get up. The boy took his time coming
over to the fire. He stood there a minute, then sat.

"I'm sorry I said what I did. I had no right to speak to
you in such a manner, sir. It just . . . seemed to come out."

"Uh-huh." Clay could hear the relief in the boy's voice.
He knew it hadn't been easy to get that out.

"I'd say we've both been under a considerable amount
of stress," Clay said. He looked at Patsy for the first time.
"I have to say this, boy, I cannot think of anything you
could have come up with would've riled me any more."

"Yes, sir. I guess that's so."

Clay poked a stick in the fire. "What in tarnation made
you *say* a thing like that, Patsy? Why something about my
father, a man you never even—"

Clay stopped and peered at the boy, sensing something,
seeing something he hadn't seen before.

"You didn't make that up, did you, Patsy? I thought you
did but I see that's not so. Someone *told* you to say that.
To say that to me. I'm guessing that'd be Scully Flatts."

"No, sir. No, sir, it wasn't, either." Patsy shook his
head, the curls of his Irish red hair catching the light of the
fire.

"You're partial right, Dr. Macon, but it wasn't Mr. Flatts
said it, and it wasn't anything myself was truly supposed
to hear."

Patsy paused, turned the coffeepot upside down and found it empty. "I overheard it is what I did. That Faro, one of the genul'men works for Mr. Flatts you an' Mr. LeSec pounded on pretty bad? He was talking to Dancy, another of Mr. Flatts's minions whom I don't believe you've had the pleasure, sir, not that a pleasure it'd be— Anyway, he was talking to this Dancy, and that's when I heard the terrible thing I realize I shouldn't have been re-peatin' to you at all."

Clay closed his eyes a moment, then looked past Patsy into the woods. "No, it's something I want to know about—I want to know *why* anyone would say a thing like that. Why Scully Flatts or his people would be talking about my father."

Patsy shook his head. "That I couldn't say, sir. All I know is what I heard, and I know that for sure."

There's likely a reason for this, Clay thought. He had considered the problem during the search for Patsy, and it had come to him that LeSec had been in town long enough to let the fact slip that Clay's father had been in the Yukon as well. He had mentioned this to LeSec before supper— and told him what Patsy had said. Jordan had been ap-palled. He swore he hadn't mentioned anything of the sort, and couldn't imagine what Scully Flatts could gain by mak-ing up outrageous stories about Randal Macon.

"I'd say the boy overheard *us*, Clay, and took it from there. There's a lot more reason in that than in anything else."

Clay said nothing more, but he knew it was possible Jordan had let something slip out. Ordinarily, this didn't happen. Still, though he would never bring it up, it had happened a time or two before, when drink had held sway over his partner's good sense.

"Just remember the conversation of this . . . Faro fellow,'' Clay told Patsy. "Everything you heard, as best you can."

"Oh, I can recall it all, sir," Patsy said. "I've a memory like none you've ever seen."

I can well believe it, Clay thought. "That's fine, then. Please go ahead."

"Faro said, 'He can call himself a doctor and a fancy Southern gent till he's blue in the face. He's still Black Jack Foster's boy plain as day. Isn't nothing goin' to change that.'

"Then this other fellow, this Dancy, he took to laughing, sir. At what Faro had said. Dancy says to him, he says, 'Wouldn't you figure, now. The Butcher made widows and orphans for nothing and his boy does the same thing for a hefty fee!' "

Clay's face clouded. "He really said that? He said my father was a killer, a . . . a *butcher*?"

Patsy bit his lip. "You . . . recall you told me to say it like it happened, sir. That's what I did, I told it true."

"I know, and I don't hold it against you," Clay said. "Where did all this happen, you recall that? When you heard Faro and Dancy talk?"

"I know when and where it was for sure, sir. It was while you and Mr. LeSec was in the town jail. And where I heard it was at one of the back tables at O'Toole's."

Patsy lowered his eyes. "I was sweepin' up, I was. I help out Jack-boy sometimes, when he's too much work to do."

Clay looked at Patsy across the fire. "I don't guess you ever told me how come you to be up here in the North, Patsy. And how you came to take up with a man like Scully Flatts. I'm not trying to intrude, you understand. I'm just asking, is all."

Patsy looked almost surprised at the question. "I'd have

tol' you if you'd ever asked me, sir. The thing is you never did. I *have* to work for Mr. Flatts, Dr. Macon. Scully Flatts has got my sister. I don't do what he says, he'll sure as Satan do awful things to her, sir!''

FIFTEEN

MORNING BROUGHT MUCH the same sights that it had the day before: northern sunlight, dense woodlands, and gray mountains behind a veil of clouds. The men heading north were indistinguishable from the weary, bearded prospectors Clay had seen when they'd left the trail to make camp.

And they'll look the same tomorrow, he thought. *And the day after that as well.* He could no longer think of himself as a member of that faceless army. *That's not me. That's not Clay Macon and Jordan LeSec.* He did not want to be like them. He did not want to look as if nothing but a dim and dreary future waited for him at the end of the trail. Maybe it did, maybe he was really no different from the rest. But it was not a thought he would let take hold in his mind.

Clay had talked with Jordan, and told him that he wanted to stay on the Lake Bennet route a day longer than they'd planned. Maybe they could spot the riders Scully Flatts had sent to follow in their tracks. Maybe the men would get lazy and careless, and he and LeSec could pretend to make camp, lead the riders in a false direction for a while and finally slip away. It didn't seem much of a plan, but it was all he could manage at the time.

There's too much here for my liking, Clay thought, leading his burro along the smooth, well-worn trail. Scully Flatts, the crazy old coot that had tried to gun him down . . . and Patsy's talk about his father as some kind of . . . of drooling maniac loose in the North! It was about as fanciful as Patsy's story about himself. The boy was a wonder, for sure.

Sitting across the fire from Clay, Patsy had spun his yarn about the misery and tragedy that had brought him to the North. Patsy's last name was Rabbitt—that part unlikely enough to be true, Clay decided. His sister was named Fiona, and she was scarcely eighteen, younger than Patsy himself. Their parents had passed away, the mother in Dublin, the father later in Chicago. Patsy hadn't cared for the poor section of Chicago, which seemed as dreary and hopless as the place they'd left behind in Ireland. When Patsy's father died, he took Fiona and what money they had, and they worked their way up to Skagway on a boat. Not to look for gold, Patsy assured Clay. They did cleaning and cooking and laundry, and planned to save enough one day to put up their own rooming house.

"Like Mrs. Poldofsky's, where you yourself stayed, sir."

The rest of the story was simple enough. Patsy got tired of saving pennies, and decided he would raise himself and his sister up to riches overnight. After two disastrous hours in a poker game at O'Toole's, he'd lost everything he'd brought to the table—and a great deal more than that—to Scully Flatts.

"How much?" Clay asked, recalling he'd put the same question to Jordan LeSec. "How much did you lose, Patsy?"

"More than an honest man can ever hope to repay," Patsy said.

"An honest man. And who might that be?"

Patsy looked pained. He held a hand against his heart.

"The craft of thievery is not a profession I chose, sir. I had no say in it at all."

"I've heard that excuse before."

"I'll grant you have, sir. But what I tell you is true. It was thrust upon me, Dr. Macon. And I'm not ashamed to say it was my own dear father himself what taught me his trade, which it is a father's duty to do, God rest his soul. I stopped it entirely when we came to the North. For Fiona's sake, if you want to know. She never took pride in the game, like me an' our mum and dad."

Patsy raised his shoulders and sighed. "My father neglected to teach me the art of cards. I learned that game myself."

"And not overly well," Clay added.

"No, sir. I did a poor job of it indeed, sir. Though after you showed him up as a cheat, I'm thinking I may have done better than I thought."

"And I take it it was Scully Flatts made you start stealing again?"

"He did, sir. And I got to keep only twenty percent of the money I took. The rest went against my debt."

"And you always turn in the proper amount, no doubt."

Patsy looked shocked. "No, sir, I certainly do not. Why would I give that low-down crook what's rightly mine? Where's the justice in that?"

"I don't know why I didn't think of that," Clay said.

Fiona was on a farm outside of Skagway. Doing honest labor on one of the many properties Scully Flatts had bought cheap or stolen. She was not speaking to her brother, who had gambled her into servitude. Patsy said he was allowed to go and look at her now and then, to assure himself she was still intact. Patsy never missed a visit, and never handed in less than a reasonable amount of what he stole to Scully Flatts. Scully had made Patsy's condition perfectly clear: Patsy Rabbitt would continue to do exactly what he was told, or the lovely and innocent young Fiona would find herself in less desirable employment upstairs at O'Toole's.

Clay gave a great deal of thought to Patsy's story, watching him across the low fire.

"And that's why you're tagging along with Jordan and me," he said finally. "Because Scully Flatts told you to. I can understand that, with your sister's honor at stake, and the whole being no one's fault but yours. What I cannot swallow is that you're betraying Scully Flatts in favor of me. And risking your sister's fate to do it. That doesn't ring right, boy. I know you're the world's biggest liar and a second-rate felon to boot, but I *don't* think you'd put your own sister in such a danger. You're young and you've taken a crooked path, but I think you're more of a man than that."

Patsy stared at him then, struck dumb for a moment, a look in his eyes as if Clay had reached out and struck him in the face. Shock turned just as suddenly to anger, and Patsy's features twisted in pain. He stumbled to his feet, and all his feelings burst forth in a flood of open rage.

"I thought y-you'd *help* me, is what," he cried out. "I know what I am, and I know I can't ever get her free by myself. I can't stand the l-likes of Scully Flatts. You *stood up* to the man, and I never seen anyone do that. I thought if I come to you you'd help me, Dr. Macon. I th-th-thought you'd show me how to get my sister free!"

"Patsy—"

Clay tried to stop him, but the boy was already gone, covering his face with his hands so Clay wouldn't see the tears already streaking his dirty face.

Clay felt a mix of emotions he could scarcely comprehend. He was stunned by Patsy's words, by the fury and the sorrow he couldn't have guessed were there. And, more than that, he felt a sense of regret he couldn't understand.

He was sorry he'd set the boy off like that, but this was something else. He felt he'd somehow betrayed Patsy, lost his respect, and he was surprised and bewildered to find it was important to him how the boy felt, important that he didn't look bad to the boy; to find that he wanted to keep Patsy's regard for him intact.

Clay was puzzled by such feelings and quickly thrust them aside. *What do I care what a mop-headed Irish boy thinks? I don't need his approval—he should be grateful if he ever earns mine!*

This is what he told himself, but the words seemed hollow somehow. The totally *unreasonable* idea that *he* bore some guilt in this business refused to go away. When he finally dozed off after the fire had burned low, sleep did him little good at all, and he felt much worse in the morning than he had the night before.

"I'm at a loss to know what to say," Jordan told him. "I can't guess the worth of a story like that. The boy's unreliable, for sure, but still . . ."

"Still what? What were you going to *say,* Jordan?" It was a habit that irritated Clay no end, people simply stopping talk somewhere and waiting awhile, or leaving the whole thing dangling and not going on at all.

"I'm not certain what. That's what I'm telling you, Clay." Jordan shaded his brow to watch a crowd of crows rise up from the trees ahead. "The way you say he acted when this business of the sister came out . . . that sounds real enough to me."

"Of course it sounds *real,*" Clay said, frowning at his partner. "Your truly accomplished liar always sounds more convincing than a man who tells the truth."

"He does?"

"Well of course he does. It's a . . . a known psycholog-

ical behavior. I expect that Freud fellow has something to
say on that.''

''Freud.''

''You ought read a book now and then, Jordan. Mental
stimulation is as important for the mind as exercise is for
the body.''

''I've heard that.''

''Well, then. There you are.''

LeSec looked puzzled. ''Yes, I suppose we see eye to
eye on that.''

After discussing it with Jordan, Clay was even more uncertain how he felt about the incident the night before. He
certainly didn't intend to share the conflicting part of his
thoughts about the boy. Not until he understood them a
great deal better himself.

Patsy kept away from both Macon and LeSec for the rest
of the day. He would do his share of guiding the mule and
any other jobs he was given to do, but when he was free
he wandered off alone. Clay understood the boy's feelings—he felt the strain himself. There wasn't much you
could do about it though except leave it alone, let it play
itself out. He wished the boy wouldn't wander out of sight,
but he didn't want to risk any more bad feelings by telling
Patsy so.

The day seemed longer than it should, and by the time
Clay's watch said four, he wished it were closer to six. The
afternoon seemed awfully quiet. There were usually signs
of wildlife about, but even the rabbits that darted in and
out of the brush had apparently gone to ground. The jays
and crows were gone, and the squirrels had stopped their
chatter and ducked into their holes.

Nature's uneasy, Clay thought. *Even the wind's got the
sense to lay low. Everything's waiting, everything's holding
its breath out there . . .*

And when it finally happened, when he saw Patsy stumble up the slope, saw the color gone from his face, heard the terror in his voice, Clay knew at once that it was worse than whatever he'd imagined it would be, what he'd feared about the day.

Without a word he dropped the mule's reins and started down the hill at a run, gripping the Sharps before him, knowing without looking back that LeSec was on his heels.

Patsy's mouth moved but the words stuck in his throat. All he could do was point, and by then Clay's nose had told him where to go. The sickly sweet odor of death was unlike any other smell in the world, and once a man knew it he could never mistake it for anything else.

He found them at the base of a big fir tree. The story was laid out plain in the shady hollow, as easy to read as the words on a page if you knew the savage language of the wild. The two prospectors had slept off the trail before, the same as Clay and Jordan and the boy; only luck had deserted this camp sometime in the night. The bear had plucked one man out of his blankets and slammed him against a tree. The force of the blow was so terrible that part of the man's skull and brain had been driven into the bark of the tree. The man was strung out a good ten yards up the slope, his body still gruesomely attached, looking at first like the man had been impossibly tall.

His partner was crumpled on his knees, and Clay knew from his posture he had tried to get up, had tried for the Winchester still at his side and never made it any farther than that. His eyes were locked open in shock, horrified for an instant at the pain, the knowledge of his death. The bear had left the man's face alone, and slashed and clawed at the rest, leaving shreds of a fur-lined coat and California denim trailing from the bloody mess that crawled with a million tiny creatures of the earth.

Clay could hear Patsy wretching, gasping for breath, and

could see no shame in that. The cadavers at medical school had been almost pleasant companions compared to the grisly sight here.

"Last night some time," Jordan said. "By the Saints, it could have been us."

"Could have for sure," Clay said. He was scarcely listening to LeSec. His doctor's eye was taking him through the ghastly event, showing him what had happened here. The dead men still had most of their meat left. The larger muscle masses, the legs and the chest were still intact. There was no gnawed bone, no leftover strips of gut or sinew. Raw muscle was the first thing a carnivore would tear off its prey—it was protein, salted down with fresh blood. The predator had savaged his victims, but left the good meat alone.

Now, why would that be? Clay wondered. The hair stood up on the back of his neck and he knew what the answer had to be. This was a bear that was out of its natural mind—angry or hurt or maybe both—even its basic instinct for food forgotten in its terrible animal rage.

"Jordan," he said, without turning around, "get the boy and get up the hill. Get back to the trail . . ."

"No, Clay, now, I won't do that." Jordan saw his partner's expression and sensed his meaning at once. "I'll send Patsy back, sure, but I'm staying here—"

"And do what," Clay said sharply, "scratch that creature's back with that toy gun of yours? Get *out* of here, LeSec. *Do it now!*"

"We don't have to stay here, Clay."

"I do," Clay said.

"Listen to me—"

"I have to stay here because it's too late for anything else and I've got the only weapon that he'll pay any mind—" Clay suddenly stood straight and sniffed the air. "By the saints, Jordan, *get the boy out of here!*"

Jordan started to speak and then Clay heard the thing clear, heard the huff of its breath against the ground, heard the dry wood crack beneath its great paws and there it was, loping black and ugly down the hill, closer than Clay had imagined it could be, and he remembered hunting in the Rockies and the old-timers saying there was nothing on earth that was meaner than a grizzly out of sorts, and when Clay finally saw one, he heartily agreed. And had continued to until now. Now he knew the stories he'd heard in the North were true: that the Kodiak coming down at him was a monster out of his worst nightmare, bigger and meaner and harder to kill than a grizzly ever hoped to be . . .

SIXTEEN

IT HAD HAPPENED to Clay before . . .

It was that rare moment when ordinary senses seem to fail, when darkness is closer than the light, and time seems to pause and hold its breath.

The bear was a creature of shadow, ripped from the color of the night. Clay could smell its stink, feel its awful roar in his belly and his chest. It rumbled down the hill straight at him, tearing gouts of mud and snow, snapping small saplings in its path. Clay raised the Big Fifty, sucked in a breath and let it go. The bear was in his sights. His heart slammed hard against his chest. Jordan LeSec would be behind him, backing him with the Winchester, but Clay knew his partner might as well throw rocks; the Winchester would irritate the monster, but it wouldn't bring it down.

Patsy screamed, took a step backward and tripped on a snow-covered root. The boy flailed his arms for balance, fell and tumbled down the hill.

The great Kodiak stopped in its tracks, jerked its shaggy form in Patsy's direction, raised itself up on two legs, threw back its head and bellowed in a terrible rage.

God preserve us, thought Clay, the hair crawling up the back of his neck. The Kodiak blotted out the sky. The pads of its feet, its terrible claws, were red with human gore.

Patsy cried out aloud. The Kodiak slashed the air in reply. It stood there, its leathery snout sniffing the wind, head swaying from side to side.

Clay could have squeezed the trigger of his weapon anytime. The .50-caliber slug would rip through the Kodiak's chest and tear at its heart. Still, Clay hesitated. Something was wrong, something was distracting the creature. It was waiting, showing its strength. It clearly preferred to scare the intruder away instead of going for the kill.

Then Clay saw it, from the corner of his eye. A movement behind the Kodiak, another patch of darkness against the snow. He had suspected it from the start, from the moment he'd seen the condition of the dead men. He watched the smaller shadow, saw it take form, and let out a silent breath.

The cub came down the slope, taking slow and awkward steps, sniffing toward its mother. The Kodiak knew her young was there, and growled out a warning over her shoulder.

That would do it, Clay told himself. Nothing but a mother's protective instinct would push a creature of the wild into such a rage that it would kill and leave the meat untouched.

He could see the cub clearly now, and it looked as if the mother's protection had come too late. The cub was badly hurt. Its fur was stained with blood. It huddled in a patch of snow and trembled its life away.

What sort of men would be so heartless—and downright ignorant—to do such a thing? Clay wondered. Lord a'mighty! Shooting a springtime cub, and the mother almost surely nearby! It'd be a lot quicker, and a lot less painless, to simply put a gun to your head.

"Dr. Macon, help me—d-do something!"

Patsy's fearful cry cut through the cold air. The Kodiak rocked on its heels, turned its eyes on Patsy and roared.

"Shut your mouth, boy," Clay said softly. "Keep quiet and keep still. Jordan?"

"I'm here."

"Just stay there. Don't do a thing unless you have to."

"You may trust me on that," LeSec said. "I'm in no great hurry to make that monster any madder than she is."

Clay raised his rifle and fired a shot in the air. The sound rolled through the trees. The bear jerked her head up straight. Dark hackles flared at her hulking neck. She looked right at Clay and didn't move.

"Back up," Clay told Patsy. "Back up real slow like, don't get off the ground. Can you do that?"

"Yes, sir. I . . . think I can."

"It's got to be better than that, boy. You hear what I'm saying?"

"Yes, sir."

"Fine. We're all settled then. Jordan, edge over real easy toward Patsy. I don't give it much play, but we're all going to try and walk away from this business if we can."

Jordan didn't answer. Clay knew his partner was moving very slowly to his right. Clay knew Patsy might stand up and bolt, and he wouldn't much blame him if he did.

Clay backed up a step, thumbing a new round in the Sharps's chamber. The Kodiak sniffed the air, dropped on all fours, shaking the ground with her weight, then rose up again, bared her teeth and roared.

Patsy couldn't take it. He jerked to his feet and ran. The Kodiak moved in a blur, throwing its mass at the boy. Clay fired, half a second slow. A bullet sliced through the Kodiak's shoulder. The bear bellowed in pain and fury and turned on Clay, its forepaw raking the air inches from Clay's head.

Clay took a step back. He heard the Winchester bark behind him, again and again. The bear didn't stop. Clay groped for another shell. It slipped through his fingers to the ground. He jammed a second cartridge in the chamber, raised the Big Fifty and squeezed off a shot. Blood fountained from the Kodiak's throat. A paw as big as Clay's head raked his shoulder, slamming him to the ground. Jordan cried out. Clay, sprawling on his back, scraped a shell off the snow, pushed it in the Sharps and fired. The great beast swayed, then dropped like a tree.

Clay came to his feet and stood above the dead creature. This close, the bear's stink was almost more than he could stand.

"Your arm," Jordan said. He gently eased the jacket off Clay's shoulders. "You got yourself a nasty cut there, partner."

Clay didn't answer. He turned and looked for Patsy. The boy had disappeared. "Lucky I didn't lose a head. Damn me, Jordan, that boy's got no sense at all, not a lick that I can see!"

"I don't guess he's ever seen a Kodiak she-bear bigger than a two-holer outhouse, Clay." LeSec showed him a sober grin. "Matter of fact, neither have I."

Clay shook his head. "No, I expect you're right about that. I doubt Patsy's tried to lift a wallet from anything near the size of that."

Jordan wanted Clay to rest, and let him take care of the bear, but Clay wouldn't have it. He asked Jordan to bury the dead men, and washed out his wound in the creek and bound it up. Patsy was off to himself, pretending to straighten up the camp, determined to stay as far as possible from the dead men and the hulking corpse of the bear.

Clay stood across the clearing from the boy, sharpening his skinning knife. He knew Patsy was miserable, ashamed of his behavior, and too young to figure what to say next.

Clay found another blade in his pack, gave it a critical

eye and tossed it in Patsy's direction. The knife quivered in the ground at the boy's feet.

"Let's go," Clay said. "That meat'll go bad we leave it sitting out there."

"What? What's that, sir?" Patsy looked appalled. He knew very well what Clay meant. It was a dilemma he couldn't solve. He couldn't refuse Clay Macon, and the last place he wanted to be was anywhere near that bear.

"Yes, sir," he said, "I'm coming. I'm coming right now."

"I don't suppose you've field-dressed a great many bears," Clay said. "Just keep your eyes open and throw up any time you like. You'll catch on right quick."

"Yes, sir," Patsy said, "I'm sure I will, sir." His voice sounded peculiar, a boy trying his best not to breathe.

The meat came off the bone in big strips. Patsy, as Clay had predicted, threw up until there was nothing more to give. Clay silently admired the boy's gumption, but wasn't about to tell him so.

When they were done, they heaped stones on the waste of the day's kill. Jordan, finished with his own gruesome task, joined the pair as they tied up the dripping chunks of good meat and hung them high in a tree. Clay showed the boy a couple of Choctaw tricks that would help protect the meat they intended for themselves. He laid aside loops of intestines for the carrion eaters, to distract them from the rest of the meat. The wounded cub had dragged itself off into the brush to die. Patsy found it, and Clay gave him the task of slicing the poor creature open and scattering its innards about. The boy did what he was told without complaint.

Patsy kept to himself, doing his share around the camp, cleaning up after supper and feeding the mule without being told. Earlier, Clay had watched him go down to the creek to wash himself clean of the smell of death. He went after Jordan and Clay had gone down and come back, as he always seemed to do. For a brash and forward lad, Patsy had a shyness about his personal habits, a trait Clay couldn't object to at all. It merely confirmed what he'd suspected all along: Patsy Rabbitt was about half bluff. He needed friendship and trust, and he scoffed at those qualities because no one had ever given him reason to believe they could exist in his world.

Patsy looked somewhat cleaner when he came back from the creek, but in Clay's eyes, he still resembled a circus clown in his baggy, outsized clothes. Where in all creation he'd found—or more likely stolen—such an outfit, Clay couldn't imagine. He made himself a promise to get the boy into something that fit whenever the occasion arose. That might be some time, considering the neighborhood, but there was little he could do about that.

Jordan had taken a walk toward the bluff and down into the hollow to see if anyone was taking an interest in their camp. It was clear enough to Clay that Patsy had been working himself up to talk. He'd stand and put a branch on the fire, check this or that, cough or clear his throat, then back off again. Finally, he walked up to Clay and folded his legs on the other side of the fire.

"I'm guessing you'd be some put out with me, sir," Patsy said. "I wouldn't be blamin' you if you were. I didn't act proper and I know it. I flat lost my wits is what I did, sir, I'll own up to that. I never saw people tore into bits, never in a nightmare even, sir. And then to come face-to-face with the unholy creature itself—"

"Patsy . . ." Clay held up a restraining hand. "I've seen many a dead man in my profession, but a thing like that is not the same. It goes beyond the act of dying, and into something else. And as far as that bear is concerned . . . God is my witness, boy, I have never seen such a devil in my life. A man'd be a fool if he wasn't afraid of that.''

Patsy blinked. His mouth fell open in surprise. ''Truly, sir? What you're telling me is so? The creature frightened you, she did, set terror in your heart, set you fair quakin' in your boots? Bless you, sir, that's a wondrous thing to hear.''

Clay frowned. ''I do not believe I said anything about terror of the heart, or any quaking of the boots, Patsy. I don't recall that.''

''I don't suppose you did exactly, sir, but that was the spirit of your words, I do believe . . .''

''It was nothing of the sort, boy. Not anything of the sort!''

Clay was more than a little irritated. Why, you couldn't say a word without this redheaded imp twisting your meaning somehow. Of all the ridiculous notions, quaking in his boots!

''I swear, Patsy, you can't get one thing straight before you're off on something else. I never said— What I *said* was, I said . . . I said a man has a right to be afraid when he faces a fearsome sight. Such as an extremely large bear, for instance, something such as that. I did *not* say, and certainly never would . . .''

Clay paused to catch his breath. Patsy was looking at him across the fire, his expression as innocent as a babe's, not a thing there you could take him down for. And yet there was something in his eyes, something at the corner of his mouth . . .

By damn, there better not be, Clay thought, *there better not be the barest trace of a smile there, boy . . .*

''Sir, is something wrong?'' Patsy looked alarmed. ''Is something disturbin' you, Dr. Macon?''

''No, nothing is disturbing me,'' Clay said. ''Not in any way. Get some sleep now. We're getting up and out of here at first light.''

"Yes, sir. And a most pleasant night to you, sir."

The boy stood and unfolded himself, and walked into shadow beyond the camp. In a moment, Clay saw him wrap himself in his blanket and turn his back to the fire.

Clay sat and watched the dying embers. He stood and stomped around, poured himself a cup of coffee, found it too cold and too bitter and spat it out.

Now, how in blazes did I let myself get into that? It's him should be explaining his actions to me and not the other way around . . .

He muttered to himself, waiting for Jordan to return. Maybe LeSec could explain it, tell him how Patsy Rabbitt seemed to pull every fool stunt in the book, and come out on top of the heap every time . . .

SEVENTEEN

CLAY MACON COULDN'T sleep.

He sat with his blankets wrapped tight about his shoulders and watched the amber sparks of light. The silent forms of Jordan LeSec and Patsy were shadows against the greater dark. Nightbirds called, and a panoply of impossibly bright stars filled the clear Northern sky.

Maybe it was the excitement of the day, he decided. A close brush with death was enough to set any man's nerves on edge and keep him wide awake. That, and the knowledge that they were never alone out here, that Scully Flatts's men were out there somewhere, dogging their trail.

As ever, the thought made Clay furious. Why? Why was that louse-ridden bastard doing this, and what did he *want*? Not for a minute did Clay believe that lame story Flatts had passed along through Fullerton Ash. Ash seemed an intelligent man, and Clay was next to certain he didn't credit the tale himself. Scully Flatts hadn't tossed them in his jail, then fattened them up and set them on their way, just to get them out of town. There were quicker, less troublesome ways to make a man disappear. No trouble at all for a man like Scully Flatts.

Something moved through the woods and Clay sat up straight. He waited, but whatever it was went away. A stray wolf, likely, or some other scavenger after the remains of the bear and her cub.

Clay dozed for a while, and woke to find the stars had made a half circle through the sky. A little of the night had passed him by. It was still and deathly cold. He thought about lighting the fire, but decided getting up would simply chill him all the more.

Jordan LeSec turned over in his sleep, mumbling to himself. Likely dreaming of a sloe-eyed Southern belle, or a lady with a lesser pedigree. Like that lovely woman in Skagway, what was her name? Clay couldn't bring a name to mind, but he could not forget the woman herself.

Patsy hadn't moved twice through the night. He slept with the innocence of youth, though *innocence*, Clay decided, wasn't exactly the word he was searching for.

Blowing a cloud of frost in the air, Clay lay back on the hard ground and tried to make himself small. It came to him at once that there was scientific proof—along with the proof of some personal experience—that two people generated more heat than one. And, setting the science part aside, it was much more pleasant as well.

He felt the color rise to his face as a vision of Adele Garnette came to mind. They had never shared a bed on a chilly night, and now they never would. Nevertheless, Adele's lovely image was there, and it stubbornly refused to go away.

You surely are an odd mix, Clay Macon, I do declare . . . one part a bookworm with those silly glasses on your nose, and another part off on a pirate ship somewhere!

She had been sixteen when she'd told him that, and he'd been twenty-eight. Still, there was never any question in his mind—or in hers, at the time—that they would belong to each other someday.

And they would have, he knew, if tragedy hadn't come between them, a tragedy of such terrible dimension it had set Adele against him, shaken her so badly she had shut him completely and forever out of her life . . .

It was the finest summer of his life, a summer of beautiful women in fancy gowns, of ballrooms and soft golden light. It was also a summer of fine hunting mornings in the Louisiana swamplands, days made all the more glorious for Clay because Adele was his companion, Adele and her older brother, Washington, a man with a spirit as lively as his sister's. It amused Washington to get lost now and then, to pretend he didn't know the bayous, though he'd wandered through nearly every mile of them half his life . . .

It was no surprise to Adele when Clay declared his love. They'd be married, he said, and he'd keep her and protect her forever. Adele said yes, without hesitation, and the kiss that followed seemed to go on forever. They were both sure nothing could ever come between them, ever drive them apart . . .

It was only a month after they'd announced their plan to marry that Washington returned from a hunt with a sickness that would soon strike him down. It was the yellow fever, the dreaded malaria that took so many lives at the time. Adele was beside herself. During her brother's sickness, she never left his side. And Clay, confident that love and the science of medicine could never let him down, promised her he'd make her brother well, that he'd have him on his feet as good as new. It was a foolish promise, and one he couldn't keep . . .

Adele fell into deep despair when her brother died. She might have found the strength to go on if her father's health hadn't failed him less than six weeks after Washington passed away. Even as Hastings Garnette slipped into a final coma, Clay Macon fought to bring him back. "Are you going to save him, too?" Adele asked him. "Is he going to be good as new?"

There was no sense of reason to her words; reason was far beyond her now. In her grief, in her awful desperation, she had put her faith in Clay instead of in higher powers. Clay had promised her and failed her, and her father and her brother were gone.

"I did all I could," Clay told her, "there was nothing more I could do, nothing anyone—"

The day began to brush the eastern sky. Clay drew himself up, bleary-eyed and sore, and gathered wood for the fire. It wasn't the first night's sleep he'd missed in his life, and likely wouldn't be the last. There was nothing for it but to get on with the day and hope for a better night. There was nothing like a long day trekking through the wilds to bring a man back to blessed rest.

The bear meat had survived the night. Clay had been right—predators had eaten every innard in sight and clawed at the rocks for the rest. The parts they'd hung high, however, had come through intact.

With Patsy's help, Clay and Jordan took time to prepare the Kodiak's enormous hide for proper curing, just in case they ever had the time. When that job was done, the meat all packed and the camp cleared away, the Yukon sun had passed over the mountains and was blazing in a chill blue sky. With the sledge full and ready, Clay led the way north. Patsy seemed curious that they hadn't returned to the well-worn trail, which was a far sight easier than hacking out your own. Clay explained that they were, indeed, still headed for Bennet Lake and the Yukon Trail; they were simply taking a parallel course in hopes of losing Scully Flatts's followers along the way.

Patsy accepted that, and Clay saw no reason to tell the boy that he had no intention of going to the Yukon—that their true course was west, toward a destination known only to himself and LeSec.

"We'll have to tell him sometime," Jordan said. Patsy had gone up ahead on the trail, guiding the mule over a rocky stand of ground. "Patsy's a city boy, but he can tell where the sun comes up. He's going to know when we quit heading north."

"When it's time, then we'll tell him," Clay said. He stopped and looked back at the dark mass of forest down below. They had climbed a fair way, and it wasn't yet noon.

"It's not the boy I'm worried about, Jordan. Even if he's selling us a lie about Scully Flatts, and I don't feel he is, it doesn't change a lot. We know Flatts has his men on our tail. That's a plain fact, Patsy Rabbitt or not."

LeSec shook his head. "I've figured it seven ways to Sunday, Clay, and I can't see the sense in it at all." He pulled a big bandanna from his pocket and wiped his brow. "The man doesn't *know* anything, he simply can't. There's two of us have your father's map in our heads—and even Scully Flatts can't see in there, I know that."

"No, he can't. But if he keeps on dogging us, it doesn't much matter what he does or doesn't know." Clay stopped and faced LeSec. "Unless we can shake those riders, we've got us a standoff, friend. We can't go anywhere *near* where we're headed as long as they're hanging around. And they can do that just as long as they like. They can dog us till the skeeters chew us up, till our food runs out. They can watch us till winter sets in and you and me and the boy are frozen solid as sticks."

Jordan shrugged. "I don't see that'd do 'em any good. If we don't *go* anywhere . . ."

"No, it wouldn't do 'em any good at all," Clay said. "But I think Scully Flatts knows we don't intend to wander around up here till we fall into a hole. I think he knows we'll make a move and try and leave his people behind."

Jordan showed him a weary grin. "He's right, isn't he?"

"You better believe he is," Clay said.

The way grew steeper and the trees grew thinner as the day wore on. Golden meadows and green valleys offered a brief respite from forests where the trees grew so close together they often formed an impenetrable natural fence.

After a quick stop at noon, Jordan stayed with the mule while Clay went ahead with Patsy Rabbitt. After the incident with the Kodiak bear, the boy wasn't keen on furthering his hunting career, but Clay assured him they'd try for smaller game. Patsy was to watch, keep relatively still, and try and learn some about the wilds.

Clay wasted little time getting himself back in the hunter's mode. This way of living was his heritage, the way he'd been brought up. Making his way through the trees or a grass-covered field was as natural as breathing to Clay. He loved being in this vast, new land he'd never seen before, and knew he could spend a lifetime seeing just a part of this Northern paradise.

So far, the Yukon held few surprises as far as the creatures there were concerned. He'd heard a faraway screaming one time, a sound he couldn't identify, an almost human cry that grated on the nerves. Still, he'd heard wildcats that sounded more human than the entire Louisiana State Legislature, so there was nothing to concern himself with there.

He kept his senses keenly alert, sometimes stooping to run his hands across a carpet of grass or taste the water from a spring. There were signs everywhere that told a man how the world around him lived and breathed. He just had to know how to look.

In a stand of brush, he surprised a nest of Northern quail, fat brown birds not used to the ways of man. A job for the scattergun, clearly. And, Clay thought, a good time to learn if he could safely turn his back on the boy.

Facing away from Patsy for a moment, he quickly ejected the round from the Big Fifty's chamber and slipped it into his pocket. Turning again, he handed the weapon to Patsy.

Patsy looked bewildered. Clay pointed at the brush and brought a finger to his lips. He stepped back against the rough bark of a fir and kept his eyes on the spot where he'd seen the birds flutter. In a moment, one bird gave a startled cry and flapped noisily into the air. Clay didn't move. He held the scattergun against his chest and let the bird go by.

"What was wrong with that one?" Patsy whispered. "It seemed a very fine bird to me."

"Be nice to have a dog," Clay said.

"Huh? What for?"

"So they wouldn't come out of there one at a time like they're doing right now."

The boy's bewildered look told Clay Patsy hadn't been lying about being a city boy. He couldn't imagine growing up without the thrill of watching a fine Louisiana hound trembling at the point.

"How's your pitching arm?" asked Clay.

"My . . . my what?"

"Your pitching arm, boy. The one you throw with."

Patsy grinned in sudden understanding. "I can throw as good as anyone you ever seen, and that's the truth, sir."

It is, is it? thought Clay. "Let's see you, then. Toss a stone right over there in the brush."

Patsy leaned down and studied the rocks at his feet, as if he'd been selecting fine stones all his life. He raised up and concentrated, frowned at the brush, and then threw. His first pitch landed nowhere near the quail. Clay let out a breath. Patsy turned red and bit his tongue. The second throw was perfect. Clay raised the scattergun in a blur and shifted the weapon from left to right in a smooth and prac-

ticed arc. Two birds dropped in the first flurry out of the
brush. Then Clay bagged another on the wing, as a big hen
left the cover late.

The gunsmoke tasted good to Clay. It tasted like a filling
dinner, like a slowly roasted quail.

Patsy gave a low whistle. "I swear, you Dixie boys can
shoot! That was fair something to see, sir, I'll tell you
what!"

Clay acknowledged the compliment with a nod. No use
shaking the boy's faith, telling him he'd witnessed an ordinary shot. There wasn't any sense in doing that . . .

He decided not to take the time to dress the birds there,
that could be done at their leisure back at camp. He added
four small quail eggs from the bottom of the stand, seeing
no reason to leave them for the foxes to suck on after dark.

Retrieving the big Sharps, Clay set off downhill with
Patsy at his side. The boy seemed to be taking to the wild
in spite of himself. His red hair was bright as brass in the
sun, and his cheeks were flush with the health of outdoors.
Maybe there was hope for him yet, Clay decided. It stood
to reason if you took a thief out where there was nothing
to steal, he'd have to find something else to do.

After the noise of the shotgun, Clay had little hope of
flushing more game. Still, he continued to move from
shadow to shadow, as a good hunter should at all times.
Besides, it was good practice for the boy.

At the edge of the woods, he harvested half a dozen
handfuls of mushrooms, taking care to carefully examine
each specimen he picked. He'd learned that practice from
his father, and his father's Choctaw guide, a man with a
face of old leather and undetermined age. Between them,
those two had left Clay with as much backwoods lore as
any man in New Orleans. A poison mushroom looked the
same whether it grew on the Mississippi Delta or in the
headlands of the Yukon.

Patsy watched patiently as Clay picked some wild mint and spinach. Nuts or edible seeds would have added spice to the meal, but it wasn't the proper season for such delicacies. He remembered his father raiding a squirrel's lair in a rotten oak, coming up with a handful of tasty walnuts. Nothing had tasted as sweet and tender since.

What happened to you up here, Father? You knew the natural world as well as any man; your heart beat the same as the creatures of the wild . . . I'd bet my life it wasn't a force of nature that crushed your spirit and brought you down. Men might break you, but never the land . . .

"You enjoy it out here?" Clay asked Patsy. "I know it takes a while to get used to the outdoor life, but once it gets in your blood—"

"Ah, I'm thinking it's already workin' its magic on me, sir," Patsy grinned, "I believe it truly is. I can feel it pulsing through my very veins, even as we speak."

"Well, I doubt it's acting quite that fast," Clay said, clearing his throat. "But I'm pleased it's working on you well."

"Indeed it is, Dr. Macon, sir. I'm looking forward to my next chance to experience adventure in the great outdoors."

"I'm glad to hear it."

"And when d'you think that'd be, if I might be asking, sir?"

Clay clapped the boy on the back. "Why, you won't have to hardly wait at all. There's high adventure waiting for you now, soon as we get back to camp."

Patsy blinked. "You wouldn't be teasin' me, would you, sir?"

"I certainly would not. I am giving you an opportunity few young men have ever had before, even those who've spent their lives outdoors in the States."

"Truly, sir?"

"Truly, indeed. You'll have the unique experience of

defeathering and dressing these plump Northern quail. I doubt there's many have ever had a chance like that. I wouldn't be surprised if you recalled this day all your life.''

Patsy's face fell. ''Aw, sir, that's a cruel joke to be playing, it surely is . . .''

Supper was a triumph. Though Clay had brought in the food, and Jordan had cooked the meal, Patsy took credit for the quail, the bear and the mushrooms as well. It was such a fine evening and the food was so good, Clay didn't have the heart to admonish the boy. And, after all, it was Patsy who scraped the hard black shell off the frying pan, where Jordan had added a special honey sauce.

Clay had no trouble getting to sleep. He scarcely remembered easing himself to the ground and turning away from the fire.

At just after three in the morning, Patsy proved he'd learned at least one piece of useful wood lore on the trip. It was Jordan LeSec and Clay Macon who slept the sleep of the dead, and Patsy Rabbitt who first heard the riders coming softly up the trail . . .

EIGHTEEN 18

CLAY COULD SEE them now, four of them, lighter shadows against the dark. They had left the horses on the back trail and were making their way up the slope on foot. Clay, Jordan and Patsy had been watching them for the past quarter hour from a heavy stand of fern and brush just outside the camp. The intruders were in no great hurry. They were content to take their time, moving up the hill on three sides, coming as slow as the night.

"They know exactly where we are," Jordan said. "They're just trying to do it right. I'd say they're waiting for the dead hour just before the dawn to make their move."

"And what move do you figure that'd be?" Clay gripped his partner's shoulder and peered into the dark. "If those riders belong to Scully Flatts—and I don't know who else they'd be—why are they making a play for us at all?"

Clay turned his gaze on the boy. "They don't mean to harm us, they just want to know what we're up to out here. Isn't that right, Patsy? Scully Flatts wants us alive and well, he doesn't want us dead?"

"Sir, it's the *truth,* it is!" Patsy drew in a breath and held it. He hadn't missed the question in Clay's voice. "That's what was told to me, Dr. Macon. Scully Flatts, he says, he says, 'Keep a sharp eye on 'em, Patsy lad, that's what you've got to do.' I swear it, sir, on my dear mother's grave.''

"I don't think we need more of that," Clay said. "You ran out of mothers and graves a great many miles back. I just want the truth, Patsy. If you haven't been totally honest with us before, I'd suggest you do so now."

"Seeing as how you appear to be up here with the rest of us targets," Jordan added.

"Dr. Macon, sir, Mr. LeSec—it's the truth, for certain it is. If you think I'd put myself in league with that . . . that ugly slab of blubber Scully Flatts!"

"Keep it down," Jordan said. "They can hear you in Seattle, boy."

"Sorry, sir, I just—"

"What I think," Clay put in, "is two things, Patsy. One, I'm most inclined to believe what you say. On the other hand, two, I can't help recalling you've a sister in Scully Flatts's hands . . ."

"Sir—"

"I didn't say I'm set on number two, boy, all right? As a fact, I'm inclined to take you at your word. Your sister in peril or no, I feel you're with us, Patsy." Clay glanced at Jordan LeSec. "If that agrees with you?"

"Good enough," Jordan said, and nodded at the boy.

"Here, then." Clay thrust the shotgun into Patsy's hands. "You're an official—and armed—member of this band, and as such, I expect you to carry your share of the load."

"I'm . . . more than grateful, sirs." Patsy's eyes shone. "I truly am, and I won't disappoint you. I swear that I'll—"

"Don't," Clay said. "Just do what you're told and keep your head down."

Clay motioned for the others to stay put. He bellied out of the brush and moved silently down the hill, across the forest floor, remembering the Indian way, that he was not an intruder here, but a part of the natural order of the wild, a creature who belonged, whose motion, shape and sound were as much a part of this Northern night as the nesting birds above or the whisper of the grass.

It was no great effort to find them all. They were lackeys, hired hands. One of them could follow a trail, but the others were more at home in the smoky atmosphere of a saloon. They knew the smell of sweat and stale beer, but a bear could creep into their bedroll and never wake them up at all.

There were four men on the slope—the fifth man was back down the draw, holding the mounts. The one who was flattened against a boulder halfway up the hill was the one who'd been out in the woods before.

Some, anyway, Clay thought. *He's out of practice, though, or I wouldn't have smelled his whiskey thirty yards away . . .*

That wasn't a good idea, climbing up a hill with the wind at your back and stopping for a nip now and then. To Clay Macon's sensitive nose, the man betrayed his presence with sour-mash whiskey, body odor, stale cigars and a sour stomach. All the woodcraft in the world was useless in face of such an assault on the senses.

"I don't want us to have to kill anyone," Clay told Patsy and LeSec, "but it's still pitch black out there, and no time to worry about where your bullet lands. Those fellows are bringing whatever they get down on themselves, so shoot whatever comes at you, and don't stop to think about it being a man."

This speech was mostly for Patsy, who hadn't engaged in this sort of business before. Clay wasn't worried about LeSec. His friend was no bloodthirsty killer by any stretch, but he had a deep religious conviction about keeping his hide intact.

"I'll be just fine," Patsy said, "you wait and see. The

Irish are a savage lot, as you know, sir. We've the blood of ancient warriors in our veins. When I'm through with those louts, they'll wish they'd never heard the name of Patsy Ra—''

"Fine, that's enough, I get the picture, boy. Jordan—if you will, take your position ten yards to the right. You'll have the cover of that outcrop overlooking the slope. I'll be left at the base of the big fir."

Clay looked at Patsy. "You'll be fine here. The brush is good cover and you've got a natural trench to hunker down in. You know how to use the shotgun and how to load it up again."

"Yes, sir."

"You're all right with this, then?"

"I am," Patsy said, and for once, Clay noted, the boy didn't feel the need to make a speech about something he knew nothing at all about. Maybe he was learning, getting a little sense in that stubborn Irish head. From experience, Clay knew there was nothing like the sudden understanding that he might be dead before dawn to get a man to thinking right.

It was as good a defense as any, Clay decided. The three of them close, facing out in a rough triangle, they'd each have a clear field of fire. You didn't want to stop and think with bullets flying through the dark—this way, they could all three shoot at anything they saw and know they had a friend to their left and to their right.

How would they do it, Clay wondered, draw fire to see where everybody was, or come blazing up the hill to try and take them by surprise?

Feeling out the enemy's position was the best thing to do—maybe find a weak spot somewhere. Clay knew if he was down there he'd try a diversion first off. Make a lot of noise on one side and send the bulk of your force the other way. "Bulk," of course, was four men out of five in this case, not exactly up to battalion strength, but neither were the defenders on top . . .

As if in answer to Clay's question, the sharp crack of a rifle echoed up the hill. Three rapid shots followed the first, then another, this last one from the west, down the slope from the boy's position.

Hold on, Patsy, don't let them spook you, stay where you are . . .

A single shot came out of the night below Clay; a twig snapped overhead, and pine needles showered on his back. Nothing more reached him after that; the fire was heaviest on Patsy Rabbitt and LeSec. They were hitting two-thirds of the hill, guessing the defenders would have to spread out somehow, covering as much as they could.

Clay inched forward and a little to the right. He carried Jordan's old 1857 Colt, having left the Sharps behind. One shot from that awesome weapon would have killed every one of the intruders, if he could have gotten them to line up straight, but it was an unwieldy piece for the close-up work he'd face that night.

One man shouted, then two, and both tore through the underbrush, making more noise than they should. A dozen bullets whined overhead. Clay grinned to himself. They were going to try the diversion, then. He approved of the maneuver, but they weren't real subtle about it, yelling and thrashing about.

They stomped up the hill on Jordan's left, squeezing off wild shots into the night. LeSec was no fool. He stayed under cover and didn't fire back. The gunfire stopped. Clay silently counted to ten. This time, one of them came in between Jordan and Patsy, the other to Patsy's right. Someone ripped off a yell and emptied his revolver inches over Patsy's head.

That was all Patsy could take. The shotgun roared twice, the muzzle flash lighting up the night. Clay wasn't overly surprised—the boy's nerves had to give; it had simply been a question of time.

All of the gunmen opened up at once, loosing a withering volley in Patsy's direction. Clay heard the boy cry out, even over the deafening noise. He bellied quickly to his right, knowing it was risky to leave his position, knowing he had to see if Patsy Rabbitt was frightened, hurt or dead.

Two spears of light arced through the darkness to his left—two shots from Jordan's Winchester, followed by a curse and a sharp cry of pain from down the hill.

There you have it, gentlemen, it works both ways . . .

Patsy had given away his position, but the intruders had shown theirs as well, and LeSec had made them pay the price.

"I'm over here," Clay said softly. "Cover my back a minute, Jordan."

LeSec didn't answer, but Clay knew he was there. He used his elbows to pull himself across the cold ground. Patsy was lying facedown, trembling like a dog left in the rain. His hands were clamped tight above his head, as if that might keep the danger out.

Clay felt a mixed sense of anger and relief. He crawled up close, grabbed the boy by the collar and shook him hard. Patsy yelled and tried to get away. Clay slammed him down again.

"Get yourself together," Clay said, "right now. Reload your weapon and hold your position. You're responsible for *my* hide as well as yours. Don't you forget that, mister. You do and you'll answer to me!"

Patsy's face was dead white. "Yes, sir, I will, I just—"

"Don't talk about it, *do* it!"

Clay turned away and crawled off before Patsy could open his mouth again. Talk wouldn't cut it now. What the boy needed was a cold bucket of water in the face. He

needed to be more afraid of Clay than he was of those
shooters down the hill.

Jordan was a shadow to his right as Clay moved back to
his post beneath the thick trunk of the fir. There was occasional fire from below, but the men down there weren't
as anxious now that one of their own was down. There was
nothing like the sight of blood that could have been his to
dampen a man's enthusiasm. They'd likely think twice before they—

Clay had to eat his words at once. A dark patch of night
suddenly rose straight up not twenty feet away. Clay
squeezed off a shot and knew at once he'd aimed high. The
figure loomed before him, firing off rounds as fast as he
could, bounding through the night like he was crazy or
bulletproof or maybe some of both. The harsh light blinded
Clay's eyes. He threw himself aside, felt powder sting his
face and fired the ancient Colt. The gunman cried out,
stumbled, caught himself and raised his pistol again.

*You and me aren't ever going dancin' again, mister—
that's about enough of that . . .*

Clay stepped aside, went low and buried his fist in the
man's gut. The gunman gagged and bent double. Clay
slammed the Colt across his skull, stepped back and let the
man slump to the ground. He squatted down, touched the
shooter's throat. Clay's bullet had cut a slice of flesh off
the inside of his arm. His pulse was steady enough, but
he'd wake up with a real fine goose egg on his head. Whipping the man's rawhide belt from his waist, Clay hogtied
him quickly and rolled him into a ditch.

*Should've gotten up close, partner. You don't want to go
boltin' out into the night . . .*

"Clay—that you over there?"

Clay didn't answer. He checked the darkness, sweeping
his gaze from left to right. One man had gotten up close;
another man might have done the same.

He went low and headed for Jordan's position. LeSec was on his belly, the barrel of his rifle pointing steady in Clay's direction. He recognized his friend with some relief and lowered his aim to the ground.

"Figured someone was taking a trophy back there. I was hoping it was you."

"I'm grateful for the thought. Anything happening down there?"

"A lot of deep concern, I'd imagine," Jordan said. "They've got one down, and in a minute or so they'll know that another one isn't coming back. That ought to give 'em pause."

Clay Macon grinned. "It'd give me the shakes is what it'd do." He turned and checked his back again. "Patsy all right?"

"He's still there; he hasn't gone away. What'd you do to that boy?"

"I didn't do a thing. I just promised him I would."

Someone down below fired off a shot, but it was clearly just for show.

"There's two of them," Clay said, "and one staying with the horses." He glanced up at the sky. "If that was me down there, I'd let you keep watch and get an hour's sleep. When it was light enough to see, I'd make sure no one got off of this hill alive."

"That's a cheery thought," Jordan said.

Clay shook his head. "I'm not saying that's what these boys'll do. Me, I wouldn't have come charging up a hill I'd never seen before in the first place."

"How come it's me? How come it's not you?"

"How come what?"

"You said if we were down there, you'd catch some sleep and I'd stay awake and watch. Why not the other way around?"

Clay looked at his partner. "It's a hypothetical question,

LeSec. We're not down there, we're up here."

"Taking a nap's not anywhere close to hypothetical to me. It's a real and serious event. If we were down there, Clay, the only fair thing to do would be flip a coin and see who gets to sleep."

"We could do that," Clay said.

"All right, fine."

"If it ever comes up, that is."

"Well, something like that, you don't ever know."

"If it does, we'll be using my coin, we won't be using yours."

Jordan looked hurt. "Well, I'll be whipped, Clay. Why would you go and say a thing like that?"

"I was with you in that tavern in Baton Rouge, Jordan . . . when you were doing your little act for those two fellas off the *Lady B.*?"

Jordan cleared his throat. "I don't rightly recall the incident."

"You think a minute and you will. I distinctly remember that Morgan dollar of yours is somewhat deformed. It's got two heads, and it's lacking a tail."

"Well for heaven's sake," Jordan said, "why you'd remember something as insignificant as that I couldn't say."

"I'll bet those two ol' boys in Baton Rouge recall it even better'n me. I reckon they—*Get down, LeSec!*"

Clay shoved his partner roughly aside as lead whined over their heads. He caught the blur of motion from the corner of his eye and saw the three figures coming at him, spread out and low, raking the night with heavy fire.

Three of them . . . the two shooters left and the man who'd stayed with the horses, too . . . moving up the slope right at Patsy Rabbitt, as if they sensed there was a weak spot there, as if they knew . . .

Clay and Jordan moved without talking, Clay to Patsy's right, Jordan to the left. Jordan snapped off three shots in the dark, spacing them out in a spread. Clay sprawled down next to the boy. Patsy's features were rigid, his cheeks peppered with sweat.

"Just take it easy," Clay said. "Don't shoot at anything you can't see, wait until you—"

Patsy let go with both barrels. Scattershot rattled through the leaves, and a man cried out down the hill.

"Good shooting!" Clay pounded Patsy on the back. "You're all right, boy!"

"Lord forgive me," Patsy said, "I hope I didn't hurt nobody, sir. I just meant to scare 'em off, I did . . ."

"I don't know if you're aware of this or not," Clay said, "but that bully boy down there doesn't feel the same about you."

A bullet plowed across the lip of the depression, showering dirt in Clay's eyes. He raised up quickly, squeezed off a shot in the direction of the flash and turned on his back to reload.

Patsy looked terrified. He tried to force a shell in the shotgun's chamber, but dropped it every time.

Jordan fired into the brush. Clay raised up and loosed two shots down the hill. Someone answered back.

Then, as if a storm had suddenly swept in off the mountains, the night was filled with a thunderous volley of fire. Muzzle flashes lit up the dark; the clean, sharp crack of Winchesters merged with the deep-throated bellow of shotguns, and the bark of revolvers.

Jordan looked at Clay. Clay peered down the hill. What in blazes was happening? Three men were suddenly making noises like an army—there was a *war* going on down there!

Everything stopped. The night was deadly still. Clay drew in a breath. Patsy shut his eyes tight. Jordan bent to reload.

"You on the hill up there. Is that you, Mr. Macon? Answer if you will, sir."

Clay frowned. The voice sounded vaguely familiar, but he couldn't place it right off.

"Who are you?" Clay called back. "What are you doing here?"

The voice laughed. "Thank the Lord you're all right, Mr. Macon. This is Fullerton Ash, your shipmate on the *Queen*, and a few good citizens of Skagway. What we're doing here is saving your hide, if I may be so bold as to say so, sir!"

NINETEEN

"I MUST APOLOGIZE again, gentlemen, for taking so long," Ash said. "We lost their trail about noon and had the devil to pay picking it up again. They found a spine of granite and flat disappeared without a trace. I curse myself for not bringing a Chilkot along. Little fellows can sniff out a mouse in a blizzard. Can't trust 'em, though. Never can tell what a red Injun's thinking."

"Don't apologize for the service you've done us, sir," Clay said. "It was a brave and selfless act, and we are grateful for your help."

"Nothing, nothing at all. Pleased to be able to take some action, Dr. Macon."

Fullerton Ash leaned close to the fire. The heavy buffalo robe did little to hide the man's gaunt, near cadaverous frame. Clay figured a man with so little meat on his bones must be miserable cold all the time. Ash would be better off sweating down on the Rio Grande, than traipsing around up north.

The four men Ash had brought with him sat across the fire drinking scalding coffee and filling their tin plates with bacon and beans. In the early morning light, Clay could see they were decent-looking men, townsmen with honest jobs, or hardworking farmers or loggers. They didn't look at all like the shooters who'd ridden for Scully Flatts.

Three of those men were now wrapped in blankets just down the hill, every one of them dead and growing cold as the earth beneath their heads. Only one was still alive— the man Clay had punched, pistol-beaten and hogtied on the hill. You never could tell with a lot of wild shooting in the dark. A man could come out without a scratch, or catch an ounce of lead between the eyes.

Fullerton Ash had told them most of it moments after the fight was over and the casualties stowed away. It was Clay Macon's doing himself, Ash said. Ash couldn't forget Clay's blunt remarks the morning Clay and Jordan had left town: If the citizens of Skagway didn't like dancing to Scully Flatts's tune, why didn't they do something about it?

"I guess this is your answer, Dr. Macon. I guess you could say we're starting now . . ."

"I'd say you are," Clay told him.

Ash held his coffee mug tightly between his hands. The sun was burning the tops of the mountains, and the light turned Ash's face a rosy pink, giving the man a momentary illusion of vigor and health—an illusion that would pass as soon as the dawn turned to day.

"I don't have proof that'd stand up in court," Ash said, "even if we had an honest judge within a couple thousand miles. Still, I know for damn sure it's not the first time Scully's dogged a prospector's trail. It's a regular habit of his, and everyone in Skagway knows it. He'll keep a look-out for a man appears he knows what he's doing, or a fellow maybe talks too much. Plenty of times, of course, nothing comes of this. But when it does . . ."

Ash let his words trail off. He tossed the dregs of his coffee at the fire, and the embers hissed at him like a snake.

"I expect I know what you're saying," Jordan said, "but

I don't like to believe it. The man is a devil, sir. Satan himself!''

"Believe it," Ash said. "And you might want to not insult the devil by linkin' his name to Scully Flatts."

"He follows a party out then," Clay said, "and if they make a decent strike, Scully takes it away from him, and one of his cohorts stakes a claim. And the men that found the gold—"

"They manage to disappear is what they do," Ash said. "No one ever sees them again."

Ash paused and let out a breath. "I am not too proud of the fact that I have taken no action against this monster before. Same goes for the others you see here. I can only say, speaking for myself, that it's easier to excuse tyranny when a man has a great deal to lose. I have a number of thriving mercantile enterprises and a bank. Those have become more important to me than—I'll say it, and be damned with my pride—more important than my self-respect."

"You're to be admired for your courage, Mr. Ash," Jordan said. "Truly you are, sir."

"Courage late is better than none at all, I suppose." Ash shook his head. "There's a lot to be done. I know the man. Scully Flatts is more resourceful—and more dangerous—than you could ever imagine."

Clay felt he would have no trouble imagining that overweight Attila associated with any sort of criminal enterprise—from cheating at cards to cold-blooded murder. There was supposed to be some good in everyone, but who'd take the time to search it out in Scully Flatts?

Clay looked up as Patsy Rabbitt walked up the hill with an armful of dry firewood he'd gathered down below. Leaving the kindling within easy reach of the fire, he filled himself a plate and took his breakfast back into the grove of trees south of the camp. Clay watched until he was out of sight. The boy never looked in his direction, where he sat next to Jordan and Ash. It was clear he wasn't comfortable with Ash and his friends.

For good reason, too, Clay thought. Ash couldn't know Patsy had admitted Scully had sent him here to spy, but he did know Patsy had worked for the man in Skagway. Patsy was likely a little unnerved in the presence of a man like Ash.

"I expect you're curious about the lad," Clay said. "I should tell you Jordan and I share that feeling ourselves. He showed up at the pass with some story about a rich man making trouble over a wallet. Said the temperature in Skagway might be too warm for a while."

Ash glanced at the woods where Patsy had disappeared. "And do you believe that, sir? You're aware of the boy's association with Flatts."

"I am, of course. If he's up to no good, he is surely bright enough to know Mr. LeSec and I would not be taken in by a ruse as foolish as that. Still, we decided if he was by chance working for Flatts, it would be to our advantage to keep him in sight."

Fullerton Ash frowned at that. "A sound idea, certainly. I don't need to tell you to have a care. The boy's slippery as an eel."

"Advice well taken," Clay said. He squinted past the morning sun, at the blood-colored clouds in the east. A hawk was etched against the sky overhead. It seemed suspended there, with no hint of motion at all.

"One thing puzzles me greatly," Clay said, filling Ash's empty cup. "I'm sure it's crossed your mind as well, especially in light of what you've told us about Scully's habit of following gold seekers. Why would his riders attack us now, when we're still on the trail and not even close to the gold fields? As far as I could tell, those men were intent on gunning us down, and I'm wondering what in blazes *for*?''

"Yes, well, there is that, sir. One could question that . . .''

Clay gave Ash a curious look. "If I may say so, I'd put it a little stronger than that. I think it's downright peculiar, and then some. I'd say it might very well be worth my *life* to find an answer to a question such as that."

Ash peered into his cup. "I can give you an opinion, Dr. Macon, for what it might be worth. I can't swear it's more than that, but I'd guess there's merit in it."

"Please do," Clay said. "I'd be grateful for your thoughts."

Ash nodded. "One of the, uh . . . One of the deceased down there was a man named Faro." He glanced at Jordan. "You met him once, Mr. LeSec, in a manner of speaking. You knocked the fellow down during that memorable poker game."

"I may have," Jordan said. "I didn't get the man's name."

"Faro was close to Scully, I know that. His number one man. Scully trusted him as much as he trusts anyone, which isn't saying a great deal. Still, I know Faro to be a sluggard, and he's as crooked as his boss. I'd wager a dollar to a dime the man decided he'd rather be in Skagway drinking bad whiskey than dogging you through the wilds and sleeping on the ground. Might be he meant to do the deed for his personal gain. I kind of doubt that. I'd be more inclined to think he'd kill you to impress Scully Flatts. Faro was mean as a hungry dog, but he was an ignorant man, and a coward to boot. He wouldn't have the gumption to cross Scully Flatts."

Clay exchanged a puzzled glance with LeSec. LeSec shrugged, and Clay looked at Ash.

"You've lost me, I'm afraid," Clay said. "This . . . Faro

fellow decided to jump the gun because of what? I don't believe you've made that clear.''

Ash hesitated. Clay was sure his eyes darted off to the mountains and back. The man was uncomfortable, and Clay wondered why.

''I'm . . . guessing it would have to do with a *map,* Dr. Macon. I don't know that, of course, but that's what I'd think, given the circumstance. Perhaps the fellow—Faro, I mean—perhaps he felt it would be a coup to remove you abruptly from the scene, simply take your map from you and give it to Scully Flatts.'' Ash spread his hands. ''No bad nights on the trail, no long separation from the, uh . . . delights of Skagway town.''

Clay leaned closer to the man. ''And why do you imagine these louts thought we *had* such a map in the first place? Why would they presume such a thing when neither I nor Mr. LeSec have ever spoken of a map?''

Ash looked at his hands. ''They could not know that, of course. It's just that . . . well, a great many gold seekers do make use of a map of some sort . . .''

''I've seen a lot of empty pockets up here,'' Jordan said. ''I'm guessing that reflects a lot of fairly worthless maps.''

''And you would be exactly right, sir,'' Ash replied at once. He looked intently at LeSec. ''A study of . . . geological conditions and the art of mining would serve a man far better than a map from some dubious source. Yet many a man would rather stake his life on a scrap of paper than engage in the hard work that—''

Ash cut himself short. He could see both Clay and LeSec staring at him, that both men were aware that he was talking too loud and saying very little at all. The color rose to his face and he ran a hand across his brow.

''I'm sorry, gentlemen, I had no intention of rambling on like that. I . . . believe the heat of the morning has put me down . . .''

"No, sir," Clay said, "I don't believe it has. I believe it is something more than that." It had struck Clay at once—the man's posture, his nervous manner. He was a man who had talked himself into a corner and saw no way to get himself out.

"I'm going to try and cut through all this, and save us both the trouble of outguessing one another," Clay said. "There's something I expect you know, Mr. Ash, and you're unaware that I know it, too. A man came to me in New Orleans, some time after my father's death. He told me he'd been to the North and was aware of certain matters concerning Randal Macon. It was his opinion that I should give him a great deal of money not to discuss these matters in the city where my father was known and respected during his life. After he had his say, I convinced him it would be wise of him to forgo such payment and forever keep this information to himself."

Fullerton Ash paled. It was clear he wished he were somewhere else, anywhere but here with the son of Randal Macon and his friend.

"I hold you blameless," Clay said, reading the look on Ash's face. "You didn't wish to offend me with such a tale, and I appreciate that. But as soon as you launched into this story of a map, I had an idea you'd heard about my father. I expect a great many people in the Yukon know these stories as well. Including, of course, Scully Flatts."

Fullerton Ash let out a breath. "You are right, Dr. Macon. And I would never do you the dishonor of repeating these . . . stories you're referring to."

"But that is just what I'm going to ask you to do," Clay said. "I have heard only one version of those events, and considering the man who repeated them, I cannot credit everything he said. It is important to me that I know as much about my father—about the man known to you as Black Jack Foster."

Clay found it hard to say the name. The words stuck in his throat, but he forced himself to say them with no expression at all.

Fullerton Ash seemed to breathe a little easier now. He wiped the sweat from around his collar and pinched the bridge of his nose.

"How much do you know?" he asked Clay. "I shouldn't like to . . . overstate the matter."

"I only know what I was told in New Orleans. I'd be grateful to hear what you can tell me, sir."

Clay exchanged a quick look with LeSec. Ash couldn't know there was no such person in New Orleans—that what little he knew had come from Patsy Rabbitt. Ash's mention of Faro had brought the name to mind at once. It was the man Patsy had overheard in Skagway. Faro and a man called Darcy. Clay wondered if Darcy was also one of the casualties of this night.

"I met your father several times," Ash said. "I can't say I knew him well. I was just getting started in business up here and I had several enterprises in the town of Fortymile, and along the Klondike and Stewart Rivers. There were plenty of men who knew Jack Foster. That was— It was the name he used up here, you understand. He came into the country in an unusual manner—up Yakutat Bay and over the St. Elias Mountains, through the Dawson Range. He and his partner—I don't recall his name—prospected all along the Stewart River, and pretty well went flat, as a number of men did at the time."

Ash paused and licked his lips. "I mean no offense, Dr. Macon, and you've asked me to relate what I know. Your father . . . changed a great deal after his failure. He became somewhat moody—depressed, I guess you'd say. He took to strong drink and I know for certain he was not a drinking man before. He was not easy to get along with at the time.

Even his partner could do little with him, though I do know that he tried.

"A merchant named Toby Huxley befriended your father when he needed help the most. Toby took him in and literally got him on his feet again. Toby Huxley was a fine man, and he had recently taken a somewhat younger woman as his wife. The first Mrs. Huxley had passed away four years before of fever and complications, and perhaps the misery as well. A number of women, and men, too, for that matter, succumb to these ailments up here. The young Mrs. Huxley, Meridel, was a fine Christian woman, and much in love with her husband. She was an extraordinarily beautiful woman, and I believe that beauty was a reflection of the purity in her heart."

Fullerton Ash hesitated. In spite of Clay's assurance, it was clear he would just as soon end the story there.

"Toby Huxley staked your father and his partner to another try at the gold fields. This time your father headed west. It was the general opinion at the time that he traveled toward the Tanana River—though of course there's no one knows for sure. He was gone for nearly a year. When he came back to Fortymile, he came back alone. His partner had died in the wilderness, he said. Jack Fos— Your father returned a very rich man, sir. He had a sackful of gold that would make a man cry. Not your raw ore with a trace of the stuff, but gold pure as the sun. I saw it myself, a beautiful pair of nuggets Toby Huxley displayed in his store."

Ash looked at Clay. "There's little more to tell, Dr. Macon, but the rest of it's the worst, I'm afraid, as you already know, if your man in New Orleans spoke true. I know what happened, as I was there. You know the tragic ending, but I doubt you could fathom the feelings in Fortymile at the time. There was an— It seems there was a . . . connection of some sort between your father and Meridel Huxley, though I don't think anyone to this day believes Meridel was anything but blameless in the matter. More than once, people heard harsh words between your father and Toby. More than harsh—violent, I'd say.

"Then, Toby Huxley was found dead in his own home. Murdered—strangled and cut up in a terrible way. His . . . his face was swollen up like a melon, and black as pitch. Your father and Meridel were gone. Vanished with all your father's gold, and all he'd given Toby, plus everything of value Toby had.

"Not long after that, the killings and the robberies began. All along the river, men murdered for whatever they had, killed in cold blood in the same manner as Toby Huxley. Cut and strangled till their faces turned black. That's where the name came from, of course. Black Jack Foster. There wasn't any proof your father had killed anyone but Toby, but— Well, as you might imagine, not a lot of proof was called for after the way the victims had died.

"Your father was never seen again, Dr. Macon, nor was Meridel Huxley. Until you returned to the North, not a soul knew who Black Jack Foster really was . . ."

Clay sat up straight. "Until *I* arrived? And what did my arrival have to do with anything? You said yourself Randal Macon never used his name up here."

Fullerton Ash squinted at the sun. "A man accosted you in the alley only moments after you landed in Skagway, sir. I know you must recall that event."

"Yes, I surely do. But what does—"

"The old man told several people what he'd seen. One of them, at least, took the information to Scully Flatts. As near as I can tell, this took place after you and Mr. LeSec were incarcerated. The man who stopped you on the street was Baxter McKay. Not wholly competent now, and he has not been so since his youngest sister disappeared. That was Meridel. Baxter McKay lived with his sister and her husband in Fortymile until a week or so before the tragedy there. When he saw you, he imagined he'd seen a ghost. You do resemble your father, Dr. Macon. I couldn't see it at the time, nor could anyone else in Skagway—except Baxter McKay. Baxter lived with his sister and her husband when your father was staying there as well, and I can see how he might be more . . . inclined to make the connection than another. He— Forgive my saying this, but perhaps a man so obsessed would also be more perceptive than the average observer . . .''

In spite of the growing heat of the day, Clay felt a sudden chill. ''And Scully Flatts let us out of jail and set us up first class in his hotel after the old man said his piece.'' He looked at LeSec. ''God help me, Jordan, the brute thinks I have a map to my father's gold. That's why he's after us. He thinks we'll lead him there!''

''I'm afraid that's the truth,'' Ash said. ''Your father never filed a claim when he returned to Fortymile. And, of course, after the tragic event, he couldn't very well show up anywhere.''

''The gold belongs to anyone who finds it,'' Jordan said.

''Or anyone who kills the man who finds it,'' Clay finished.

Fullerton Ash looked straight at Clay. ''I would not judge a man for his father's sins, sir. And I cannot in all honesty say you should, or should not, profit from what he's done. That's not my place to say. I'm here because I'm determined to rid the land of men like Scully Flatts. We are approaching the twentieth century, Dr. Macon. The time for his kind has come and gone.''

Clay held Ash's gaze. ''His kind . . . and my father's kind as well?''

Ash saw something he didn't want to see and he turned away at once.

''I believe I've said, sir, I don't feel it's right to blame the sins of the father on the son. I, uh . . . I do not hold with that.''

"It looks to me like everyone north of Seattle has already sat in judgment of me *and* my father,'' Clay said. "Without a word of good from anyone. And I don't hold with that, either, Mr. Ash . . . I don't hold with it at all . . .''

TWENTY

FOUR DAYS—SOME good, but mostly bad—had passed since they'd left Fullerton Ash and his men. Clay had done his best to stay clear of the primary route to the North. He had kept his party well away from the larger tributaries of the Yukon River, avoiding the chance of running into strangers. The main road was hazardous enough—hacking your own way was a hardship that was often too much to bear. The sledge was heavy and awkward on the high, treacherous slopes, and the mule was sometimes more trouble than it was worth. Add in a razor-sharp wind, mud up to the knees and skeeters that would drive a grizzly mad, and many days seemed twice as long as the last.

From a high upland ridge, Clay paused to watch the bright stream below twist through the green carpet of springtime grass. Caribou grazed there, eating their way from one bend in the river to the next. The Dawson Range rose up in splendor in the northwest. And slicing through its far, unseen slope was the Yukon River, and the Stewart and the Klondike past that.

More than once, Clay thought of the endless line of prospectors to his east, taking the easier, well-traveled path. Even though the warming weather occasionally made for partially pleasant days, it also posed a problem. As the ground's ice cover grew thinner, the mud turned to an often impassable slush. Every day, it was harder to move the sledge. A great deal of time was spent gauging the best way to shift the heavy load, or angle the runners to make things easier on the ever-weary mule.

They were well past Bennet Lake now, high above a network of the Tagish feeder creeks. Clay was certain he was looking at a spot that had seldom if ever been seen by white men. Western hemlock and red cedar grew thick as reeds on a lake. One tree was home to a magnificent, sharp-eyed eagle. As Clay watched, this awesome bird left its perch and stroked the air with powerful wings. Its high-pitched screech echoed across the valley and sent chills up Clay's spine.

He allowed himself at least a partial sigh of contentment. There were hard days to come, but the map in his head told him their destination wasn't that far away—at least as the crow flies, or an eagle who didn't have to worry with sledges and a mule. North of Whitehorse lay the thumb-shaped Lake Laberge, and north of that and west . . . He couldn't let himself dwell on that, but he couldn't put it away. There was a dragon's spine of gold thrusting out of the ground up there, a great ridge of wealth beyond the dreams of even the greediest of men. All he had to do now was find it . . .

Jordan LeSec and Patsy Rabbitt made no argument at all when Clay announced they'd make camp on the high ground overlooking the greening plain. It wasn't close to stopping time, but if Clay hadn't noticed, they didn't intend to bring it to mind.

If the two had known what Clay had in his head, they might have wished he'd go on. Clay announced that he had a fine idea for making life easier on them all. It would take a little work, of course, but the benefits would far outweigh the effort itself.

"Sure, and I knew there'd be a catch to it," Patsy said. "Just once I'd like to see good times comin' for free, without there being hard labor lurking somewhere close by."

Clay couldn't repress a grin. "You're not well enough acquainted with Mr. Hard Labor to shake his hand, boy. Unless you call lifting wallets heavy work, and I can't see how that's much of a strain."

Patsy looked pained. "I don't think it's fair of you to say that, Dr. Macon. I've put that shameful practice behind me, as you know. Besides, it's a far more tiresome job than you might imagine. There's hazards of every sort involved, and they can wear a person down."

"I won't argue that," Clay said.

"If I were you," Jordan said, "I wouldn't even try."

Clay's idea began to take shape just after an early supper. Working in shifts, Clay and LeSec felled a big fir, then carefully cut and shaped four foot-thick slices from the lowest and fattest part of the trunk. Patsy dragged branches out of the way, and offered more supervision than Clay felt was necessary. When the job was done, he stepped back proudly and announced that they now had four fine wheels, though this was easy enough to see.

In the morning—much too early, Clay admitted to himself—they began to shape a pair of axles, and after that they had the sometimes maddening job of fitting the axles to the wheels. It was Patsy who came up with the concept of applying generous measures of bear hide and bear grease—then reminded Clay and Jordan of his contribution every two minutes or so.

A little after noon, their former sledge wore wheels, and the whole apparatus looked something like a wagon—a machine, Clay assured the others, that would be far better suited to the terrain and the weather ahead.

"If it works," Jordan said under his breath.

"I heard that," Clay said, "and it sorely wounds me, old friend, that you doubt me on this. The Macons have had a way with mechanical things for generations past. We've a special knack for it, there's no denying that."

"I never heard you speak of this before," Jordan said. "Of this special aptitude."

"It may be that I haven't. I'm telling you now."

"I don't guess we even need a test run then. We can just load up this contrivance and be on our way."

Clay cleared his throat. "I'm confident we'll be just fine. However, I have no objection to a test run."

Patsy piped up. "I believed in you all along, Dr. Macon. I never had a doubt. It's a pure marvel, sir, it truly is."

Clay gave Patsy a thoughtful look. After all this time, he was still not sure when Patsy was being sincere, or when he was simply exercising his Irish talent for spreading sheep manure.

Jordan LeSec was perfectly sure what *he* thought, and laughed aloud.

It worked. It held together and rolled. The axles squeaked with a wagonlike sound, the straps and fixtures held, and the wooden linchpins were solid as iron.

"I knew it was sound," Jordan said. "Anyone could tell from the start it had the makings of a vehicle of quality and craftsmanship."

"Thank you," Clay said. "Without your constant support, it would have truly been an impossible task."

Even though they'd traveled above the waterways and steered clear of the rare cabin or crude shelter, Clay and his party did not go entirely unnoticed. Twice they spotted the rising smoke of another campfire and, certain the others had spotted them, hallo'd the men around it and talked barter.

Five pounds of Kodiak meat fetched a good crosscut saw on one visit. Another group was amazed at Clay's knowledge of native plant life. All along the trail, he had stopped to pick the edible greens and roots that had begun to stir in the warming spring topsoil. He'd also spotted herbs that were good for making tea or warding off scurvy. He found men would pay a good price for the chance to eat something besides meat, beans and hardtack.

Clay was not totally at ease with the travelers he met on the trail, but he felt they'd attract more curiosity by trying to hide their passage. Still, before approaching another camp, he looked over the group through his telescope. Then he posted Jordan behind a stand of brush or on a high outcrop with the Winchester, until he was sure of his reception.

Once, two native traders came out of the woods, catching the three completely by surprise—phantoms very much at home in their own thick forests and uplands. They called themselves ''Koo-Chin,'' and they dealt in pelts and primitive, gleaming jewelry that gave ample proof of the territory's mineral riches. They knew all about Kodiak bears and were greatly impressed with Clay's kill. They took a small portion of meat and gave Clay a necklace of pale green stone and white quartz.

At the end of the day, after they'd met the Koo-Chins, the trip nearly ended in disaster. The converted sledge was running fine, bouncing over the rough trail behind the mule, with Patsy at the animal's side. No one was ever sure what spooked the creature, a snake or its mulish imagination, but it happened at exactly the wrong place and time.

Clay heard Patsy yell, jerked around and saw the mule bolt, its eyes wide with fear. Patsy hung onto the traces, trying to settle the animal, but the mule was too frightened to stop. Clay watched in horror as the brand-new ''wagon'' teetered on the edge of the rocky cliff. The ground vanished beneath the rear wheels, and stones rattled into the depths below. Packs, tools, tenting, bedrolls, food—everything they needed to survive—began to slide toward oblivion, as Patsy fought the mule, and the mule fought just as hard to break free.

"Never mind the mule," Clay yelled, "cut loose the *food*, Patsy, don't lose the food!"

Patsy didn't hear, or was too stubborn to quit. Clay watched, dumbfounded, as the boy pulled himself up on the mule and started frantically kicking its sides and jerking its ears. The mule kicked out, gave a terrified bray and nearly shook Patsy free.

Patsy held on. The rear wheels slid farther over the edge and Clay knew he couldn't make it, knew he couldn't get there in time . . . He could already see it in his mind: the wheel giving way, the wagon and Patsy and the mule going over, the boy screaming out and flailing helplessly in the air . . .

The mule made a noise Clay had never heard before—not from a burro or a mule, or a horse of any kind. It was more like the screech of a mountain cat crying in the night. The mule trembled, bucked and took off like a Louisiana thoroughbred. The wagon wheels jerked off the ground, sending a cloud of dust and gravel in their wake. Before Clay could blink, the wagon was ten yards up the trail on solid ground.

Jordan LeSec ran up and braced the wagon's wheels with stones. Clay jerked Patsy off the mule and sat him firmly on the ground. He didn't wait to loose the traces, but slashed them with his knife in case the animal bolted again.

"That was good work," he told Patsy. "You saved us an awful lot of trouble." He looked Patsy up and down. "You hurt any, you all right?"

"I'm fine, Dr. Macon. As good as can be."

Patsy looked a little shaky, but all in one piece. Clay

glanced past him to the mule. It didn't look as if it planned further mischief—in fact, it looked walleyed and subdued, and it was clearly keeping its distance from Patsy Rabbitt. Clay frowned. He studied the mule then looked at Patsy again. Patsy was grinning like a fool and the color was rising to his face.

"What's so funny?" Clay asked. "If you'd gone over that cliff . . ."

"Nothing, sir." Patsy's smiled vanished. "Why, you're right as rain, there's nothing funny at all."

"Patsy—"

Jordan LeSec threw back his head and laughed. Clay stared. LeSec couldn't stop.

"Now, what's the matter with *you*?" Clay was plainly irritated. "I guess I'm the only one who didn't hear the joke."

"You heard it," Jordan grinned. "You just don't understand mule talk." He jerked a thumb at the animal and Clay walked over to its side.

"I don't know what the poor beast said," Jordan told him, "but I doubt it would please Preacher Bill at the First Presbyterian Church."

Jordan held the mule's head straight. The mule's eyes were wide with fright. Clay saw it, then, on the tip of the animal's right ear. There was a bloody half circle, and the clear indentations of teeth.

"The good Lord help us," Clay said. He suddenly understood how Patsy had coaxed the mule into action, and why it had made such a loud and painful sound.

"Why didn't you go ahead and bite it off?" Clay said. "It wouldn't take much."

Patsy tried to look alarmed. "Now, that'd be an act of cruelty, sir. I'm shocked to hear you say such a thing, and you a medical man, too."

Jordan started laughing again, then caught Clay's expression and stopped. Clay muttered under his breath and stomped off. Maybe he could take the incident lightly later on. Now, though, his belly was wound up tight; the image of the wagon and the mule going over the edge, Patsy spinning helplessly in the air, was still clear as death in his mind . . .

Just before sundown, the dangerous trail eased off into a hidden mountain valley, a steep and grassy meadow with a grove of dark trees that sheltered a pleasant creek. The place was a natural campsite—close to firewood and water, and sheltered from the wind and the sight of passersby.

As he did at the end of every day, Clay met the night with mixed emotions. Fullerton Ash and his men had relieved them of the burden of Scully's riders, but Clay was not foolish enough to let down his guard. He considered Ash's actions a reprieve, and nothing more. Before they'd parted, Ash told him, "Look for a different Skagway when you come back, Dr. Macon. We're going to change a lot of things down there."

Fine, if that's the way it happened, Clay thought. But Scully Flatts was no ignorant lout, in spite of his manner and appearance. When his men didn't return, he'd likely recall that his poker companion, Fullerton Ash, and several other townsmen had been out of Skagway at the time. Did Ash think Flatts would be easy, after all he'd done to create his criminal empire? If he did, he was in for a most unpleasant surprise.

Clay remembered the very wry hunter's rule his Uncle Beauregard had taught him: "If you want to chase a grizzly outen his den, first thing you got to remember is *the bear, he don't exactly want to go . . .*"

"I've thought it up one side and down the other," Clay said. I've chewed it till I've got a belly full, friend. If I live to be a hundred and ten, nothing's going to make me believe my father was a cold-blooded killer. I don't care what Ash or any fool says, Randal Macon didn't strangle anyone, or run off with another man's wife. It didn't *happen,* Jordan—you know that as well as I do!''

''Of course I do, Clay. There isn't any question of that, not any at all.''

''Damn right there isn't. There's not a . . . a rational man alive who'd credit such a thing . . .''

''Changing his name, now I can see that,'' Clay said, going over ground Jordan had heard several times before. ''He was a proud man, Jordan, you know that. Maybe a little too proud, but that's how he grew up, that's the man he was. What I think happened is, he didn't want anyone up here to know he was a man who'd been duped by his partner and lost every cent he had. He wanted to start over in the Yukon. I'm not saying he didn't call himself Jack Foster, there's nothing wrong with that . . .''

''Be perfectly natural if he did,'' Jordan said.

''Well now, it would. It'd be just like him to.'' Clay ran a hand through his hair. ''I'm guessing most parts of the story could well be true. Father found the gold, and Adam Carlyle did die in the wilderness, though Randal Macon certainly didn't kill him, as the tale implies. It could also be so, his making friends with this Toby Huxley and his wife. And I'll tell you this—I'm dead sure my father paid the man back handsomely for his help. The rest of it, now . . .''

Clay shook his head and went silent. This was the part where it was hard to go on. Every time he went over the story, aloud to Jordan or in his head, he stopped right there. Right before the horrors he refused to believe, wouldn't let himself imagine. Randal Macon the drunkard, the murderer, the man who'd murdered Toby Huxley and stolen his wife. That, and the other men cut and strangled, their faces turned black.

*He was different when he came back home . . . He wasn't
the same after that, after being up here . . . This country
could do things to a man, awful things you wouldn't
believe . . .*

Once more, Clay swept the haunting visions from his
mind. He felt miserable, overcome with shame that he
could dwell on such thoughts. No matter what had happened to him here, Randal Macon of New Orleans, husband
and father, a man respected by all who knew him . . . No,
he could never have been that other man, he could never
have been things like that . . .

Clay stood abruptly and walked away from the fire, toward the dark grove of trees. Jordan didn't ask where he
was going. He already knew. His friend was going to look
for a moment of peace with himself, for some comfort to
his soul, something Jordan was afraid he wouldn't find.

The night was unseasonably warm in the saddle of the high
valley. The clear air was rich with the scents unleashed by
Clay's passing, the smell of grasses and herbs, the heady
aroma of the wakening earth itself.

He listened to the nightbirds and the sound of running
water close by. The wind rattled the tops of the trees. A
small creature froze at his coming, then escaped in a rush
through the grass. A three-quarter moon was halfway up
the sky, so bright it dimmed the stars.

In spite of the torment within, Clay felt this was one of
the most beautiful places he'd ever seen in his life. A man
could stand in this very spot forever and find perfect satisfaction with his world. There would be no questions un-
answered; he would know all he needed to know.

Walking deeper into the grove, he could see the water
clearly now, see the moonlight flashing on the surface
through the trees. He wondered how this place would be in
the dead of winter. Not at all like it was now, of course,

but it would take on the special chill beauty of the season. The valley might be protected a little by the cliffs soaring up on every side. Still, it would be numbing cold; there was no place in the Yukon you could get away from that.

Clay stopped. Something moved up ahead, a shadow against the trees, a flash of white. What could be out there, what kind of wildlife that size?

He relaxed then and grinned at his own foolishness. With the disturbing thoughts of his father on his mind, he'd clean forgotten Patsy Rabbitt. As ever, Patsy's youthful modesty had led him to bathe apart from his companions. He had wandered off down here after supper, while Clay and Jordan sat by the fire.

A peculiar time to go for a swim, Clay thought. Even if there was a little warmth in the air, the water would be icy cold at night. He shrugged and backed away from his spot beside the trees. The last thing he wanted to do was intrude on the lad's privacy, make him think someone had—

A dry twig snapped beneath his feet. In the quiet of the grove, it sounded like a shot. Patsy, only a few yards away, quickly turned and faced him. He was frozen in a shaft of moonlight, pale as a marble statue, water foaming white about his ankles, staring right at Clay.

Clay's heart nearly stopped. His throat constricted and he couldn't get his breath. The answers to a great many questions raced through his mind at once. Patsy's slight build, the penchant for privacy and that ridiculous, outsized baggy clothing that had effectively hidden Patsy's secret till now, a secret that was hidden no more:

Patsy Rabbitt wasn't a *he* at all. Patsy was very definitely a she . . .

TWENTY-ONE

"THIS IS APPALLING," Clay said, "it's . . . it's *unnatural* is what it is. I cannot imagine that you'd do such a thing to me!"

"I haven't done anything to you, sir," Patsy said. "I've not harmed you in any way."

"You've deceived me, Patsy. You have misrepresented yourself. You have led me, and Mr. LeSec, to believe that you're one thing, and we learn you're something else."

Patsy thrust out her chin. "I am not a *something*, Dr. Macon. I am a person, like yourself."

"Hah! Oh, no you're not. You said you were like me, but you are definitely not like me at all."

"I'm a woman. That's the only difference I can see."

"That's all? Well, that may not be a great difference in your mind. It is a quite a difference to me."

Patsy rolled her eyes. "You didn't even know it until last night. Now all of a sudden I'm a . . . a freak of some kind."

"You are not a freak. Nobody ever said you were a freak, Patsy." Clay felt the heat rise to his face at her mention of that encounter by the creek. He didn't even want to think about that. If he let that scene come to mind . . .

"Besides," he said, "you're exaggerating again. You're

not a woman, you're a . . . a girl. I believe that's the official designation of an underage female. A child who has not reached the status of womanhood.''

Patsy forced a grin. ''You think I'm a child, do you?''

''Yes. I most certainly do.''

''Well, you didn't get a good look then, I guess.''

Clay stared. ''I didn't get *any* kind of a look. I didn't— I wasn't even— Tarnation, I will not engage in talk like this with you!''

''I am twenty-two, for your information,'' Patsy said. ''I'll be twenty-three in September.''

Clay held up his hand. ''See, now, that's another lie. You told me eighteen once before.''

''I never did.''

''Eighteen is what you said.''

''You're mistaken. I said no such thing.''

''You look fourteen, you ask me.''

''I don't believe anyone did. I don't recall inquirin' how old I look to you.''

''Eighteen. I distinctly remember that. I have a very good memory. You don't get through the difficult years of medical training without an excellent memory, I assure you of that.''

''Fourteen, you think.''

''Fifteen, perhaps. I couldn't say for sure.''

''Then you've no cause for concern, Dr. Macon. A child is a different issue entirely. Your morals are in no danger at all, you'll be happy to hear.''

''My *morals* were never . . . were never an issue, not in any way . . .''

Clay let out a breath. Patsy was perched on a rock at the edge of the camp. The morning sun sparkled on his—on her fiery red hair. Clay was miserable. Everything was fine, then everything was wrong, everything was upside down. Patsy didn't even *look* right anymore. The same baggy clothes, the pug nose, the sassy attitude, but—it just wasn't right. Nothing was the way it ought to be.

"The position you have put me in is fraught with difficulties," Clay said. "I don't see how we can proceed on this venture with you being a . . . a . . . being what you are. On the other hand, I can't very well turn around and take you back."

Patsy drew herself up straight. "I've no desire to inconvenience you, sir. Just don't concern yourself with me."

"Will you stop *saying* that, please?" Clay felt his hands shaking at his side. "I do have to concern myself, Patsy. You are a . . . young lady in the wilderness, in the company of two men."

"I wasn't yesterday."

"What?"

"I wasn't yesterday. Just skip the part about the creek, sir, and we'll go on from there."

Clay stared at Patsy a moment, then turned and walked off, muttering to himself. "I assure you, that is not at all satisfactory to me . . ."

Jordan grinned at the scene from the edge of the grove where he was packing up the mule. He felt sorry for his friend. He had seldom seen Clay Macon so flustered in his life. Angrier, yes, and certainly in darker and sadder moods. But for downright bewilderment, the discovery of the true Patsy Rabbitt took the cake.

He had known something was wrong when Clay stalked back from the grove the night before, kicked the cooking pot halfway to Seattle and wrapped himself up in his blanket without a word. A few minutes later, Patsy returned from the grove as well, picked up a bedroll and dragged it as far as possible from Clay. Whatever had occurred out there, Jordan LeSec was sure it wouldn't make for a pleasant day.

Clay woke him early, long before the light, and made

him walk around in the cold—without his morning coffee—
and listen to him rant and rave about the treachery of females in general, Patsy in particular, and the sad state of
world and national affairs. After that, Clay had walked back
to camp, choked down his breakfast and waited for Patsy
to rise. That had been two, nearly three, hours before, and
the pair had been at it ever since.

Jordan shook his head and tightened the mule's harness.
He knew Clay Macon very well. Clay did *not* think women
were treacherous creatures. He liked and respected them,
and was attracted by their charms. He had not entirely put
his feelings for Adele Garnette aside. The wound was still
fresh, but it would heal. Jordan knew exactly what was
going through his friend's head now. He had come to like
Patsy Rabbitt, come to enjoy his companionship, even his
devil-may-care attitude. His, not *hers*. He liked Patsy Rabbitt as a male. Now that he wasn't one anymore, Clay had
no idea what to do. He couldn't very well retain the friendship, could he? That wouldn't be proper at all. And if he
couldn't, then what? He'd have to treat Patsy like a woman,
and he couldn't even imagine such an outlandish circumstance.

"Good luck to you, friend," Jordan said to himself. "I
hope you don't walk off a mountain while you're working
this out in your head."

"She *claims* a good part of her story's true," Clay said,
"but how can I credit that? Dozens of lies so far, one on
top of the next—how are we supposed to guess what's true
and what's not?"

"It's not all that many lies," Jordan said. "One rather
large one, yes, and a few half-truths. I would not go so far
as *dozens,* friend."

Clay blinked at LeSec. "You're what, then? Taking his—
taking her side of this?

"I'm just saying. I am not taking anyone's side."

"It sounds like taking sides to me."

"Well, it isn't, all right? You might try and get ahold of yourself, Clay. Think about something else, get a proper perspective on things."

"Huh! Tell that . . . person over there. Get *her* proper perspective on things. I'm not the one making fools of folks, pretending I'm something else . . ."

Clay was quiet for a moment, a condition Jordan knew wouldn't last. They had climbed out of the valley, back to familiar rocky ground. The sun was nearly straight overhead. Clouds piled up on the far side of the Dawsons, signaling a possible afternoon rain.

Patsy walked ahead beside the mule. Jordan tried to look at her from a purely objective view. That was still Patsy Rabbitt up there. Nothing had changed at all, really. Except that now Jordan saw a gesture or so he couldn't quite recall. A manner of walking, certain indefinable qualities he hadn't noticed before. He decided Clay definitely had a point. There was ample reason for confusion here.

"She says the part about Chicago's true," Clay said. "She and her sister Fiona left there after their father died. They took what money they had and worked their way west then up to Skagway on a boat. The only thing different is— *she* says—they decided two young ladies couldn't possibly travel alone. So one of 'em had to be a brother. No one looked askance at that. They told anyone who asked that their parents were dead and they were going to live with an uncle who was a famous retired lawman from Dodge City, Kansas."

"Which one?" Jordan said.

"What are you talking about?"

"Which former lawman was it? She happen to say?"

"I don't know, Jordan." Clay looked at his friend. "That

was something she just made up; there isn't any uncle anywhere.''

''I know that. I just wondered if they had the good sense to pick somebody real.''

Clay made a face. ''Those two haven't *got* any sense. At least the one we know. Apparently, that story about the poker game is true. I'm inclined to believe Patsy Rabbitt could get in debt to a sharper like Scully Flatts, and that he'd haul the sister off to a farm somewhere to make certain Patsy didn't run. Which he—she would, we both know that. I swear, Jordan, I can't get used to saying she and her. It just doesn't sit right with me.'' Clay slapped at a mosquito that was sucking on his arm. ''He was such a fine lad, too. Showed a lot of promise understanding the outdoor ways.''

''Still does, I'd say.''

''What?'' Clay looked puzzled. ''How can you say a thing like that? Patsy Rabbitt's a woman, Jordan. Sometimes you flat bewilder me, you truly do.''

The breeze off the mountains was cool enough, but the sun was uncommonly hot. Clay was wringing wet by noon; sweat the color of mud stung his face, and he could scarcely stand his own smell. With all the confusion and surprising revelations of the morning, he'd forgotten to shave again, and now he sported a two-day beard peppered with red mosquito bites.

Glancing up ahead, he saw Jordan's rangy form bent to the trail. The back of his neck was dirty, his pants were badly torn and a big streak of bear fat stained his shirt.

Clay wondered what the good folks of New Orleans would think if they could see the city's fair sons now. The Camerons and the DeWills. The snooty Widow Johnson, whose family line was so elegant she wouldn't speak to anyone at all.

And the Garnettes, of course. Adele, and a bevy of cousins, aunts and uncles, was still left in what many imagined was New Orleans's third finest family. Adele would know him, but the others wouldn't recognize him a foot away. If old Hastings Garnette, Adele's father, were still alive, Clay knew he'd laugh his head off and slap him on the back. Hastings had all the money and family he could manage, but he'd never lost touch with the world. He'd been everywhere and done near everything, and nothing much impressed him anymore.

"It's all the same," he'd told Clay once over a glass of Kentucky whiskey. "Everywhere you go it's just people, boy. People livin' on top of one another, and stinking up the Maker's green earth."

Hastings was an enigma to most people—including his own family—but Clay had been fond of the old man. An engineer with an Oxford degree, he'd traipsed through China, South America—everywhere there was a dam or a bridge to build. He had a spear wound from Morocco, a medal from Queen Victoria and an itch to get out and start all over again.

In 1862, the Yankee Admiral Farragut sailed up the Mississippi toward Vicksburg and shelled the Garnette plantation along the way. The house was reduced to rubble, but Hastings simply built it again, bigger and better than before.

Clay had seen portraits of Adele's long dead mother, and he knew where she got her quiet beauty and smoldering black eyes from. But her lively spirit and bold sense of daring definitely came from Hastings Garnette.

I dreamed about your beauty, but I fell in love with your spirit. You should have stayed with me, Adele. We needed each other. It would have worked out real fine . . .

Clay caught himself and shook off his thoughts. He looked up at the mountains and drew in a breath of chilly air. It simply wasn't so, and he knew it. It wouldn't have worked out at all.

It was a bitter truth that men and women in love often chose to ignore. They wanted everything to be perfect, and turned a blind eye toward any barriers that stood in their way. Clay had tried to ignore what had happened between them, but he knew, in his heart, that when he walked out of the Garnette mansion that night he was walking away from Adele for the very last time.

And maybe that was the way it was supposed to be, he decided. If there was a grand plan of some kind, as he truly believed, he and Adele were no part of it at all . . .

"Clay—over here!"

Clay looked up to see his partner some twenty yards ahead. He was standing in a shallow depression by the wagon, his hand on one of the wheels. Patsy stood out of the way beside the mule. She met Clay's eyes for an instant and looked away.

"What you got?" Clay asked. "I hope that left rear wheel isn't splitting. If it is—"

"The wheel's just fine, Clay; it's as good as it can be."

Clay caught the tone of pleasure in Jordan's voice, looked at him again and saw LeSec straining to keep from grinning from ear to ear.

"Down here," Jordan said. "Take a look and tell me what you see."

Jordan squatted down by the wheel and Clay joined him. The wheel was mired six inches deep in a furrow of yellow sand. The furrow was filled with water, perfectly clear water, and as Clay watched, he could see more water trickling in.

"Taste it," Jordan said, "go ahead."

Clay cupped his hand in the chill water. He brought a drink to his lips, but he already knew what he would find.

"It's fresh," he said. "Springwater, Jordan, or I'm an Alabama dog."

Jordan didn't try to hold his excitement any longer. He

laughed aloud, and Clay joined in. Patsy Rabbitt watched the two, bewildered by their actions. What was so all fired wonderful about water? There was plenty of water everywhere.

Jordan LeSec and Clay Macon were likely the only men in the Yukon who thought springwater was the finest sight they'd ever seen. The map they shared in their heads, the site of Randal Macon's gold, was surrounded by freshwater springs . . .

TWENTY-TWO

THERE WAS NO question about it: fresh springwater, a stream not ten inches wide, flowing directly across their paths. Snowmelt wouldn't taste as sweet, and it wouldn't contain itself in such a small but steady stream. Spring runoff would cause a wider, swifter trough.

And if that wasn't proof enough, the plant life growing along the stream told a story all its own. The ferns and grasses were definitely year-round growth. They would never get enough nourishment to thrive during the short life of a runoff stream.

"The springs should form a nearly closed horseshoe," Clay said, "the closed end being where we are now." He nodded to the northwest. "If the place we're searching for is anything like I'm thinking, it'll be something like that valley we camped in last night."

"Shut off from the outside," Jordan agreed. "Only more so, I'd wager. I think you could walk right past it real easy, if you didn't know where to look."

"I hope you're right," Clay said. "I hope that's exactly how it is."

A day, maybe two, Clay thought. They had to be close. Everything seemed to fit with the picture his father had painted in his head. Keep to the uplands then, north by northwest. Maybe they'd spot another spring or two, but it wouldn't much matter if they did. The springs were *there,* they knew that for certain, and their presence pointed the way.

The grade ahead was steady, but not too steep. They were climbing higher now; Clay could look back the way they'd come and see the dark ridges they'd crossed since the morning and, far beyond that, lost in the afternoon mist, the thick band of trees that hid their camp of the night before.

That seemed a long way back, and the event that happened there farther behind him still. He had very much hoped to keep it that way—but to make sure he didn't forget, Patsy Rabbitt was walking toward him, red hair shining like copper in the sun. She still wore her baggy overalls and still looked like an unemployed clown. Somehow, though, the effect wasn't the same anymore.

Patsy fell in beside him without a word, matched his long stride as best she could. Clay pretended she wasn't there. What you didn't think about, what you kept out of your mind, would most likely go away. At least, she hadn't said a thing about the freshwater spring, and he was grateful for that. He had no intention of sharing his father's knowledge with the old Patsy Rabbitt—much less the one who'd suddenly appeared on the scene.

"Mr. LeSec said he'd lead the mule and the wagon for a while," Patsy said. "He's real good with the creature, he is. Me and the animal don't get along so well, not like we did before."

"I shouldn't wonder," Clay said, almost to himself.

"What's that again, sir?"

"Nothing. I didn't say anything at all."

"You'll forgive me then. I plainly thought you did."

"Huh."

"I expect you'll not be speakin' to me often again. That's how it's looking to me."

"I'm sure we'll find it . . . necessary to communicate at times," Clay said. "I've no objection to that, as long as it's something that has to be said."

"Such as what, sir?"

"I beg your pardon?"

"I'm not wantin' to exceed the limitations of my speechifying, sir. So I'd be grateful if you'd give me some guidelines of a sort, what kind of things you'll be wanting me to say. I'm guessing 'Hello' and 'Good evening' and the like are out of bounds, as it were. Whereas, if I was to say, 'Dr. Macon, sir, there's a precious large snake up there where you're about to place your boot,' I'm thinking that would be permissible to say."

Clay looked at Patsy and frowned. "I'd say you're being impertinent is what I'd say. You seem to find something humorous in this . . . in this matter, and I fear that I don't."

Patsy looked away. "It might be you're wrong, sir. You don't know everything, Dr. Macon, even if you like to think you do."

Clay stopped abruptly. Unless she wished to go on without him, Patsy had to stop, too.

"If you've got something to say, just go ahead and say it; don't beat around the bush."

"Anything I have to say, I doubt you'd care to hear, me bein' what I am and all, the female not having near as fine a brain as the male—"

"Stop it, Patsy. Stop it right now!"

Clay turned on her in a fury, and Patsy took a step back, frightened by his sudden burst of anger. It was true she'd meant to bait him, but she knew at once she'd gone too far.

"I'm sorry," she said. "I didn't mean to rile you. Truly I didn't, now."

"Yes, you did, too." Clay shook his head and studied the ground. He was nearly as surprised at his outburst as she was and regretted the fact that he'd let her see him lose control.

"You meant it, but I had no business reacting as I did. I'm— This has been . . . an unusual thing to happen—I don't think you'd argue that."

"No, now, I couldn't very well disagree with you, sir. And if it's any help at all, I'll say I wouldn't have deceived you and Mr. LeSec for a moment. As you know, the deceit was already under way for the protection of myself and Fiona. It's hard to stop such a thing when it's begun."

Patsy kicked at a bed of ants. The creatures scurried frantically about in all directions, sounding the alarm.

"I thought it was a lark for a while. Playing at being a lad. It got old quickly, I'll tell you that. It isn't like your actor on a stage. You can't let it down for a minute—if you do, someone'll likely find you out."

"I hadn't thought about that," Clay said. "I'd guess it's a trying thing to do."

Patsy held his gaze a long moment, as if she truly wanted him to understand.

"You said this morning it's an unnatural thing, and you were right about that. I'm a woman. I'm not a man, and I've no desire to be one. I feel like I'm walkin' about in someone else's skin, and I don't like being in there, I don't like it any at all."

"Then why don't you stop?" Clay said. He let his hands sweep the sky, the broad horizon. "There's no one here you need to fool. No one to keep you from being who you are."

Patsy opened her mouth to speak, then quickly turned away. "I'm flat scared to, I am. I . . . don't know if I can. What if I was to try an' go back to being me and there's nobody there? What's to become of me then?"

"Patsy—"

She was gone then, running up the slope toward Jordan and the mule. He thought he might have seen a glitter in her eyes, maybe perspiration from the heat, maybe a single tear. Or maybe, he decided, it might have been nothing at all.

Jordan believed he'd found another freshwater spring, but if he had, it had dried up some time before.

"I don't care if it's dry or not," he said, "a spring's a spring."

"Not if there isn't any water," Clay said. "That's the thing about a spring, there's always that telltale sign of water. That's how you can tell."

"Huh!" Jordan pulled his hat down over his eyes. "You see a . . . a volcano, it doesn't have hot stuff spewing out the top, it's a what? It's still a volcano is what it is."

"That doesn't make sense."

"And why not?"

"Because it doesn't. Because it's not the same thing at all."

"A person of reason is bound to see it is." Jordan looked at Patsy. "You understand what I'm telling him, right? A spring is still a—"

"No, sir," Patsy said, holding up both hands, "I've got no opinion on the subject, I wouldn't know the first thing about volcanoes of any kind."

"That's all right, neither does he," Clay said. He turned to LeSec. "I don't suppose you've a spare cigar down in your pack somewhere, one that hasn't been slept on or dropped in a spring? A smoke'd be a comfort right now."

"I might have," Jordan said, "but I'm not real sure I'd care to share it with a man too stubborn to admit he's in the wrong."

"If you won't give it to me, I'll buy it."

Jordan frowned. "You think I'd be so crass as that? To sell you a cigar?"

"I think you would."

"How much would you give?"

"I'd go as high as half a dollar, considering the location we're in."

"Two dollars."

"What?"

"Two dollars and it's yours. And it's not broken, either. It's in fair condition, only the slightest bit of flaking on the end."

"Two dollars is outrageous. Do I have to pay you now?"

"Certainly not. A man of repute, especially a medical man, always has credit with Jordan LeSec."

"What a pleasure it is to have a friend," Clay said.

"Words to live by, Doctor. That's as true as it can be."

Clay sat up straight; he had dreamt of Adele again. The night air chilled the beads of sweat that peppered his brow. He felt his heart slam against his chest.

Pushing the blankets aside, he sat up and took deep swallows from his canteen, then slipped into his boots. Jordan and Patsy were shadows beyond the dead fire. The night was bright under cold Northern stars. Clay guessed it was a little after three.

He walked away from the camp, up the side of the hill where he could look down into the dark and silent world below. The forest there was an almost impenetrable barrier, in every direction except the way they'd come. In the morning, he'd have to try and find a way around it—hopefully a route that wouldn't take forever and lead them far off their path.

The heavy woods concerned him. The springs he was expecting were there, and the high, grassy terrain. He felt his father would have mentioned such a prominent obstacle as the woods that lay before him. Maybe they weren't as close as Clay thought. What if they weren't *supposed* to cross the woods, if they'd taken the wrong way when they left the sheltered valley and headed this direction?

He couldn't let himself think about that. If they had to go back, check the landmarks again, it might be days, more than that, before they could—

Clay went rigid. A chill that had nothing to do with the Yukon night touched the back of his neck. Something had moved down there. Something at the edge of the woods. Not a deer or a caribou or any other creature that might be out in the dark. This was something that walked on two legs, paused for an instant in the starlight, then vanished in the forest. again . . .

TWENTY-THREE

CLAY WOKE THE others quietly, keeping low and moving up between them, speaking their names just loud enough to bring them out of sleep.

"Don't get up," he said. "Don't move. Stay where you are and listen to me."

Patsy looked sleepy and scared. Jordan got the message loud and clear. He touched the stock of his Winchester and nodded at Clay.

Clay told them what he had seen. He said he was certain it was a man down there and not some animal or the shadows playing tricks.

"Oh, no!" Patsy drew in a breath. "It's Scully Flatts and his crew come to murder us all!"

"Stop that. *Now.*" Clay quieted her with a glance. "And keep your voice down. Sound carries in the cold night air."

Patsy looked subdued. Clay paused and listened. There was nothing to be heard at all out in the dark. He looked at Patsy and LeSec. Their breath appeared in little puffs of white.

"We're well enough off where we are," he said. "The outcrop gives us good cover, and we won't be exposed until it's light. Jordan—belly down there with the mule and the wagon. Find yourself a spot. Whoever's out there, I don't think it's thieving they're up to, but you never can tell."

"I'm on my way," Jordan said. He took his .44 rifle and a canteen and slipped down the hill. Clay watched him vanish in the dark. Moments later, he heard the faint call of an owl and knew that his partner was in place.

"If you've got any questions, I can't answer 'em," Clay told Patsy. "I saw a man. One. Which means he could be by himself or have a dozen friends." He caught the look in Patsy's eyes and shook his head. "That doesn't mean it's Scully Flatts. We don't know that."

"I'm sorry I went and lost my head, sir. It won't be happening again."

"I know that," Clay said. "You'll do just fine."

Motioning for Patsy to stay where she was with the scattergun, he crawled on his elbows to the side of the low stand of rocks where they'd built the fire the night before. The outcropping sheltered the camp on the north; the rocks angled off to the east and disappeared underground. He kept his eyes on the spot where he'd first seen the man, using the hunter's trick of looking slightly off center so his peripheral vision would pick up any movement nearby. He would have been greatly surprised if he'd spotted anyone in the same place he'd seen them before. Whoever was out there had to be smarter than that.

Clay glanced up at the sky. Close to four, and a long time till first light. Who was it down there? In spite of what he'd told Patsy, Scully Flatts's riders were number one on his list. Ash's attack had staved them off awhile, but Clay had never imagined Flatts would simply give up and go away. Gunmen were cheap enough. Lose one bunch and you could always hire more.

Maybe they'd gotten smart, he decided. Maybe they'd come out this time with one of those Indians Ash had talked about. It wouldn't be hard for a real good tracker to sniff out three people walking, a mule and a wagon.

If they are there, will they wait for first light? Will they come up then?

More than likely, they knew what had happened to the first crew of raiders in the dark and wouldn't care to try that again.

Clay bellied down to check the southern approach. It was too steep to climb, but he checked it anyway. Jordan had the west, so they were all right there.

He let out a frosty breath. *All right* wasn't exactly the way to put it. Three of them, with four directions to cover, and all points of the compass in between. If there weren't more than two or three blind and lame shooters down there, why they'd be just fine.

He couldn't recall a longer night. It seemed to take the chill Northern day forever to appear. He greeted the first pale glimmer of light with anticipation and dread. They'd come now if they were coming; there was just enough night to blur their movement, enough of the day to pick a target out.

Clay was proud of Patsy. She had stayed awake and kept her post without complaint. He knew she was scared. Now and then she had turned to face him in the dark, as if to make sure he was there. Each time he'd returned her glance with a cheery thumbs-up, a gesture she'd answered with a smile.

The first green spear of morning finally broke through the trees. Moments later, the land was swept with buttery light.

"All right, then," Clay said, squinting against the glare, "enough is enough."

He slid past Patsy to her left. Jordan was bleary-eyed. The mule was asleep on its feet.

"I'm thinking no one's down there," Clay said. "I'm going to circle in past you and have a look-see."

"Come back whistling 'Dixie' or I'm likely to shoot. It's been a right irritating night."

"I'll do that," Clay said. He wiped the dew off his Colt revolver and bent into the brush.

"Nothing. Not a broken twig, not a footprint in the grass." He shook his head and sipped scalding hot coffee. "I *saw* a man out there. I didn't dream him up."

Jordan frowned. "I was thinking last night. When you saw this fellow, you kind of assumed he'd seen us—that he knew we were there. It was, what—three in the morning? Maybe he didn't, Clay. Maybe he passed us by."

Patsy looked hopeful at that. "Sure, I'll bet that's the answer, sir. It was just some prospector, that's all in the world it was."

"I'd like to go along with that," Clay said, "but a man up in these parts, spooking about in the dark alone? And not leaving any sign at all?" Clay shook his head. "I'm afraid that doesn't work for me." He shook off the question in Patsy's eyes. "I don't know who it was, I haven't got any idea. We're carrying arms at the ready today, and we're staying up close. Anyone has a better idea, I'm all ears."

"When's the next boat back to New Orleans?" Jordan said.

Clay grinned. "If I knew that, I might race you to the dock, friend."

The going was easy and hard, easy and hard in a steady repetition, up and down steep hills creased like an unruly carpet across the earth. Clay was concerned. The hills were such an obvious feature in the land, they should have been in his father's directions. Unless—as he'd thought when he saw the thick woods the day before—unless they had gotten off the trail somehow and were wandering off the mark.

There should be a shallow valley, and high granite

ridges sharp as the edge of a blade, sabers that scrape the sky . . .

Only there weren't any valleys, only the folded, rocky hills, so steep going up it was all the three of them could do, along with the mule, to get the wagon to the top. And, going down the other side, there was always the danger everything would give way and the animal, the wagon and all their goods would go racing downhill to be smashed in a million pieces. It had almost happened before, and Clay remembered the countless shards of broken timber, scattered wheels and skeletons of burros and mules that littered the treacherous passes on the way from Skagway. In this lonely corner of the world, your life could end quicker than you could blink.

At noon, they came to the steepest hill yet. Clay looked up the slope with dismay. They were already weary, whittled to the bone. The hill up ahead might as well have been a snowcapped peak of the Rockies.

Clay asked Patsy to stay with the mule and wagon, while he and Jordan climbed the hill. It was rough going, even without the burden of a pack. Still, the two ran the last few yards to the top, anxious to see what the rest of the day had in store.

"By all that is holy," Clay said, staring at the awesome sight below. "I'd like to say I'm surprised, but there's little about this trek that could surprise me anymore."

Jordan didn't answer. He peered over the ragged edge of the hill. This was the end; there was no place else to go. Even if they could empty the wagon and carry loads up to the top, there was no way down the other side. The hill ended abruptly, a few feet from where they stood, the landscape plunging straight down. It looked as if some giant had taken an enormous bite out of the earth, chewed it up and spit it out again. The deep rift, yawning over five hundred feet below, was filled with rocky rubble. The tops of dead trees poked through the debris.

"I don't have the least idea where we are," Clay said. "If this disaster happened before or after my father was here I can't tell. I don't even know that he came this way at all. There's nothing around here that's where it ought to be."

He glanced down at Patsy and the mule and the wagon below. The folds they'd crossed were choked with thick growth on either side. There was no way to go but back the way they'd come. He thought about the long and weary hours behind them, manhandling the wagon up and down the rocky hills.

"Unless you've got a better idea, I say we've got to do it," Clay said. "I don't see us going through all that again. There isn't any other way that I can see. We take what we can carry and leave the wagon here. We either find our way or we don't. The goods'll likely be safe where they are."

Jordan's expression mirrored Clay's distress at this decision. In the wilderness, it was never a good idea to abandon your supplies, even if you meant to come back. Anything could happen to cut you off, keep you from finding your way again.

"There's no use thinking about it," Jordan said, "let's go."

The mule was used to pulling the wagon and balked at the idea of carrying a load on its back again. Patsy didn't give the beast time to argue. She explained in no uncertain terms that mules had two ears, and the other could be chewed off as easily as the first. The animal gave Patsy a baleful eye and seemed to understand.

When it was done, when they'd taken everything they could carry, they started back up the way they'd come. No one cared to look back at the wagon, still loaded with most of their precious supplies. They'd be back soon, they told themselves, this was only temporary.

Clay Macon had no intention of covering every inch of ground they'd crossed since morning. The more he thought about it, the more certain he became that they hadn't really strayed that far from Randal Macon's route. If the landmarks weren't there, it was simply because they'd missed them somehow, or they didn't look quite the same now. Maybe his father had passed this way later in the year, not at the beginning of spring. If he'd come through here in winter, say, then *nothing* would look the same.

"If we don't see anything familiar by nightfall," Clay said, "I'd like to try and find a way through those thickets to the west. It can't be as hard going as it looks. There has to be a break somewhere."

"And why's that?" Jordan asked.

"Why's what?"

"Why does there have to be a break somewhere? It doesn't stand to reason that just because you'd like to find a way then we will. I mean, it's very possible we won't."

Clay let out a breath. "Jordan, I can think of a dozen unhappy surprises on my own. I don't need any help from you."

"Well, just trying to be *logical*." Jordan shrugged. He stopped to mop his face. "No sense fooling ourselves in the face of adversity, Clay. Might as well face up to it now as later on."

"Let's not," Clay said.

"Not what?"

"Let's not face up. Let's fool ourselves. I think I'd like that."

"Whatever you think," Jordan said. "For myself, however—"

The first rumble of thunder cut off Jordan's words. The distant sound shook itself through the Dawson Range to the east and rolled off every hill and hollow in between. Almost at once, a chill wind sliced across the rocky face, bringing the smell of rain. The sun disappeared, the land grew dark, and the first black, roiling clouds swept into view.

Clay felt his throat go dry. He glanced at the sky, then ran toward his friends. "Don't try for the top," he shouted, "get to the thicket. Patsy—hold onto that mule!"

The animal was already wild-eyed, its nostrils flaring with fear. Lightning crackled out of the sky, striking the ground nearby. The heady smell of ozone filled the air. The rain hit with no warning, slamming into the hill like a solid wall. Clay yelled at Jordan, his words lost in the deafening noise. He'd been caught in mountain storms before; he knew how quick and deadly they could be. Water was rushing by him now, small rivulets coming together, each gaining strength from the next, until a torrent roared into the hollow below.

Patsy cried out, lost her footing, then caught herself again. Clay came to her side to help. She shook him off and forced a smile. Rain plastered auburn hair to her face. The rain ran in her eyes and mouth and she ducked her head and bent into the wind. Lightning struck less than twenty yards away, sizzling across the stony earth. The mule went wild and ripped the halter from Patsy's hands. Jordan stretched out and caught the animal before it bolted.

With Patsy hanging on, Jordan struggled up the slope with the mule, forced the animal into the thicket and secured it tightly to a tree. Clay joined them a moment later. The heavy tangle of branches overhead took some of the brunt of the storm, but not enough to help. Clay wished they'd thought to bring their slickers from the wagon, but there were other items more valuable than that.

Thunder shook the ground, and the lightning seemed to lash out in one continuous burst of light and sound.

"I've never *seen* anything like this," Jordan shouted,

close to Clay's ear. "Now I know what they mean about coming down in buckets!"

"This isn't buckets, this is barrels. You should've gone to Colorado with me. The rain fair drove you to the ground; a man couldn't stand up."

Jordan made a face. "You don't mind, I don't care to hear any more about Colorado. This right here is good enough for me."

"Dr. Macon, over here!"

Clay and Jordan turned at once. Patsy was bent beneath a narrow strip of tarp she'd discovered in her pack. Rain was streaming down her face, and the tarp wasn't helping at all. She tried to speak, but her mouth wouldn't work. She stared at Clay and LeSec and pointed dumbly toward the rocky slope where they'd stood only moments before.

Clay moved past her and squinted into the rain. The hillside was a waterfall now, roaring into the hollow below. And beyond, past that, in the woods on the other side . . .

The thicket across the way angled down from higher ground. The trees and undergrowth had disappeared in a raging flood of muddy water; earth, stones and great firs and cedars swept by in the runoff from a hundred hills and promontories. Clay saw it, and his stomach tightened into a knot. Jordan saw it, too. He swore in a rapid string of Cajun, words seldom heard outside of the deep bayous.

Perched atop the naked roots of a tall tree, their wagon and former sledge rushed by, rolled once and vanished in the dark and swirling waters.

TWENTY-FOUR

THE RAIN ENDED as quickly as it had begun. Clay had seen it happen many times before. In mountain country, you could look right through the edge of a storm, see the end coming, and watch the sun appear again.

"There's no use thinking on it," Jordan said. "There isn't anything we could've done. We'll be just fine. People get by in the wild on a lot less than we've got in our packs right now."

"You're right," Clay said, "they surely do."

He wondered who LeSec was trying to convince. His partner looked like a wet and miserable dog who'd lost his last friend.

"I'm missing coffee some," Jordan said. "Other than that, I've no complaints at all. I don't like starting the day without a little coffee inside."

"If we had some acorns, sir, I'd fix you a fine hot drink," Patsy said. "Why, acorn coffee's near as good as true coffee itself."

"It is?" Jordan gave Patsy a hopeful look.

"It surely is, sir, I promise you that."

"She's right," Clay said, "it's not bad at all."

"Well, then . . ." Jordan's face split into a smile. "Could

we possibly make some now? It's not mealtime, I know, but we could overlook that.''

Patsy chewed her lip. ''I don't see how I could, Mr. LeSec.''

''And why not?''

''No acorns, sir.''

''What?''

''I don't have a single acorn, not a one.''

''We could gather some then. We could do it right now.''

''No, we couldn't,'' Clay put in. ''You've been in the woods before, Jordan. You may recall acorns grow from oaks. We're too high up for oaks.''

Jordan stared. ''All of those . . . trees, you're telling me not one of them's an oak?'' He gave Patsy a painful look. ''Then what did you bring it up for, Patsy? Here I am almost tasting this . . . this acorn coffee, and— Oh, never mind. I doubt if I'd like it anyway.''

Clay watched his partner stalk off into the thicket to get his pack. He still looked like a wet dog; now he looked like a wet dog that had lately been whipped.

''He does like his coffee in the morning, that's a fact.''

''He does that, sir,'' Patsy said.

''We're not exactly out. I saved a small sack from the wagon.''

''Say, now that's fine, sir.'' Patsy grinned. ''Mr. LeSec'll be mighty pleased!'' Her smile suddenly vanished. ''If that's so, then why did you not tell him so? It'd bring him great pleasure to know.''

''Right now, he doesn't see a chance of having coffee until we reach civilization again. He'll brood for the rest of the day, and that'll be that. If I tell him I've got some on hand, he'll be delighted, but he'll want to drink it now. Then it'll all be gone and he'll start complaining again. So the longer we put it off, the longer he'll be at peace, and the longer you and I won't have to listen to him. And that's why you'll not mention that there's any coffee within a hundred miles of here.''

Patsy stared, her mouth open wide. ''I'm purely humbled in the face of your wisdom,'' she said. ''I'd never have thought of such a thing, Dr. Macon, it would've never crossed my mind.''

Clay hid a smile, almost willing to believe this blatant Irish blarney.

''Jordan and I have known each other near forever,'' he said. ''If you can't do a dear companion a favor now and then, well, what are friends for?''

''You're surely right in that,'' Patsy agreed.

The runoff on the hillside had diminished to a trickle, but the rocky surface was still slick as glass, and some of the stones had been loosened by the rain. Clay kept his crew close to the thicket, where the grasses still held the soil. It was fairly slow going, but a slip in the wilderness could break an arm or a leg, and even a minor fracture could prove fatal so far from any help. He could set a broken bone just fine, but if the bone should pierce the skin, or infection set in . . .

''Just watch your step,'' he told the others. ''I'm not in the mood to do any doctoring out here.''

It was Jordan LeSec who spotted the ravine. If they'd been climbing straight up the hill, as they had before the storm, they would have passed it right by. LeSec was leading the mule up close to the woods when he saw the patch of white through the trees. At first he thought it was the sky, but he knew at once it was too low for that.

Tying the mule to a tree, he bulled his way through the thick tangle of vines and second growth a good ten yards into the trees, gathering cuts and bruises along the way. Even so short a distance was a strain, and the effort left him gasping for breath. Then, after he tore a veil of undergrowth aside, there it was: A fault line had thrust up through the earth, leaving a narrow, V-shaped ravine, a declivity twenty feet high on either side. The near impenetrable thicket formed a tunnel of green overhead, but the great upthrust of granite kept the trees and undergrowth at bay.

Clay felt the discovery was some compensation for the storm and losing all their goods. The ravine ran nearly level and due northwest. It was like finding a convenient doorway through a solid brick wall.

"I know what you're thinking," he told Jordan. "There isn't any such place in my father's directions, but those swayback hills weren't there either. I'm for taking it easy for a change, see where we end up. We can't be any more lost than we are right now."

Jordan patted his pocket for a cigar that wasn't there. Patsy was out of earshot down the draw, easing the packs off the mule for a while. Jordan looked down the ravine, but his thoughts were farther away than that.

"You think we'll find it, Clay? I'm not saying anything, you understand, I'm just asking what you think."

"I think we're flat lost, like I say. I think we found one of the springs right where it's supposed to be. I don't know what we did wrong after that." He felt his partner's gaze. "There's only two things to do, same as there ever was: Go ahead or go back."

Jordan looked appalled. "For the life of me, Clay Macon, you're wrong about that. There isn't any choice but one, and you know it!"

"I never thought there was," Clay said.

It was almost too easy, he thought, but he wasn't about to complain about that. Rain, spring runoff and years of erosion had formed a dirt-and-gravel pathway through the fault. It was much like walking down a well-kept city street. Only the occasional boulder stood in the way, and none were too large to let a person or a mule go by. Even the foliage from either side of the ravine seemed to add to the traveler's comfort. The branches met and entangled to form a canopy of shade.

Climbing the folded hills, abandoning the wagon and re-packing stores had taken a large part of the afternoon. Running from the storm had eaten up the rest of the shorter Northern day. Evening came quickly in the hollow of the ravine, and Clay and his crew had been on the trail less than two full hours before the light began to fail.

With the darkness came the chill, a sharp and biting cold that always took newcomers to the Yukon by surprise. Supper was hardtack and pan bread, and the last of Clay's greens. The fire was more than welcome, and, for once, there was an abundance of dry wood nearby.

For the first time in many nights, there seemed no reason to worry about intruders. The foliage was so thick over-head, no one fifty feet away could spot the fire, and the smell of smoke would dissipate quickly in the heavy undergrowth. Clay figured anyone who could even *find* the ravine was a woodsman who'd put Daniel Boone to shame.

The day had been full of hazards; Clay, Jordan and Patsy Rabbitt were aware of the fact that any or all of them could have easily not survived to sleep that night. There was little talk around the fire. No one had anything to say.

Jordan and Patsy were breathing easily under their blankets long before the embers began to die away. Clay took his usual turn around camp, a much shorter stroll this time; it was nearly too dark in the ravine to see his hand before his face.

He crawled into his bedroll and dropped off to sleep without a thought. If he dreamed, the dream faded, and sooner than he wished, he opened his eyes to the light.

Clay was irritated that the night had seemed to vanish without the illusion of passing time. A night like that didn't give a man a feeling that he'd gotten any real rest at all.

There was only the palest touch of light in the ravine. He lay still and listened for the first sounds of morning. It was unusually silent, even for a Yukon dawn. Maybe the birds were cold, too. Maybe they figured to wait until the sun worked its way through the canopy overhead . . .

Clay sat up, immediately alert, grasping his blanket about his shoulders, his senses suddenly sharpened by a feeling he could neither see nor hear. Cold or not, there ought to be birds; it was light enough for that. The Yukon wasn't that different from anywhere else. The birds had to—

The sound pierced the silence, a deep-throated thrum, and a fraction of a second after that, a hum like angry bees. Clay froze, every muscle and tendon in his body twisted up tight. The arrow whined past his cheek and ripped through the fabric of his blanket, jerking it off his shoulder and pinning it to the ground . . .

TWENTY-FIVE

"JORDAN—TO ARMS!"

Clay Macon shouted out a warning as he tore free of the blanket and threw himself at Patsy Rabbitt. Patsy screamed, coming quickly out of sleep; Clay scooped her up and sprawled against the far side of the ravine.

A second arrow sang overhead, sparked on granite and snapped in two. Another whined in the shadow of the first, struck the dead fire and showered the mule with smoking embers. The mule made a terrible sound, snapped its tether and bolted out of sight.

LeSec cursed under his breath. He hugged the back of the ravine, his Winchester at the ready.

"That volley was too fast for one man," Clay said. "Got to be at least two of 'em."

He hesitated and listened; pointed past Jordan, jabbed at himself, then at the packs. Jordan nodded and moved off down the draw.

Patsy looked at Clay in alarm, guessing what he had in mind.

"Sir, you mustn't do that," she said, grabbing at his sleeve. "You won't get a foot and a half out there!"

"Those boys can punch the eye out of a gnat," Clay told

her. "If they wanted to kill us, we wouldn't be standing here now."

He handed her the Colt and peered up the rocky wall. "Stay here and stay flat. One thing they *can't* do is get close enough to shoot down. If one of 'em tries it, start firing that thing and don't stop." He looked at her a long moment. "I know you can do it, I saw you do it before."

Patsy forced a smile. "I'll do well enough, I will."

Clay took a breath and nodded at LeSec, ten yards down the ravine. LeSec stepped back and loosed a rapid volley at the rim overhead. His hand worked the lever in a blur. In the same instant, Clay leaped from cover, grabbed up their packs on the run and sprinted back to the wall. A single arrow thrummed out of the brush, but Jordan had shaken up the intruders, and Clay reached the wall without a scratch.

"You're all right, then," Patsy asked. "You're not hurt, Dr. Macon?"

"I'm fine," he told her, handing Patsy her pack, "piece of cake."

He slid the straps of his own pack over his shoulders. The big Sharps was tied to the back with leather thongs. He felt a great sense of relief to have it back. It wasn't any use in the narrow ravine, but he wasn't about to leave it sitting behind.

Jordan came up beside him, slipping fresh shells in the rifle.

"That looked like fun," he said.

"No problem," Clay said, "safe as a Sunday walk."

"And where would that be? The Little Big Horn?"

LeSec retrieved his pack. Clay got the revolver back from Patsy and checked the loads again.

"I still say there's no more'n two. You all right with that?"

"I'd reckon so," Jordan agreed.

"I was telling Patsy I figured they were good enough to do us all in if that's what they had in mind. I'm thinking they're saying 'you folks aren't welcome here.' "

"They're getting the message across to me," Patsy said, "and I can't speak a word of Indian, sir."

Jordan caught Clay's eyes. "It was one of them you saw in the woods back there. They tracked us to here."

Clay nodded. "I'd bet on it and give good odds. If they don't want to kill us, they want us out of here," he said, "and I don't much care for trekking back the way I've been."

Patsy piped up. "Me neither. It's flat humiliatin', and I won't stand for it, sir."

"My thoughts exactly," Jordan said and grinned.

Clay looked into the tangled canopy overhead. "Let's see how serious these fellows are. It's easy enough to find out."

As Clay had said, there was no problem putting the Indians to the test. Still, it was hard on the nerves—every time a curve in the ravine gave the bowmen a target, their arrows flew with such frightening precision it was hard to imagine they weren't aimed to kill. Jordan raised his foot in disgust and looked at his boot. An arrow had scoured a narrow groove in its heel.

"I'm impressed," he said under his breath. "You all like to quit doing that now?"

Clay was pleased when the ravine straightened out again half an hour later. The Indians were enjoying themselves, cutting their misses pretty thin. The "game" they were evidently playing presented a dilemma. If one of the Indians showed himself, Clay, Jordan or Patsy would have a quarter second at best to decide if they dared risk returning the favor. And what if the Indians changed their minds? Someone'd have an arrow in his gut before he could start to blink.

Why do they want us to turn back? Is their village nearby, or what?

Clay tried to remember whether he'd heard the northern tribes had sacred burial grounds like their brothers to the south. Maybe that was the problem; Indians got real riled up over that. A bigger question was why this bunch bothered to spare three travelers at all. Drop the bodies in a hole somewhere, who would ever know?

Something was making these fellows itch. The Indians they'd met along the way, the Koo-Chins, were certainly friendly enough, but this group didn't want to trade beads— this bunch wanted to play games where a man could get himself dead.

The massive, fault-driven walls of granite that had ground themselves together to form the ravine came to an end as quickly as they'd begun. Clay signaled the others to a halt as the pathway vanished abruptly in a head-high tumble of fractured stone. The path was a dead end ahead and to the left. To the right, however, a new route twisted off and downward in a sharp and steady decline.

Clay could guess what had happened. The granite ravine became a river during the heavy rains and spring runoff from the snows. Flood-driven boulders jammed up where the rock face ended, and the water flowed off to the right. Over time, it had worn its way through the softer stone and formed a twisting, narrow cleft, scarcely four feet wide. The walls were slick as a wormhole and striated with a dozen shades of orange, brown, yellow and white.

Clay looked up at the narrow expanse of sky. The Indians knew exactly where the intruders were. If they liked, they could sit up there and command the way in and out with no trouble at all. They wouldn't even have to waste arrows. They could toss down rocks and hold a small army at bay.

He glanced at Jordan and Patsy. Their expressions told him all he needed to know. There was only one direction: straight ahead.

It was cooler in the wormhole, sheltered from the sun. The slick stone was damp to the touch.

"We've been heading down since we left the thicket," Clay said, "but nothing like we're doing now. It's getting steeper all the time."

"I'm hopin' it'll end somewhere," Patsy said. "I don't like narrow places, Dr. Macon. I feel like everything is closing in."

"There's an end," he told her, "I promise you that." He touched her arm and pointed at the sandy floor. "That's our mule's tracks, right there. And those real shallow ones are Indian moccasins, headed the same way we are. This place has been used a long time."

Patsy raised a hand to her throat. "I'm not certain that's the answer I cared to hear. I was hopin' maybe we'd found a secret way."

"There's plenty of secret ways up here," he told her, "but I'm guessing our friends out there know them all—" Clay stopped abruptly and motioned the others back. "Look at the light—we're coming out!"

Jordan had seen it, too: the brightness, the sudden expansion of the rim overhead. He levered a shell into the Winchester and stood at Clay's side.

Clay drew the revolver and walked cautiously ahead. The wormhole leveled out into a grassy hollow surrounded by a grove of tall pines. Bright red runners and yellow blossoms of silverweed clung to the massive boulders that had tumbled down from above.

Clay motioned the others to him. There was no use trying to stay in cover now. The Indians would be perfectly at

home in this clearing and were likely watching from somewhere at that very moment.

No one spoke as they walked through the clearing and
into the grove of trees. There was no underbrush here, only
a soft carpet of moss and green fern.

There's water here, Clay thought, *and plenty of it* . . . He
could smell the heady scent of the loamy earth, almost feel
life stirring in the soil. The air was clear and clean, but it
was much warmer here than on the rocky heights they'd
crossed the day before, or in the ravine itself. He sensed
the valley was protected; they were still quite high, and it
shouldn't have been as mild this far to the north . . .

And then the trees began to thin, and he walked out of
the grove and into the warmth of the sun . . . He saw it,
then, the sheer, dizzying heights of gray-pink stone that
surrounded the valley, a great unbroken wall like the spires
of a thousand cathedrals, rising nearly a quarter mile high,
their tips lost in a mist of white clouds . . .

Below him stretched a valley so green and lush it almost
hurt his eyes, and he knew at once he'd found it, that this
was his father's valley, that Randal Macon had stood where
he was standing now . . . and, Clay was certain, he had
gazed at this place with the same sense of wonder, knowing
that he'd somehow stumbled on a Northern paradise . . .

Clay was overcome with the thrill of discovery, with the
knowledge that all of it was here, exactly as his father had
said it would be. And if this part of it was true, then it
stood to reason the gold was here as well. Randal Macon
had brought gold back to Fortymile, and this is where he'd
found it. Here was the site of that dragon spine of riches
that had thrust itself out of the earth to rival the brightness
of the sun.

He strolled down into the valley, all thoughts of Indians
or any other dangers put aside. Clay Macon of New Orleans
was here, and nothing could stop him now. He laughed as

he saw their lost mule, grazing far below, filling its belly with more soft grasses than it had ever dreamed of before.

He saw the springs, then—not one, but three—blue pools that shivered in the light, fresh water bubbling up in their centers, spreading in perfect circles to sandy shores. *The good Lord help us,* he thought, *no wonder the valley is green! There's enough fresh water here to—*

The arrows buried themselves to the hilt, inches from his feet. Clay stopped. From the corner of his eye, he saw Patsy reach for the scattergun, saw Jordan raise the .44.

"No," he said softly, without moving his head, "don't. Let them make their play. They'll tell us where we stand soon enough."

He could see them clearly now, two shadows watching from the trees, fresh arrows nocked and ready. He turned to face them, his hands spread and empty in the universal gesture of peace. The Indians didn't move. Clay wanted to take a step forward, but decided to hold his ground. He didn't know what they were thinking, what they might take as an aggressive move against them . . .

"*Clay!*"

"I see it," Clay said. He took a deep breath and held it. "I see it, but I don't guess I believe it."

The woman walked out of the trees. The Indians parted to let her through. She took two steps into the clearing, then came to a halt and whipped the shotgun from behind her long skirts. Holding it steady at her waist, she swept the double barrels along the line of Clay and his friends.

"Don't move a muscle, any of you," she said. "I'd just as soon drop every one of you on the spot."

She spoke perfect English, likely from the Midwest, Clay thought. Ohio, and maybe Indiana. She was tall, slender, dressed in all black. A gray bonnet all but obscured her features.

"You don't have to point that thing at us," Clay said.

"We're not looking to cause any trouble, ma'am."

"Hah! Now, is that right? Don't want to cause any *trouble,* just kinda passing by."

"If you could let us talk—" Clay took a cautious step forward.

"Stop!"

The woman raised the weapon and fired. Black smoke and a yellow tongue of flame exploded from one of the twin barrels. The shot was deliberately high, but Clay, Jordan and Patsy ducked and covered their heads. The sound of the gun echoed like thunder, rolling across the high walls of the valley.

"Might be that'll answer any fool questions you got in your heads," the woman said. "And no more talking, hear? Just drop those weapons to the ground, real easy like."

The three did as they were told. For the first time, Clay got a look at her weapon. It was an old Remington 10-gauge. He hadn't seen one in a while.

The woman turned and rattled off a string of harsh, throaty sounds. The Indians emerged from the trees, weapons at the ready. Clay stared at the pair. Behind him, Jordan muttered to himself. They were Koo-Chins, as Clay had figured they'd be, but they were anything but the fierce "warriors" he'd imagined when their arrows were whipping by inches from his face. One was a man, and the other was a woman, and neither could have been any younger than sixty or sixty-five. Not that it mattered anymore. Their bodies were old, but apparently their eyes were dead true.

The woman walked to one side, the Remington steady in her hands. Clay didn't have to look; he knew the Koo-Chins were behind. He heard them retrieve the weapons, and hoped they'd handle them well. He intended to get them back.

He glanced at the woman. He couldn't imagine who she

could be. What was she doing out here, alone in this valley, with two ancient Koo-Chins?

Clay checked himself. He was taking a lot for granted. He had no reason to believe there weren't others here. There might be a whole clan here, and very likely was. If there were, they might have reason to hole up here—and even more reason to make sure strangers didn't go back to reveal their whereabouts.

Clay felt a sudden chill. Lord a'Mighty, in the excitement of the moment he'd forgotten that whoever they were, they'd for certain found the gold—*his* gold, the treasure his father had found that now belonged to him! The heat rose to his face. They couldn't do that, not now, not after all they'd been through: Scully Flatts and his shooters, the hardships, the storm that had swept their wagon away. They had no business, no right to take what was his! No right to—

Clay Macon froze. He felt his knees give way; stumbled, caught himself and stared. The corner of a house had appeared past the trees, and, seconds later, more than a corner, a doorway, a gabled roof, windows, a garden leading up along the steps ... It was a grand, impossible house, perched on the grassy heights in the shadow of the awesome stone wall. It wasn't just any house, it was his. Clay Macon's. The house he was born in, the house Randal Macon had built for his bride in faraway New Orleans ...

TWENTY-SIX

CLAY WAS STUNNED—staggered—by the sight. It couldn't be, and yet it was. *His* house, here in this lost Northern valley, as far from the hot and sleepy city on the Mississippi Delta as a man could possibly be.

He heard Jordan draw in a breath; he had seen it, too. Clay wanted to turn to his friend, but his eyes were locked on the scene below. He saw now what he'd failed to see in that first astonished glance. The house was incomplete, a shadowy projection of the Macon home in New Orleans. It was an unfinished dream, a ghostly vision of a gingerbread palace set in a grove of dark trees. Two sides were nearly done. The roof was half-shingled, leaving the rest of the structure open to the sky. A familiar turret crowned the single, finished corner of the house. Clay felt a chill at the sight, for the tower was exactly like the one that had held his father's private study. There, he had often worked far into the night, trying to pick up the pieces of the company his partner had left in a shambles when he fled the country with his Creole beauty, leaving his family behind.

"Heaven help us, Dr. Macon," Patsy said beside him, "what kind of place is this, sittin' out in the middle of nowhere?"

"That's going to take a while to answer," Jordan said, "and I don't think I'd ask him right now."

Why, Father, why did you do it? Why did you rebuild your world up here, when all we wanted was you back home with us!

The woman came to a halt. "Stop right there and sit. Right now." She raised the twin barrels of the Remington an inch and a half—just about right, Clay thought, to tear off his head if she happened to pull the trigger or the thing went off.

"Meaning no offense," he said, "but you want to be real careful with a weapon like that. It can—"

"*Sit!*" The barrels dropped a foot. Great, Clay thought, it's a gut shot now. He lowered himself and sat.

"What do you think she's going to do with us, sir?" Patsy said. "Are we goin' to be all right?"

"I don't know," Clay said softly, trying not to move his lips. "I'm not getting any real friendly feelings so far."

"This ground is wet," Jordan said. "The least she could do is let us have some chairs."

"Most likely she will. Soon as she serves tea and cookies."

"I am looking forward to that. I'd much prefer coffee, but tea will do fine. Tea and a fresh cigar."

Patsy winked at Clay. "I know where you might find a cup of coffee, Mr. LeSec."

Jordan frowned. "And where would that be? What are you talking about, girl?"

"She's suffering from illusions," Clay said, "same as you. I think it's the altitude."

The tall woman walked around and behind the three, lowering the weapon to her side. Clay could hear her conferring with the Koo-Chins. Whatever she was saying, it didn't sound good. The harsh, rapid words of the Indian tongue didn't lend themselves to gentle speech—certainly not to a man raised on the lazy, liquid sounds of New Orleans.

Clay looked beyond the facade of clean lines and graceful filigree that gave the house below its distinctive Southern flair. The Yukon winters had taken their toll, and the place was falling apart. Uncovered struts had gone black with the wet. Shingles and clapboards hung loose on rusted nails. Two, maybe three rooms on the east side of the structure were finished and enclosed. The rest was a hollow, skeletal shell. Another winter might see the thing sagging to the ground.

Or maybe not, Clay thought. His father hadn't likely started the place before 1888 or 1889. Surely the weather would have brought the place down by now, if the winter chilled this valley the way it did the rest of the country nearby . . . And if it did, why was everything so lush and green, why wasn't it as cold as it ought to be, even in the spring?

Is this what you saw here, Father, a haven, a paradise? A place where you could hide, where no one would find you? What happened to you, Father, what changed you, turned you into someone you could never be before?

Clay felt a flush of shame at his thoughts. It wasn't true and he knew it. Randal Macon had never been Black Jack Foster. Not ever. Would a mindless killer do this, spend himself on such a labor of love as the house he had begun in this valley? It simply couldn't be. The Bible stories of his youth taught that man couldn't handle the delights of Paradise, that he'd tainted himself and given in to greed.

But that was another time, another age, another man. It wasn't his father, it wasn't Randal Macon, the kindest and most gentle man he knew.

That's what he was then . . . You don't know what he became up here . . .

"Clay?"

"What?" Clay stared at his friend. "What is it, LeSec?"

"I thought you were talking to me. I couldn't understand what you said."

"You're mistaken. I didn't say a thing."

When she came back to face them, the woman had given the shotgun to the Koo-Chin male. He stood beside her, straight and unbowed by the years, his dark features etched with a leathery map of the Yukon and all its tributaries.

"This man is Otapah," the woman said. "His wife is Awah-Choop. She's back there behind you with her bow all ready. Otapah's a dead shot, and his wife's a sight better than he is, but we don't tell him that. If you've got any thoughts about white skin being some better than red, now's the time to keep it to yourself. I've told these two you're not to be harmed unless you do something foolish like try to run away. If you do, they'll put you down so fast you won't have time to blink."

"Ma'am, you don't have to do this," Clay said. "We don't intend to run away. As a matter of—"

The woman raised one hand. The Koo-Chin brought the shotgun to his shoulder in a blur.

"Mister, I don't need any talk from you. You understand? Don't you open your mouth again."

She pulled the bonnet closer about her face. She spoke a few words to the Koo-Chin; he answered her and lowered the Remington again.

"You," the woman said, jabbing a finger at Patsy. "What are you doing dressed up like a boy? I sure enough know you're not."

Patsy glanced quickly at Clay, then looked at the woman. "That's a . . . kind of a long story, ma'am. It's not real interesting, either, I doubt if you'd want to hear it at all."

The woman looked straight at her. Her eyes were little points of light in the shadow of the bonnet.

"You related to either of these men?"

"No, ma'am, not either one."

"They're not family at all."

"No, ma'am, they're just—"

"You *belong* to one of 'em, something like that?"

"I don't any such thing!" Patsy thrust out her chin. "I don't belong to anyone, savin' my old mum and dad, and them both being dead, I reckon I belong to myself!"

The woman paused. "Is that the truth, girl, or a lie? I'll tell you now, I won't abide a lie."

"I don't lie, ma'am," Patsy said. "I never told a false-hood in my life. I wasn't brought up that way."

Clay looked up through the trees. Lightning seldom struck from a perfectly cloudless sky, but you never could tell.

"Come on, then," the woman said, "get up. Leave your belongings where they are; you won't be needing them here."

"What?" Patsy stared. "Come on . . . where, ma'am?"

The woman shook her head in irritation. "You deaf or something, girl? You're going up to the house with me, where do you think? You might have been camping out with men before, but you sure aren't going to do it on my place. Folks behave decent here."

"I'm as decent as you are," Patsy said, "and don't go saying I'm not."

Patsy was glaring at the woman, her face on fire. Clay leaned in close. "It's all right," he whispered, "do as she says. We'll work this out."

Patsy looked straight ahead. She nodded at Clay, swallowing her fears. She stood then and stalked past the woman without looking at her, marching straight for the house.

The woman stared at Clay. "Let's get something straight right off. I can tell you've got a bunch of questions in your head. You can forget 'em. You won't get any answers here. I *know* who you are. The Koo-Chins knew it first time they saw you, when you made camp back up in the hills. I tried to turn you back because you've no business here. Jack Foster might've built this place but it doesn't belong to him anymore, and I've got nothing to say to his son.''

She hesitated and folded her hands at her waist. "One thing, and that's all. Is he alive or is he dead? I don't want to know more'n that.''

"He's dead," Clay said. "He got back home, but I think he was already dying then.''

The woman nodded. "I guess I knew that. I guess I always did.''

"You're Meridel Huxley, aren't you, ma'am? I expect you have to be.''

The woman's head snapped up. "There is no one here by that name, mister. And you won't be speaking it again!''

She turned then, black skirts swirling about her, and stalked toward the house, back straight and head held high, a woman determined to hold onto her dignity and pride, even if everything else in her life was gone.

TWENTY-SEVEN

THE CELLAR WAS built of rough-hewn pine, the chinks in the floors, walls and ceiling filled first with mud and then overlaid with pitch. Solid piers were placed every six feet to keep the ceiling intact. The house above might fall into ruin, Clay thought, but this place would survive—along with the smoked meats hanging from hooks, the barrels of apples and potatoes and the jars of preserved vegetables and fruit.

"My father built this," Clay said. "I can see his meticulous touch everywhere."

He stood in the center of the room, sweeping the light of the tallow candle along the walls. "Even if the house wasn't a dead ringer for our place back home, I'd know. I can see his hand on every board and every joint. He did everything the same, putting something together with his hands or working out a business deal. Everything had to be right."

He turned then and slammed a fist into his palm. "What I can't figure, Jordan, is why? What did he *do* this for? Putting up a . . . a house like this in the wilds, leaving it half-done and then coming home to die."

Clay stopped and let out a breath. "I know who can give me the answers, tell me everything I want to know."

"The woman," Jordan said. "Meridel Huxley. "No matter what she says, that's who she has to be.''

"Of course she is. There isn't any doubt. She doesn't expect us to believe anything else."

"Then what's the use in pretending? She knew your father, she knows who you are."

Clay turned away. He could hear the sound of branches against the house. Dust motes danced in the thin shaft of buttery light at the top of the cellar door.

"She isn't denying it to us—she's keeping it from herself. She doesn't want to think about who she was, what . . . happened to her then."

Jordan shook his head. "If something happened to her, your father wasn't responsible for it, Clay. You know that the same as I do. He never killed a man in his life, and he certainly never harmed a woman. It wasn't in him. Not in Randal Macon."

Clay ran a hand through his hair. He was too tired to stand, but too overcome with tension and anger to even think about sleep.

"That's just it," he said, "she didn't call him Randal Macon; the man she knew was somebody else. And it isn't anyone she feels real kindly about. The way she said his name, there's no mistaking that."

Jordan didn't answer. He wanted to argue the point, to give Clay something more, but there was little he could say. He felt helpless, watching his friend's misery. From the moment Clay had heard the name Black Jack Foster, he had fought to believe in his father, that he could not be guilty of such terrible crimes. Now, faced with the woman who had known Randal Macon's other self, he was tearing himself apart inside.

Late in the afternoon, the Koo-Chins brought food: dried venison softened in a stew, beans and flat bread made of corn. The bread reminded both Clay and Jordan of the tortillas they had tasted in Texas and Mexico. There was a jug of water to drink and a basket of apples. The apples were large, and as sweet as any Clay had ever tasted.

The man, Otapah, laid the food on a wooden box, while his wife covered Clay and Jordan with the Remington double-barrel.

"Otapah," Clay said, "and . . . Awah-Choop? Did I get that right?"

The man's expression didn't change, but the woman grinned. Clay wondered if she was pleased, or if he might have mispronounced her name. In most Indian tongues, the slightest stress on the wrong syllable could totally change the meaning of a word or a whole sentence.

"I don't know if you speak English," Clay said, "but I'd like you to see that we're friends. We didn't come here to cause trouble for you or Miz—for the lady upstairs."

He reached under his shirt and brought out the stone necklace he'd gotten from the Koo-Chin traders early in the trip.

"We traded these with some other members of your tribe. They were real friendly. We got along quite well."

The Koo-Chins looked at each other. Awah-Choop said something to her husband and they both exploded in laughter. They pointed at Clay, hid their mouths behind their hands and giggled all the way out of the cellar. They were still grinning and shaking their heads when they locked the heavy door behind them.

"Now, what's that all about?" Clay held the loop of his necklace and examined it with care. "This is a perfectly fine piece of work. I don't see anything funny about it."

"They do," Jordan said.

"I know they do, you don't have to tell me that." Clay looked irritated. "Everybody knows something around here but us. Tarnation, Jordan, that woman can't keep us locked down here forever. She hasn't got a right, and I won't have it."

He stopped pacing and stared at the ceiling. "I wonder what she's doing up there? What's she saying to Patsy?"

"From the way she acted outside, I'd guess she's giving her a lecture on men. What's wrong with us, why we can't be trusted, matters such as that."

"I doubt the woman will get too far with Patsy Rabbit," Clay said. "Patsy's about the stubbornest, most hardheaded person I ever met. Male *or* female."

Jordan grinned. "I might just tell her you said so. In Patsy's book, that's about the highest compliment you could give."

Just before the short Northern day vanished behind the high stone walls of the valley, the Koo-Chins returned with the evening meal. This time there was fried fish along with the cornbread and beans. Clay decided it was some kind of mountain trout. Whatever it was, it was delicious.

Before the Indians left, they tossed the pair sleeping bags and blankets from their packs. Clay tried to talk to them again, and they answered him with polite and distant smiles. Clay decided they spoke some English, but they weren't about to let him know that.

"I've been thinking about the woman," Clay said. "Meridel Huxley. Fullerton Ash said she was considerably younger than her husband. We don't know what that means, but I'm guessing he was maybe around the same age as my father when he left home. He was fifty-five, then. If Meridel's husband was the same age, she might have been . . . what? Twenty or twenty-five?"

"Or eighteen," Jordan said. "It'd just be a guess. What's the point you're making, Clay?"

"I'm coming to it. Let's say she was twenty at the time. Randal Macon came up here in 1886. That's twelve years ago. She could be anywhere between thirty and thirty-five if we're right. A woman as fine-looking as she was supposed to be would've blossomed into full beauty at the age she is now . . .''

Jordan looked up, suddenly catching Clay's thoughts. "She hides her face. Keeps it tucked in that bonnet all the time."

"Or at least all the time she was talking to us."

"You think something happened. Something's . . . wrong with her face?"

"What else could it be? A woman hides her face from a man . . .'' Clay closed his eyes and rubbed the back of his neck. "Tell you the truth, I don't know what to think about anything. I've got too much turning in my head.'' He spread out his bedroll on the floor. "And I don't like to sleep in cellars. A nice feather bed indoors, or hard ground under the sky—fine. But I don't much care for anything in between.''

He turned and faced the wall. He could hear Jordan fumbling about and wished he'd keep still. Not that he really expected to get to sleep himself, but he could at least lie awake without a lot of noise.

"Clay?"

"What?"

"You still awake?"

"What do you think?"

"I wish I had a cigar, Clay. It wouldn't have to be a good cigar. A cheap cigar'd be fine."

"Well, you don't. Get some sleep, LeSec.''

"I don't think I can.''

"You can't if you intend to keep talking all night, I guarantee that.''

"A cigar. A cigar of any sort and a hot cup of coffee. That's two things I'd like most of all. What do you suppose Patsy was talking about this afternoon—that she knew where I might find a cup? What a peculiar thing to say.''

"Shut up, Jordan."

Jordan let out a breath. "Yeah, all right. There's no use thinking about it. It just gets worse if you do."

"I'm glad you see that. Put it out of your mind. Think about something else."

Clay waited. Jordan LeSec was either taking his advice, or he'd dropped off to sleep at once. Clay wished he hadn't held back the small sack of coffee for a moment when Jordan would "appreciate" it the most. That time was certainly now, and the coffee was upstairs in Clay's pack. Meridel Huxley would certainly find it. Then she'd either drink it herself or throw it out.

Either way was fine with Clay—as long as LeSec didn't ever find out the answer to his prayers was twenty feet over his head.

TWENTY-EIGHT

CLAY SLEPT IN spite of himself. He woke stiff and hungry, stood up and stretched and squinted at the narrow band of morning that etched the cellar door. Jordan was still asleep, curled up in his sleeping bag against a barrel of potatoes. A slight smile on his lips told Clay that his partner was having better luck with his dreams than he could claim himself.

Someone was stirring around. He heard someone coming down the outside stairs. Had to be one of the Koo-Chins, Clay decided. Neither Meridel Huxley nor Patsy weighed enough to creak a board.

A beetle waddled along the cellar floor, found a mountain in its path and scurried quickly across. Jordan woke up kicking, slapping at his face.

Clay grinned. "Looks like you found a friend. A bug of the female variety, I expect."

"Speaking of which," Jordan said irritably, "I was having a lovely time. There was this lady of good family from Atlanta—"

"I don't want to hear it. Get up and wash your face and clear your head. We've got talking to do."

"About what?"

"About getting that woman's attention, making her stand

still and *listen* for a minute and a half. She wouldn't let us get a word in yesterday and I don't intend to let that happen again.''

Clay hesitated, moved to the cellar door and listened, then faced LeSec again. ''On the other hand, I'm not sure talking'll do any good. I thought about it some last night. I'm never going to believe my father murdered that woman's husband or anyone else. The thing is, she believes it, and for now that's all that counts.''

Jordan muttered something to himself. ''Maybe the woman's not . . . thinking straight anymore, Clay. The way she acts, I wouldn't find that hard to believe.''

''Maybe. All the more reason for us not to wait and see what she's got in mind for us. It might be something you and me wouldn't take much pleasure in, friend.''

''You got an idea?''

''Nothing worth talking about. All I've got's a real worrisome concern for a couple of Louisiana hides.''

Jordan frowned. ''Neither of those Koo-Chins is going to be easy to take down. I haven't seen 'em get careless yet.''

''I don't think you will.'' Clay moved restlessly about the small room. There was little light except for the stub of their candle from the night before. He didn't care for the gloomy atmosphere, and there wasn't any room to turn around. The cellar was a lot finer quarters than the Skagway jail, and it sure smelled better, but it was a lockup all the same.

''I'd like the chance to talk to Patsy. She can do more than we can, and she's had a chance to talk to Meridel Huxley.''

''Meridel Huxley's also had a chance to talk to her,'' Jordan reminded him.

''I think Patsy Rabbit can hold her own. The girl's real

good at, uh . . . deciding what to tell and what to keep to herself.''

"Lying, you mean."

"Right, that's the word I was searching for. You can count on Patsy for that."

Breakfast arrived. The usual flat cornbread and some black-berry jam. More venison jerky, only this time it wasn't in a stew, and they had to do a considerable amount of gnaw-ing to get it down.

The Koo-Chins gave them a few minutes to themselves, then opened the door again. "You . . ." Otapah jabbed a finger at Clay. "You comin'—not him."

"Absolutely fluent," Jordan said. "I suspected it all along."

Clay looked at Otapah and his wife. Awah-Choop held the shotgun steady in her gnarled hands.

"I don't like this," he told Jordan, "separating us, leav-ing one of us here . . ." He turned to Otapah. "No, we don't want to do that. You understand? Me and him. We stay here together and we go out together."

"You. Not him." Otapah's expression didn't change. Awah-Choop raised the shotgun, pulled back the hammer and aimed it at Clay's head.

"Don't let her bluff you," Jordan said. "She's not going to do it, friend."

"I have your word on that?"

"I'd say the odds are on your side. Seventy-thirty. Maybe more than that."

"Let's go," Clay told Otapah. "My partner here's the third worst gambler in the world."

After the darkness of the cellar, the bright spring morning was almost too much to bear. The grass sparkled with a million droplets of dew. Clay was struck once more by the uncommon warmth of the valley. While the chill winds of the Yukon sliced through the uplands just a few miles away, the sheer fortress of stone that ringed the valley kept the cold at bay.

Otapah walked behind him, trailing by a good ten yards. His shoulders sloped, and he kept the shotgun at his side, pointed at the ground. He seemed to pay no attention to his charge, and this irritated Clay no end. The man might be taking a nap for all the concern he showed. If his prisoner took off—well, fine. He'd get maybe two, three feet before the buckshot brought him to the ground.

The Indian said something in the Koo-Chin tongue, then added, "Up there. You go."

"Might as well," Clay said. "Arguing with you doesn't do a lot of good."

The walkway was paved with slabs of flat stone set precisely half an inch apart. A fuzz of bright green moss filled the cracks in between. The path made a gentle curve up a grassy terraced hill by the side of the house. Clay was impressed by the walkway's neat and orderly design. The pattern of the paving stones was purposely casual and yet quite precise, as if the maker had had a flair for the Oriental arts.

At the top of the terrace, Otapah called a halt. The grass here was a thick, yielding carpet of green. Mountain flowers were already beginning to burst free of the earth.

"It's a pretty sight," Clay said. "What am I supposed to do now, stop and paint a picture?"

Otapah didn't answer. He gazed out over the trees as if no one else were there.

"Look, why don't you go and get LeSec? Bring Awah-Choop, too. Gather up everyone in the whole darn place and we'll have a footrace. Yukon championship, right?

"Hell's bells, I know you understand me, *do* something man!" Clay didn't like to be told what to do. He'd been holding back his anger as long as he could, and he was losing patience fast.

"What I need to do, Otapah, instead of watching the grass grow, is talk to the lady of the house. She's going to have to do it sometime, she might as well quit puttin' it off and—"

Clay stopped. The words stuck in his throat and he stared at the girl walking toward him from the shadow of the house. Her arms and shoulders were bare, her skin fresh as cream. A pale, blue cotton gown clung to her slim and shapely form; her hair was a mass of copper ringlets, graced by a ribbon that trailed down the curve of her back.

Not a girl at all, Clay corrected himself, a full-grown woman, and a genuine beauty at that.

"I'm sorry, miss," he said, bending at the waist in a courtly bow, "I'm new here in the valley and I don't believe I've had the pleasure."

"You just stop that, Dr. Macon; you're embarrassing me to death." Patsy raised a hand to her bodice. Her fair skin colored from her throat to her brow.

"Heaven help me," Clay said, shaking his head in wonder, "I don't know what you expect me to say. You're not the lad I used to know, Patsy Rabbitt, or anywhere close."

"Miz . . . Miz Mary . . ." Patsy glanced over her shoulder at the house. "She asked me to call her that, it isn't her name, you know, but . . . anyway, it was her gave me this outfit and fixed me up lookin' nice. She says it's not decent for a girl to be looking like a boy."

"Well, she's fair right," Clay said. "It's a crime to be hiding such a— I mean, the way you were covered up and all . . ."

The more he said, the worse it seemed to get. Now it was his turn to feel the heat rise to his face. It was amazing how quickly things had changed between them. Even when he'd discovered she was a woman, it was nothing like this. There were still the baggy overalls and the dirty face, and he'd gotten fairly comfortable with that. Now, though, here was this . . . this person in a frilly blue dress and he was stumbling over his tongue, trying not to say the wrong thing.

Patsy showed him an easy smile. "Don't you be worrying now, I'm not used to me myself." She looked down and smoothed her hands along her waist. "I wish I could see dear Fiona in a dress like this. She's the pretty one in the family, you know."

"No, I don't know, Patsy. But I know for sure she's not the only one."

"Here now, don't be saying that." Patsy looked up at him, and he saw that her eyes were moist with tears. "Will we get her back, sir? You think I'll see my sister free?"

"I know you will, Patsy. I promise you that. Even if we—"

Clay looked quickly away, pretending there was something in his eye. He'd almost done it again, a natural gesture, reaching out to hold her and comfort her like he would if she was a—if she was a regular woman.

And that's exactly what she is, you old fool, as real a woman as you're ever likely to see . . .

"It's some peculiar in there," Patsy said. "It's like a museum or something, you know what I'm saying? There's two rooms and a kitchen, and little enough furniture to go around for that. What there is is old and fancy, worn down to a nub, and you can't hardly see for there's not a drape open to let the sunlight in."

Patsy sighed and bit her lip. "The place is as gloomy and hid away as she is, Dr. Macon. There's little joy in the woman at all."

They were walking past the terrace in the shade of the giant fir trees that spread a cloak of shade across the house. Buttery patterns of light danced on Patsy's pale skin, and mottled the forest floor. Otapah walked behind, out of hearing, but close enough to perform his duties as chaperone and guard.

"And she never let you see her face," Clay said, "not any time at all."

"No, never." Patsy shook her head. "She treated me well enough, or as well as I think she could. But she always bowed her head when we spoke, or turned away. The lady's in a sorrowful state, she is. She left her world behind somewhere, in a place as full of sadness as that dark house itself."

Meridel Huxley had questioned Patsy Rabbit a great deal about herself and her companions—where they'd come from, and how they dared intrude on a place where they didn't belong. Patsy had told the woman her own story, how her sister was a prisoner of Scully Flatts, and how that situation had come about. Scully Flatts meant nothing to the woman at all, but she was familiar with the kind of man he was and the evil he brought into the world.

"It's when I . . . when I might've stretched the truth a bit that I got in hot water," Patsy said. "I told her you were hunters and explorers, respected gentlemen of the Old South who were just in the Yukon on a lark."

"Oh, Patsy . . ."

"I know, and you're right in what you're thinking, it was a foolish thing to do. She told me quick enough that it was clear from the mining picks and other such notions in your packs, the kind of things a prospector carried, you were like all the others, sniffing about for gold."

"Miz Huxley *said* she knew who I was," Clay said gently. "She saw my father in me right off. I think she'd have to swallow quite a lot to believe we stumbled into a valley where my father just happened to build a house."

"I *know* that, sir." Patsy rolled her eyes. "I knew it, and I didn't stop to think at the time. I get to blabbin' as you know and forget where I'm going or where I came in. It's a fault in me, sir, I don't have to tell you that.''

Clay grinned. ''It's who you are, Patsy, same as I'm what I am. There's faults we've all got to live with. You've got yours, and I've most certainly got mine.''

Patsy cocked her head and smiled. It was a distinctly feminine gesture, and it confused Clay Macon no end. Little motions and movements he'd never given thought to before, when he thought Patsy Rabbitt was a young and still immature boy, took on a new and frightening meaning now.

They were leaving the grove of trees and walking back into the sun. The east side of the house was masked by a high, thick shrub that Clay couldn't name. Its tiny blossoms were white, and its leaves sharp and waxy as the holly that grew in the South.

''And what'd those be, I wonder,'' Patsy said, ''these faults of yours, Dr. Macon? Would you name 'em for me then?''

''I surely would not,'' Clay said. ''No one is fool enough to list all the things he does wrong.''

Patsy laughed. ''I could be giving you a start.''

''Oh, is that right, miss?''

''Of course, I'd never be so ... inconsiderate as to do such a thing.''

''Might be risky, too.''

''And how would that be?''

''Well, I might have to dredge up some fading memories of life on the trail ...''

Patsy raised a hand to her mouth in mock alarm. ''You'd not be so unkind as to speak such things aloud.''

''Of course not. I've too fine a breeding for that.''

''Well, I don't,'' Patsy said, ''but I've got good Irish sense sometimes.''

They both burst into laughter. Patsy moved closer to him, her eyes sparkling with pleasure. She laid a hand on his arm, then quickly jerked it away, as if she'd touched a hot stove. She turned from him and brushed at her hair.

"I'm so glad she . . . let you come out in the sun," she said. "It's not right, locking you and Mr. LeSec up in that place. I bet it's dark down there."

"The beetles seem to like it just fine. Jordan wouldn't mind if he could get a cup of coffee now and then."

"Oh, Lordy . . ." Patsy held back a grin. "I flat forgot about that."

"Good. Just keep on forgetting. You and I would be in deep trouble if he ever guessed the truth." Clay frowned and gave her a curious look. "Have you wondered any *why* Miz Huxley let you and I get together? After all her fine talk of propriety, I'm more than a little surprised. Even if we do have Otapah close by."

"Oh, I think I know why," Patsy said. "She . . . she doesn't think I'm too bright, you know. A young and flighty girl. I'm almost sure she believes I'll learn something from you I don't already know. And she—" Patsy looked embarrassed. "The woman almost said aloud that she'd like to give me another fancy dress. And she showed me a real pretty bracelet and a ring . . ."

Clay let out a breath. "Tarnation, if she wants to know something about me, why can't she speak to me herself? I've been trying to bring that about ever since we got to this place."

"I don't think she can. Talk to you, speak her mind. I don't think she can do that."

"And I expect you're right," Clay said. "I expect you're very right indeed . . ."

Clay hesitated, backed up a step and stopped. Something bright caught his eye, a sudden, intense flash of light through the tall stand of shrubbery to his right.

"What is it?" Patsy said. "What do you see?"

"I don't know. Something catching the sun, over by the house."

Clay stalked the edge of the shrubs until he found a spot slightly thinner than the rest. The leaves pricked his hands as he parted the branches and stepped into the thicket itself. The glare hurt his eyes. His guess had been right; the bright light was coming from a spot near the base of the house. He cursed to himself as a few drops of blood welled up on his hands, then he parted the thick cover and stepped through.

"You—no going in there. *No going in there!*"

Clay glanced back. Otapah was waddling toward him in a flat-footed gait, waving the shotgun over his head, dark eyes wide with alarm.

"Take it easy, fellow," Clay called out. "I'm not running away, just looking around."

He turned then and stared at the sight before him. Otapah was still shouting at his back, but Clay paid him no mind. It took him a moment to understand what he was seeing, and even then it was hard to believe it was real, because it simply didn't fit, it didn't *belong* here.

There were narrow rooms of clear glass, extending from the back of the house, three of them, each with a steep, slanting glass roof perhaps seven feet high at the peak, and each wing itself nearly four yards wide. The panes of glass were soldered together in crude metal frames, not perfect workmanship at all, but clearly good enough to get the job done.

It was not the structure itself, though, that filled Clay Macon with awe, but the marvels it held inside. It was scarcely spring in this Yukon valley, yet the growth inside resembled a lush tropical isle. Thick vines clung to the glass wall, bearing tomatoes red and near to bursting, as big as cantaloupes. There were immense cabbages, larger than any he'd ever seen before, the purple-veined leaves of beets and the green tops of vegetables he couldn't identify.

"God's wonder," he said beneath his breath, "this *is* an Eden, it's a true paradise."

It struck him, then, that even vegetables of normal size could not spring up overnight, not this time of the year, and certainly not here. The truth brought a tightening in his chest. There was no other answer that made a bit of sense: These greenhouses in the sheltered heart of the Yukon did not follow the growing seasons of the land, or any seasons at all. The vegetables grew and thrived here all year around.

"It's a marvel," he said, turning to see if Patsy was there. "I've never seen anything li—"

He caught a glimpse of Patsy, saw her eyes go wide, saw her mouth open to shout a warning that never came, then everything was dark and very quiet, and, for the second time in a few short weeks, someone slammed the butt of a shotgun hard against the side of Clay's head . . .

TWENTY-NINE

THE WORLD STRETCHED out forever, a long and endless plain that faded into the dark. He tried to bring something into focus, to make it stand still. Everything wavered, melted and twisted out of shape. He closed his eyes against the nausea that threatened to climb up from his belly to his throat. That was even worse. The dizzy, tilted landscape followed him into the blackness, refused to let him go . . .

He opened his eyes and tried again. The flatness stood still for a moment, long enough for him to label it as the cellar's pine floor. He was lying with his cheek against the rough-hewn boards. His flesh seemed glued to the wood. He waited a moment, then pressed his hands carefully against the floor and raised his head. His skull exploded in a starburst of pain, and he cried out and sank to the floor again.

He was cautious the next time. His head still pounded, but it wasn't too bad if he took it real slow. He wanted to retch, but the sickness teetered on the edge and wouldn't let him follow through.

All that expensive medical training, and I can't do a simple thing like throw up . . .

He leaned weakly against the wall and practiced slow, deep breaths. He already knew that Jordan was gone. He couldn't tell the time, but he guessed it was late afternoon. If he'd had a patient who'd been out that long, he'd have been more than a little concerned.

Someone had cleaned him up—washed off most of the blood that had to have been there with a blow like that— and wrapped a clean bandanna around his head. *Real nice manners they practice up here,* he thought. *They cave in your skull, then make sure you live to feel the pain.*

He heard a tiny noise and turned his head carefully to the right. There was a plate of food there, and the beetles were having their annual ball. They'd asked everyone in town; hey, come and eat your fill, and be sure and carry something home.

Sitting up was one thing; standing was something else. He took it in slow and easy stages, pulling himself along the wall, resting awhile, then going at it again. When he could walk well enough without help, he dragged an empty box to the door, stood it on end, stepped up and prayed he didn't fall. Through the crack at the top he could see green branches and a small patch of sky. He heard some birds call, heard the whispered sigh of the wind. Easing himself back down again, he sat on the box and started mehodically pounding on the door. Beat . . . rest . . . beat . . . rest . . .

It was an easy rhythm that wouldn't wear him out. He could keep it up all day. Maybe take a nap now and then.

Beat . . . rest . . . beat . . . rest . . .

He could do it forever, he decided, and the thought brought a weary smile to his face.

''Stop that,'' Otapah said. ''You stop doin' that thing, you hear? Don' be doin' that.''

''You don't like it,'' Clay said, ''open this thing and let me out of here.''

''Couldn't be doin' that. You stop. Be stoppin' right now.''

Clay continued his monotonous beat. "You could kill someone hitting 'em like that, you know? Huh? Do you? You *care* if you do or not? That matter any to you?"

Clay waited, but Otapah didn't answer.

"I don't know what's itching you, friend, but I wasn't figuring on throwing any rocks at your little glass houses, all right? You had no cause to go bashing in my head like that, not any cause at all. Where's LeSec, anyway? My friend, the tall skinny fellow I came in with, you remember him? Lord, I hope you didn't give him the same kind of tour you gave me. I hope you didn't—You listening to me? Otapah, I am *talking* to you. Don't just sit there like you're stone deaf or something, you understand? You listening to me? Say something over there!"

"He's not listening because he isn't here. A Koo-Chin doesn't like a lot of talk, he isn't used to it."

Clay sat up straight. There was no mistaking who was talking to him now. "Well, this is sure some honor, ma'am. I didn't expect to get a visit from the warden herself."

"Don't feel it's any special privilege, mister, 'cause I sure don't."

"Where's Jordan? Why isn't he here?"

"That's no concern of yours."

"Yeah, now, beggin' your pardon, it is. He's a friend of mine and I'd like to hear he's in good health, that he hasn't been knocked on the head and dragged off somewhere."

Meridel Huxley made a noise in her throat. "Don't you moan about that. You brought it on yourself, meddling where you didn't belong."

Clay had to laugh. It hurt his head, but he couldn't help himself. "I did what? I'm sorry, but I didn't see any *signs* anywhere said 'Walk in here and an Indian'll bash in your head.' If I'd have seen that—"

"Don't be smart with me. I've no interest in whimsy or wit of any sort, and no patience with it in others. You trespassed on a private place. That's *my* things back there; it doesn't have anything to do with you.''

Meridel Huxley paused. Clay could hear the slow measure of her breath, almost feel the pressure of her body against the door.

"That . . . that girl lied some to me. Trying to tell me what you were doing here and not a word of truth in that sassy tongue of hers. I went through your things. And don't call it snooping 'cause it's not. I've got a perfect right, someone comes on my place, I don't want them here. I know your name from your papers. Clay Macon. A doctor, no less. From New Orleans, Louisiana. I never was there and have no desire to see it from what I hear. Jack Foster wasn't his name, I know that. There was scarcely a man up here using the name his folks gave him. Every one of 'em came to this country wearing some kind of lie about himself.''

Meridel paused. "His last name was Macon, like yours, then. What else? The whole thing.''

"It was Randal, ma'am. Randal T. Macon.''

"Randal.'' She said the name to herself. "I guessed the South somewhere. Randal Macon fits. What's the T for?''

"Taylor. Grandmother was a Taylor before she married. Her family's kin to Zachary Taylor, the President. His son was Dick Taylor, a general in the Confederacy who fought in the Shenandoah Valley and the Seven Days. He was a West Louisiana commander after that.''

"I'm not a Southern sympathizer, Doctor. That doesn't slice any butter with me.''

"No, ma'am.''

"He's gone, you understand that? You have no rights to anything here. It isn't your home, if that's what you're thinking; it's mine.''

"I wouldn't even consider taking anything from you,'' Clay said. "Such a thing never crossed my mind.''

"Huh!" Meridel cut him off with a chilling laugh. "You think I was born last Thursday afternoon? I've seen what's in your pack. There's nothing that brings men up to this country but gold fever. That's what brought *him* up here. Greed for gold's what's caused all the sorrow I've had to bear, all I've had to live with. It's what brought death to my husband and cold murder to more souls than I can count!"

Clay didn't think of himself as a coward, but, at that moment, he was grateful that a solid wooden door stood between them. He could scarcely stand to hear the terrible things she was saying, and knew he could never face her while she named his father's crimes. Even if he didn't believe her, couldn't *let* himself credit her words, he didn't want to hear her, didn't want to know . . .

"Whatever it was that . . . I'm sorry, I . . . If you have been wronged, if you have suffered ills somehow . . ."

"Can't say it, can you? You can't." Meridel's voice was as harsh as grinding stone. "Lord God on high, you don't know the meaning of *wronged*. You don't know what it means!"

"I don't guess anyone can share another's hurt," Clay said. "I wouldn't even try to understand your feelings. I—"

"Well, that is *mighty* big of you, such a fine and noble thought!"

Clay looked at the cellar floor. "Ma'am, I don't think talking's working out too well for you and me. Maybe another time'd be better than now, I don't know. I'd be grateful if you'd tell me when my friend's coming back. I'd appreciate that."

"Don't want to talk about sin and guilt and such, that it?"

"I'll be pleased to converse with you on anything you like . . ."

Meridel made a noise in her throat. "Maybe you and

your *friend* won't be plotting to do people wrong if you can't get together. That's what comes to mind to me.''

"Jordan and I don't mean you harm in any way. How can I make you believe that?''

"You can't. Don't bother to try. I'm not any kind of fool, *Doctor* Clay Macon. I know what you're looking for here. Jack Foster showed up in Fortymile with some gold, all right, but it didn't come from *this* place. You understand that? *It didn't come from here.* He didn't tell anyone where it came from. No one at all . . .''

Clay felt a sudden tightness in his throat. Meridel laughed, as if she could peer through solid wood, see the expression on his face.

"Don't expect you want to hear that, do you? Well it's the truth. You don't believe it, fine. It's all the same to me.''

Why would you lie to me, Father? What for? Why would you lead me here if there's nothing to find? What do you want me to see?

"He was here," Clay said. "He built this place. He had a reason for that. What was it, Miz Huxley? You know the answer, and I've got a right to hear it.''

"Don't you call me that! Not ever!'' Her voice rose to a frightening pitch. "There's . . . there's no such person, don't you say there is!''

God help the poor woman, Clay thought, *she's got a great sorrow in her soul. There's a hollow place inside where a person used to be . . .*

There was so much he wanted to ask her: What did Randal Macon say to her? What did he do? What was he like? Was he someone else, then, as Meridel Huxley was clearly someone else, too? He wondered again about the extraordinary greenhouses he'd seen and the main house itself. He had no doubt that Randal Macon had built them, and likely with little help. He was a brilliant man, a man with a foot in two worlds—at home in the intricate and demanding arena of business and finance, and equally as competent fashioning a trap in the woods. Much of the warehouse and shipping district on the delta had risen from Randal Macon's combined skills as merchant prince and builder.

And here, in this valley, who was his father then? Clay asked himself. Nothing in this lush green world looked like the handiwork of a madman and a killer. It looked like the work of the Randal Macon Clay knew.

"I'd like to talk to Patsy Rabbitt again," Clay said. "If you'd let her come here—outside the door like you're doing now, why, that'd be fine."

"You don't need to see the girl. You've got no reason to."

"Ma'am, if you'll recall, I saw her before. You're the one who sent her out to see me. What's different between then and now?"

"That was a mistake on my part. It won't happen again."

Clay pressed his head against the door. "What is it you mean by that, it won't happen again? I don't understand that, and I don't care for the way it sounds. I want to see Patsy and I want Jordan LeSec back here. You've got no right to do this, we haven't done a thing to you. Why in blazes do you think we—"

Clay stopped. He hadn't heard her leave, hadn't heard her move at all, but he knew she wasn't there . . .

He would not have advised a patient with a bad head injury to sleep. Stay awake, he would say, that's the thing to do. Still, Patient Macon ignored Dr. Clay Macon's advice and fell into a deep and heavy sleep. In his dreams he was a child, in his room in his father's home in New Orleans. Giant, ugly beetles with black and shiny skulls were swarming over the house, eating stone and wood and glass in their path, pounding on the walls, fighting to get to his room and do terrible, monstrous things to the small and terrified child . . .

He sat up straight, cold sweat peppering his brow. He felt empty, light-headed, so weak that gravity seemed to drag him to the ground.

Someone was beating on the cellar door. Otapah was jabbering at him in the Koo-Chin tongue, an endless stream of words that made no sense at all.

"What in blue hell you doin' that for?" Clay said irritably. "You want in, you got the key, not me."

"You be standin' way back, you hear?"

Clay pulled himself erect. Sharp stabs of pain lanced through his head.

"All right, I'm standing. Way back, if that makes you happy. What now?"

The door swung in. Otapah stood there with the Remington shotgun pointed at Clay's belly.

"You got it all wrong," Clay said. "It's still dark outside. They don't shoot prisoners till dawn. Didn't anyone tell you that?"

Otapah looked confused. "Mizzy, she say—you watch him, Otapah. Watch him real good."

"Yeah, that figures. Can't be too careful, you got a wounded, unarmed man locked up tight in a cellar. No telling what he's going to do."

"You be stayin' back."

"All *right,* I'm back. You're up there, and I'm back. Now what?"

Otapah gave him a narrow look. Without lowering his weapon, he bent down and reached for a plate and a jug behind him, laid them on the floor and stepped back.

"Where's Jordan?" Clay said. "My friend, the man I came in with. I need to see him. I need to see him right now."

Otapah shook his head. "Otapah has . . . has struck-ed you too much." He slapped at his head and made a face. "Sorry. Too much."

Clay had to grin. "Is this an apology? Is that what it is? Well, friend, if you don't mind I've given some thought as to paying you back in spades, I guess I'll accept."

"Sorry," Otapah said again. "Struck-ed too hard."

"Yeah, I got that. You surely did, too. If you'd *struck-ed* a tad more, you could've planted me in the garden out there."

"Eat," Otapah said. He pointed at the food. "Real good."

Clay glanced at the plate. "Say, jerky and beans again. I guess it'd be too much to ask to see a menu, right?"

"Eat. Real good food."

Next time he comes, Clay thought, *I might be able to rip a stave off one of those apple barrels. If he'd point that shotgun away for a second and a half, I'd struck-ed that Indian so hard he'd—*

The flat, deadly crack of a rifle broke the silence of the night. Otapah stared at Clay, then turned and ducked out the door. Three shots followed quickly on the heels of the first. A man shouted in the dark. Another man answered with a laugh.

Clay ran after Otapah, keeping low against the side of the house. Someone in the upper window loosed a volley of pistol fire. Whoever was out there laughed again and fired twice, thunking wood over Clay's head.

Someone called out nearby. Otapah froze, holding the Remington at his side. Awah-Choop whispered from the shadows and Otapah disappeared. Moments later, they both came out of the dark, dragging Jordan LeSec by his arms. His head hung limply from his shoulders, his long hair touching the ground.

Clay's heart nearly stopped. LeSec's eyes were clouded,

half-closed. His face was drained of color and his shirt was smeared with blood.

It came to him, then, struck him like a knife in the heart . . . It had been there gnawing at the edge of his mind since they'd come to the valley, and now it rose up dark and ugly and clear . . . No one could bring in the timber and the glass and all the things a man would need to do what his father had done here . . . not through the impossibly narrow pathways Clay and his companions had come . . . There was another way into this valley, a way horses and wagons could come and go with ease, yet hidden enough to keep intruders out . . .

And it had served its purpose well until now, Clay thought, touching the cold flesh of his friend. Now, though, the way was a secret no more; they'd dogged his trail and sniffed him out and they were here.

He knew who they were; he had no doubts about that. He had heard that laugh before, in a poker game above a Skagway bar, and he was certain he'd know it anywhere.

Scully Flatts. Scully Flatts was here . . .

THIRTY

JORDAN'S BODY FELT almost weightless on his shoulders, as if the very substance of life had fled, leaving a useless husk behind. Awah-Choop led the way, Clay on her heels, taking the steps to the second story four at a time. The stairway was exposed, built against the outside of the house. Gunfire blossomed in the night; lead whined overhead and thudded into wood.

Otapah followed the others, sweeping the Remington from side to side, patiently holding his fire. The bullets were coming close enough; he didn't care to guide the shooters, give them any help.

Awah-Choop burst into the room, loosing a string of Koo-Chin at Meridel. Patsy stepped back from the window and looked at Jordan. A strangled cry stuck in her throat.

"Stop it," Clay said sharply, "I don't need that. And keep clear of that window. We don't need any more casualties than we've got."

"Is he . . . is he dead? Oh, Dr. Macon, don't go tellin' me that!"

"I didn't tell you a thing," Clay said, ripping open Jordan's shirt. "It was you telling me. Somebody get me water and some cloth. Be sure the cloth's clean. Move, now."

Awah-Choop bent low and made her way out of the

room. A shot struck the edge of the window, whined off at an angle and shattered a kerosene lamp.

"Damn you," said Meridel Huxley, "damn you every one. You're the cause of this. It's you that's brought this plague of trouble here!"

"I won't argue the point," Clay said. "I guess you'd say we did. If you want to get riled at someone, though, you might consider those fellows out there." He couldn't see her clearly. She was back in shadow on the far side of the room. "What I'm saying is, blame doesn't matter much now. Sitting here cussing each other won't help. Staying in one piece is what you might be thinking about."

"Don't you tell me what to think about. I won't have it!"

Her voice was like a rasp on wood. It would have irritated Clay if he hadn't had better things to do. The Koo-Chin woman brought him a tin bowl of water and a strip of white cloth. The bullet had gone into Jordan's left side. Clay decided it had likely cracked a rib and maybe nicked the spleen. There was plenty of blood. No arteries were hit, but the bleeding was heavier than Clay liked to see.

"The lead's still in there; I've got to get it out. Patsy, get me that short hunting knife from my pack. Hold it in a flame for a while."

The guns had gone silent. Clay glanced up at Otapah. He had the door to the stairs cracked open, peering into the dark.

Clay looked at Patsy. "What was he doing? You know? Why'd they have him out there?"

He knew better than to ask Meridel. Talking to her was a pure waste of time.

"He was—" Patsy glanced at Meridel. "She had him locked up in a little shed in the trees. You can't see it from here. Awah-Choop was taking him his supper . . ."

Clay cursed under his breath, and Patsy handed him the

knife. "How many?" He asked Awah-Choop. "You understand what I'm saying? You see how many men?"

Awah-Choop bit her lip. She held up five fingers, then two more, hesitated, and added another.

She was guessing, Clay thought; she couldn't have seen all of them in the dark. Still, she was a deadly marksman and a stalker, and the count was likely close. Eight, then. Most of them no better than the last hired shooters, a few a little better. Jordan LeSec was out of it, and he didn't think Meridel Huxley would be of much use. Patsy would do what she could. That left himself and the two Koo-Chins as effective fighters. Clay let out a breath. They'd need a break to get out of this mess. Maybe two or three.

"Otapah, over here if you will. Hold him down. Patsy, take his place at the door."

"You don't take orders from him," Meridel said. "Stay where you are."

"Otapah stopped, looked at Meridel, then at LeSec. He shook his head, almost an apology, and went to Clay. Awah-Choop held a sputtering candle close to the wound.

"All right, friend, you aren't going to like this near as much as dancing, but it's what I got to do."

Jordan groaned and his body went stiff as the knife dug into his flesh. Clay worked quickly, probing then twisting the tip of the blade with the surgeon's practiced skill. A bloody clump of lead appeared in the open wound. Clay nodded, satisfied, and stanched the flow of blood. Jordan opened his eyes, then passed out again. Awah-Choop lifted his shoulders, and Clay wrapped the bandage tightly about his abdomen and chest.

He rinsed his hands in the tin bowl, stood and looked at Meridel Huxley. She sat on a low bench against the wall. A shawl was drawn tightly about her shoulders. Her features, as ever, were lost in the shadow of her bonnet.

"I won't bother telling you again I'm sorry we brought

trouble on you," Clay said. "It's here. We've got to face it or give in. I don't recommend the last. When Patsy and I were talking outside, she told me she'd mentioned Scully Flatts to you. That's who's out there now. He wants my hide. If I thought he'd leave everyone else alone, I'd go and take my chances. Only I know he wouldn't stop at that."

Clay hesitated. "You were right about gold fever, ma'am. That's what he's here for, why he's sniffed out every trail in these mountains until he ran us down. I thought we'd lost him. I was dead wrong. I thought we had some help in Skagway, but it's clear that didn't work out. Scully Flatts . . . Scully Flatts thinks my father struck it rich here. You say he didn't, but Scully won't likely take your word for that."

Clay waited. Meridel Huxley didn't move. She looked as if she hadn't heard a word, and he knew that wasn't so. He glanced at his watch. Half past eleven. Otapah was watching the stairs. Patsy was at the window, and Awah-Choop was in the other second-floor room, looking at the night from there. No one outside had fired a shot for some time. Clay figured that was bad news. If they weren't shooting, they were up to something else. Moving up, getting in close. Planning more misery for the people in the house.

It could be some worse, Clay thought. At least they were on the second story; the two finished rooms allowed for a clear view in all directions. They could see anyone that moved in the unfinished areas below. The greenhouses were against the south wall. The three springs and foot-high grasses covering the draw were between the forest and the house. It wasn't much cover, none at all in the light of day, unless you had ice water in your veins, but men could maybe get pretty close in the dark.

Clay moved over to Meridel and sat on the floor; far enough away so she wouldn't feel threatened, near enough to talk. Meridel stiffened at his approach. She grasped her hands in her lap, as if the gesture might keep him away.

"We've got to talk," Clay said. "There isn't time for what you think about me, or whose fault is this or that. We're in for some trouble. I'll do all I can to get us out. There's some things I've got to know. I'm guessing the way Scully Flatts got in was the route I was supposed to find, instead of the one I did.

"I'm saying that because stumbling on that path through the thicket isn't something I figure could happen twice. There's another way in here, the way my father got all this lumber and material into the valley. I want to know where that is. Where it comes in, and where it goes out."

Meridel Huxley was silent a long moment. Finally, she let out a long breath, a painful breath of resignation, Clay thought, and deliberately turned away.

"It goes north from here. Cuts through the Ring Ridge. We call it the Ring Ridge because that's what it does, rings the whole valley from everywhere else. You wouldn't even see it unless you knew it was there. It looks like a dead-end canyon but it's not. It twists about nine or ten miles, always hiding behind the ridge, and the rock's too hard to take tracks. It comes out through some trees. There's a river right there, not a quarter mile away."

"Which river is that?"

"I don't know that it has a name. There's more tributaries of the Yukon than you can count. That's one of them. Your father . . . Your father would trek upriver to one of the trading posts. He'd order some of what he wanted at one, and something else at another, so as not to attract much attention. Then he'd barge the materials down here."

"I don't think Scully'll try to flush us out right yet. I think he'll worry us through the night, get the lay of the land in daylight. He's not in any hurry. And the more he keeps us holed up, the longer he figures we'll have to think about what's waiting for us.''

"He's better at that than any man I ever saw." Clay hadn't seen Patsy come up, and wondered how long she'd been there. "Draggin' out suffering, that's for certain what he likes to do."

"And what are we supposed to do while this . . . Scully Flatts is out there doing as he pleases?" Meridel asked. "We just sit here like bumps on a log? Is that what you've got in mind, *Doctor?*"

"For right now it is. That's exactly what we're going to do. It gets a little darker, those boys are getting some shut-eye, I'll go out and take a look around."

"Why, you can't!" Patsy's eyes got wide. "You can't— I mean, you mustn't do somethin' such as that!"

"I don't intend to stomp around and blow a horn, Patsy." He showed her a grin. "I'll take it quiet and easy. I've been out in the dark before."

"That . . . isn't the point, as I see it," Patsy said. "It seems to me like a risky thing to do."

"Patsy, it's risky as can be, right in here . . ."

"You're a lot of trouble," Clay said. "If I'd known you were going to go and bleed all over everything, I would've left you back home."

Jordan showed his partner a weak grin. His eyes were sunken pits and his flesh was the color of lead.

"I'll bet I . . . flat ruined that blue flannel shirt. I liked that shirt a lot, Clay. Cost me four dollars, too."

"I expect we can get you another shirt."

"Not like that one you can't. They make 'em in St. Louis. You can't even buy them anywhere else. I'm going to get through this all right, aren't I? I'm going to make it okay . . ."

"You're going to be sore is all. Didn't hit any vital parts."

"Clay? It was Scully Flatts, wasn't it?"

"Yeah, it's him."

"I can use a gun. You'll have to prop me up some but I can shoot just fine."

"Well, I sure hope you didn't think you were going to lie around here and sleep all night. I expect you to—"

Clay stopped. Jordan had closed his eyes again. Clay felt someone behind him and turned. Meridel was standing over his shoulder.

"You can go," she said. "I can take care of him." She caught Clay's expression. "The man's hurt. I don't have to like him or you either to do what has to be done."

"I'm obliged," Clay said. He stood and walked toward the window, stopped and watched her a moment, saw the way she ran the wet cloth gently over Jordan's face.

"I hope there's the chance," he said, "when this is all over, you might talk to me. Tell me what . . . what happened up here. I need to know about him, no matter what he was, no matter what he did . . ."

"You can *need* all you like, won't do you any good." Her voice was harsh and flat. "That's over, I told you that. That's done!"

He had studied every inch of the grounds for half the night, moving from one window to the next. He imagined where Scully Flatts would have a man posted, where he, Clay, might set up a watcher if he were laying siege to the house. He was worried about the sky. There was no moon at all, but the Northern stars were so bright you could read out there.

At a quarter till three, he said a silent thanks. Bright flashes appeared in the east, thunder rolled through the mountains, and, moments later, a storm swept over the valley.

Clay didn't waste a moment. He slid past Otapah at the door and dropped to the ground. The scaffolding of the outside stairway partially hid his fall, and the rain did the rest.

Counting slowly to fifty, he moved on his elbows away from the house. The grass was only foot-high, and he hugged the wet ground. The rain drummed down and he prayed it wouldn't stop. He wormed up the slight rise, toward the first of the three springs. Peering over his shoulder, he looked back at the house. He knew he was safe for the moment. If it hadn't been raining, everyone on the second floor could have seen him perfectly well. That was one of his goals—to see how close the intruders might get up in the night, where the danger zone began.

Five yards, then six. He stopped and tried to listen through the rain. He thought a man stifled a cough off to his left. He was certain he smelled tobacco smoke. Clay shook his head. Damn fool. He hoped they were all as careless as that. It would give him some odds he badly needed just then.

His hand touched water. He dipped his fingers through the grassy edge of the spring. The pure, chill water bubbling up from the earth wasn't far from freezing. In seconds, his hand was numb with cold.

Clay didn't move. The smoker had to be four, maybe five feet away. A clump of ferns over there grew close to the edge of the pool. It was only inches higher than the grass, but enough to shield a man from the house.

The watcher's position told him a lot. If Scully Flatts had a man this close, with the rain drumming down, he was running a pretty tight ship. Scully couldn't know the man was smoking, of course—if he had, the fellow would have wished he'd let his habit ride.

Clay could imagine how the rest of the intruders were deployed. He could see it in his head, how many men it would take to watch the house and make sure nobody left. You wouldn't have to commit all your men to a job like that, just enough to—

Lightning struck the tall fir and split it right to the heart. Clay looked up, startled, his eyes seared by the light. He was staring right into a bearded face, black eyes and the slash of a mouth. The man was dipping his canteen in the spring. He looked at Clay, as startled as Clay himself.

Clay went for him, his reaction half a second faster than the other's. He grabbed at greasy hair with his left, slammed his right into the bearded face. The man grunted and pulled away, splashing clumsily on his back. He grabbed the strap of his canteen and swung it at Clay. Clay ducked, took the blow on his shoulder and buried his head in the man's belly. The man was short and thick-bodied. Clay circled the man's waist and felt muscle as hard as oak. He drove one knee into the earth and jerked the man to the right. He let out a yell, flailed his arms and fell into the spring, taking Clay with him. Clay kicked out with his knee. The man pounded him on the head, finding the spot where Otapah had struck him down.

The pain nearly put him under. He fought to clear his head. The freezing water was draining all his strength; somewhere in the back of his mind he remembered the man had cried out. Someone had heard him then, even through the rain. His friends would already be on their way. Clay suddenly relaxed his grip, let the man go, thrust his hands up through the pummeling fists, and jammed two thumbs hard into the man's eyes.

The man screamed like a mountain cat. He thrashed frantically at Clay, fighting to get past him to the shore. Clay was glad to let him go. He dragged himself from the numbing cold and ran, plowing through the wet grass as fast as he could. Gunfire rattled behind him; he could hear the deadly missiles hum past his head, see the geysers at his feet. The house was a million miles away. He was running like a deer but he couldn't outrun a hail of lead.

Yellow fire blossomed ahead. Once, and then again. The sound ripped through his head; he could feel the heat on his skin. Otapah stood midway down the stairs, sweeping the deadly shotgun from left to right. Beside him, her small hands steady as a trooper's, Patsy Rabbitt emptied Jordan's revolver into the night.

Clay leaped up the stairs, scarcely touching the steps, and threw himself through the door. Otapah let out a whoop, rammed fresh shells into the Remington and blasted away again.

"Clay, Clay, oh Lord, you all *right*?"

Patsy ran to him, wrapped her arms around him and pressed her cheek to his. "I thought you were dead out there, I thought you weren't coming *back*!"

"I'm . . . I'm fine," Clay said. "I'm all right, I'm just fine."

He could smell her damp skin, her wet hair, and then she was gone, muttering to herself about a cup of something hot.

It took him a moment to catch his breath. Another to recall that that was Patsy Rabbitt he'd held in his arms. Patsy Rabbitt who'd called him "Clay" instead of "Dr. Macon" or "sir."

He was too stunned to think. He certainly didn't know what to do or what to feel. A long time back, a scallywag had tried to lift his wallet on the street. Much more recently than that, a lovely girl had pressed her cheek against his. Both these events had happened, but he was sure they hadn't happened to him. No, sir, not to Clay Macon, late of New Orleans. It must have been somebody else . . .

THIRTY-ONE

HE MEANT TO stay awake, keep watch, think about the coming morning. There was so much to do, things he needed to tell the others, things he had to warn them about.

He woke when Otapah touched his shoulder; he opened his eyes at once. The dreary light of false dawn blurred objects around the room. His body had betrayed him, drawn him down into sleep. Clay wondered if those three short hours had done more harm than good. His head pounded with pain, and he ached all over. Something warm and furry was living in his mouth.

Jordan was sleeping, breathing easy now. His head was slightly hot, but it wasn't the kind of fever a physician worried about. A little rest and nourishment and LeSec would start getting his strength back again.

You skinny jackass, if you'd gone and croaked on me, I swear I'd have never spoken to you again . . .

"He woke up once. Wanted a little water is all."

He turned and saw Meridel in the dark. She sat on the hard wooden bench, straight and stiff, the rough shawl pulled about her arms, features hidden from the light. It was as if she hadn't moved since he'd seen her the night before.

"Thank you," he told her, "it's kind of you to watch."

"It is not a kindness to do what needs to be done. I don't seek your thanks."

"Thanks are just given. You don't have to seek them out."

He didn't have to see her face; he could sense the anger there. "I have my own ways, Doctor. It is not your place to try and change them. I don't welcome your opinion or your help."

She stood then and walked quickly into the other room. Clay smelled soup and heard the clatter of dishes. Patsy said something to Meridel. At the sound of her voice, Clay felt a tightening in his chest. They'd hardly even looked at each other since the thing that had happened between them the night before. Obviously she had felt something, too. He dreaded the moment when their eyes would have to meet; they both knew they couldn't just leave it there—they'd have to do something, they'd have to talk it out.

And what happens then? What in blazes are we supposed to say?

Why hadn't Scully shown his face? Maybe his outriders had found the valley and sent word back to Skagway. If that were so, they'd be sitting holed up in the house for a week. Nothing would happen till Scully himself was there. *He's not in Skagway, he's already here. I can feel him, he's here . . .*

"They're not going to let us walk out of here, are they?"

Clay turned. He'd been leaning against an inside wall, checking the Big Fifty Sharps. Patsy walked out of the kitchen and came to offer him a steaming cup of tea. Clay reached for it and gratefully took a sip.

"You know Scully's after gold. If there's any here—and Meridel Huxley says there's not—he won't leave anyone behind. Either way, he'll keep his shirttail clean."

"You're right. I guess I knew that." Patsy looked down

at her hands. ''I guess you and me ought to talk. About . . .
you know, what happened last night.''

''Patsy, maybe now's not the right time—''

''Yeah, now, I think it is. I think I got to say this.'' She
looked up at him. ''It's my fault, I take all the blame. I
don't know what made me do a fool thing like that. I
just . . .''

Her voice faded off. She bit her lip and a tear trailed
down her cheek. Clay didn't know what to do. If he reached
out and touched her, comforted her in any way, that would
just make everything worse. If he didn't, if he sat there and
didn't do a thing . . .

''Something happened,'' he said, ''and there isn't any
need to lay blame on anyone. That was a frightening thing
to go through. I was real glad to be alive, and you showing
your concern was a natural thing to do. We were both of
us letting our feelings show, and I think there was plenty
of cause for that.''

''Not you. Me.''

''I don't understand. I was—''

''Me. *I* was letting my feelings show, not you. And I
don't want you bein' *nice* or anything, either. Saying it was
you to blame any 'cause that isn't true. I'm the one made
a big dumb fool of myself, *Dr. Macon,* not you. You didn't
know what in . . . what in blue blazes was goin' on!''

Something gave way inside. The tears burst through and
Patsy stumbled to her feet, covered her face and fled the
room.

Clay stared after her. Meridel looked at him, left her post
by the window and followed the girl into the kitchen.

''Whatever I did, it wasn't right,'' Clay muttered to himself. He thought about what he might have done, what he
could have said that would have made things better. He
went over everything twice, and nothing came to mind.

• • •

Scully Flatts took no further action during the morning.
They could smell his cooking fires, but no one showed his
face among the trees. As the day stretched into late afternoon, the rains came again, lashing the valley in a fury.
Streams formed in the heights and merged into a hundred
small rivers that surged through the heavy spring grass.
Awah-Choop took Clay to a window and showed him an
awesome sight. High above, on the Ring Ridge that guarded
the valley, untold tons of runoff spilled through the rocky
serrations in a broad, continuous veil. As the cool rain
reached the warmer temperature below, a column of clouds
billowed up toward the sky. To Clay, it was an almost
reverent thing to behold, the wonder of it suppressing the
danger that faced them here.

*If I get out of this, I'm never going to forget it . . . There
isn't another place like it anywhere . . .*

Jordan was too sore to move, and griping about it to
everyone, which told Clay his friend would be fine. Meridel
made soup with venison stock and onions. She said there
was plenty of food for a few more days, but after that
they'd have to replenish the kitchen from the garden and
the cellar. Clay wondered if she realized there were two
things wrong with such a plan: One, there was no way to
reach the cellar without getting punched full of holes, and
two, there wasn't enough ammunition between them to hold
off Scully Flatts that long. Maybe she knew, he thought. If
she did, she wouldn't show it. Displaying a weakness of
any kind wasn't the woman's style.

Clay talked with everyone about his or her part in defense
of the house, and that included Patsy Rabbit. They were
both too polite, didn't want to act that way and didn't know
how to stop.

Just before dark, Scully's men began destroying the
greenhouses. They fired shotguns from the safety of the

trees, yelling and whooping as the glass panes shattered in a million pieces, covering the ground with shards of sparkling light. To Clay, the men sounded like boys skipping school, playing harmless pranks in the neighborhood. Only these boys were grown-up men, likely with whiskey under their belts, and they'd just as soon shoot you in the belly as break a pane of glass.

"Don't return their fire," Clay said. "You can't stop 'em, and it's a waste of ammunition."

The Koo-Chins solemnly nodded agreement. They sat and listened to the shotguns and the sound of breaking glass for a while. Then Otapah went to the window overlooking the back of the house, nocked an arrow in his bow and let it fly. A man screamed in the trees, a cry of such agony it chilled everyone who heard it. Otapah laid his bow carefully aside and sat back down beside his wife.

During all this time, Meridel Huxley never moved from her bench, never showed a hint of feeling as the sounds of destruction reached her ears. She'd found a place to hide, Clay thought. Somewhere no one could hurt her anymore.

"These short Northern days never bothered me before," Clay said. "Now I want to stall off the night as long as I can."

Jordan took a deep breath. He insisted on sitting up, but the strain showed in his face.

"How long can you hold them off, partner? I'm thinking one good rush'd do it. That isn't what I want to see, but I can't figure any other way."

"Twice, maybe." Clay glanced over his shoulder to see if anyone was near. "If we're lucky, we push them back the first time. There's no blind spots, and if the night's bright enough we can bring some of 'em down when they cross open ground. If they lay down a cover fire and rush us . . ."

Jordan was quiet for a moment. "I wish I had a good cigar, Clay. A man needs a smoke at a time like this."

"Don't start. It won't do any good."

"Clay . . ."

"What?"

"I've got to tell you something, friend. It's been on my mind a long while and I want to set it straight."

"Whatever it is, you don't have to do that," Clay said.

"All right."

"I beg your pardon?"

"You said, 'You don't have to do that.' I said 'All right.' I was going to tell you but I won't."

Clay looked at him. "Let's get to it. What are we talking about here?"

Jordan cleared his throat. "That yellow-haired girl, the one who was Sarah Butterworth's cousin from Vicksburg?"

"I know who you're talking about. I'm not likely to forget a girl looked like that. There aren't a lot of girls twelve years old look like that."

"She liked you best, Clay. I thought you ought to know."

Clay frowned. "She sure had a funny way of showing it. Going off with you."

"Well, see, that's the thing."

"What is?"

"I sort of hinted—all right, what I did I came right out and told her."

Clay waited. Jordan found something to look at on the wall. "I told her you were crazy, Clay. I think what I said was, 'an unstable mental condition.' I might've said you were . . . inclined to foam sometimes."

"You told her I foamed."

"Sometimes. Not all the time."

"You told Sarah Butterworth's cousin from Vicksburg I

foamed. Then you swept her off dancing, all those night flowers blooming, those colored lanterns hanging in the trees . . .''

''It was an awful thing to do. I thought you ought to know.''

''Uh-huh. I guess I'm supposed to admire your courage for admitting what a low-down weasel you are.''

''I was hoping you'd see your way clear to forgive me, Clay, seeing as how we're facing a possible threatenin' situation right now.''

''Well, you'll be disappointed then, because I don't. I can't overlook something like that.''

Jordan nodded. ''I fully understand. I accept that.''

''Good.''

''There's one thing I'd like to say.''

''I'd just as soon you don't.''

''If I had to live that moment over, I guess I'd do the same thing again.''

Clay had an answer for that, but his words were lost in the deafening volley of gunfire as Scully Flatts began an all-out attack on the house . . .

THIRTY-TWO

THEY CAME THE way Clay might have planned it himself, blazing away from all sides, pouring lead into the dark, making every window a dangerous place to be.

He called out and swept his hand about the room. Nobody heard him, but they all knew what to do. The Koo-Chins took their places at the far side windows; the trees were thinner there, and their arrows could fly straight and true.

Levering a shell into the Winchester, Clay bent low and hurried to the front of the house. A rifle barked and stitched three holes in the wall. The fourth struck a mirror dead center, scattering shards of glass everywhere. The volley caught Patsy unaware—she cried out, hit the floor and crawled to the kitchen wall.

Clay muttered under his breath. One thing he'd tried to make clear was the location of the ''kill zones'' in the house. The intruders had to aim up to hit the second story. The closer they got, he'd explained, the more shots they'd put in the ceiling, and the easier they'd be to stop. The most effective angle for the shooters was back up on the hill, where they could fire straight into the rooms—but that took them farther away and decreased their odds of a hit.

''Unless someone out there's pretty good,'' he'd added,

"and then you're going to get your head shot off."

Outside, a gunman emptied his revolver at close to fifty yards. Clay didn't think the fool hit the house once. The flat crack of a rifle followed the shots at once. The window frame over Clay's head exploded and clattered about the room.

Awah-Choop shouted. Her husband said, "Huh-huh-huk!" which Clay translated into "Helluva good shot!"

"Clay—over here . . ."

Jordan jabbed a finger at the window, then ducked as lead whined out of the dark. Clay squatted down beside him.

"Over there," Jordan said, "by the spring. You can see 'em when they step out of shadow. That big fir with the broken limb hanging down—there, right there."

"I see them." Clay squinted. Shadow on shadow. But one of the shadows moved; came apart, then flowed back to the others again. Rifle fire opened up on the far side of the house. Bullets poured into wood like someone pounding nails.

"That one fellow just bellied down from the woods to meet the others," Jordan said. "There's three of them, I figure. Right before that, he was hunkered down with another bunch over to the west."

Clay nodded. "Working something up, you think. Maybe coming in."

The Remington thundered behind him. Patsy's position, to the right. She knew better than to try for a target at that range, but he'd told her to use the weapon if someone appeared to get close. The way those fellows were acting, someone likely did.

"They'll make a lot of noise on one side, draw us over there and send the quiet bunch in from behind," Clay said.

"We shouldn't let 'em do that."

"I don't know, I think we maybe should."

Jordan looked at his partner a moment, then grinned. "A New Orleans gentleman's supposed to play fair. That's what they always told me."

"That's real peculiar, coming from the likes of you."

"Huh? What'd I do?"

"You told that pretty girl from Vicksburg I foamed at the mouth."

Jordan made a face. "For Pete's sake, we were thirteen years old. I wish I'd never brought that up."

"The boy grows up to be the man. You plant bad seed, you get a crop of stunted corn."

"Who said that?"

"I did."

"A man's got a pretty big head," Jordan said, "he goes to quotin' himself."

Clay made his way around the house, letting the others know what he had in mind. The Koo-Chins understood. Patsy nodded. Clay waited a moment, but she wouldn't turn around and meet his eyes.

"You see what we're doing," he told Meridel Huxley. "I'm not saying it's the best idea but it's the only one I've got right now."

"Do what you need to do," she told him. "I'll do whatever you wish." She gripped the scattergun Clay had given her, the one he'd used to bring down the quail. It wasn't much good, but it was something for her to hold. "I'll do my part, the time comes. You don't need to worry about that."

"I wasn't, ma'am. I know I can count on you."

He studied the dark hillside, hunkered down by LeSec, watching the shadows that didn't belong. They came just as he'd guessed, working their way through the trees. They were quiet, but not quiet enough. He could hear their whis-

pers now and then, hear their boots sweep through the wet
grass.

When all the sound stopped, he silently counted to ten;
started on eleven as the night erupted in a deafening roar.
Timbers seemed to shudder as Scully Flatts's gunmen
loosed a withering volley of fire at the east side of the
house. Shingles went flying as lead rattled like hail in a
summer storm.

"Watch 'em," Clay called to Otapah, "keep 'em occu-
pied."

He tossed him the Colt revolver and herded the others
to the far end of the house. The men coming up the other
side raised hell, yelling and hooting and filling the night
with brilliant blossoms of fire. It sounded to Clay like a
frontier wedding or the Fourth of July.

It played on the nerves to ignore them, to let them keep
coming with only Otapah there, moving from window to
window, snapping off shots with the Colt to try and keep
the game alive.

"Steady, steady," Clay said, "they're not doing any
harm, just making a lot of noise."

Patsy stood close beside him with the 10-gauge shotgun.
He could see the pulse in her throat, hear the quickness of
her breath. Jordan was propped up in a chair with the .44
rifle, and Awah-Choop had her bow and a ready supply of
arrows.

They were all there, ready for whatever came at them,
all but Meridel, for Meridel was crouched in shadow, shaking uncontrollably, hunched up against the kitchen wall.
The moment the terrible howling and shooting began, she
had fallen to the floor, come apart, shattered like the glass
in her ruined greenhouses . . .

Clay tried not to hear her, tried to pretend she wasn't
there. He knew she would loathe herself for this, for a fear
she couldn't handle, a terror she couldn't overcome. No one

there would blame her, but that wouldn't help; nothing in the world could take away the shame that she would feel within herself.

"Wait," Clay said, "wait, let them come, let 'em get near as they can . . ."

He watched them, counting the shadows, four . . . five . . . They snaked their way up to the house, counting on the shouting and the gunfire of the others to hide their approach.

Closer, come on, you devils . . .

Clay came swiftly to his feet and brought the Big Fifty to his shoulder. The Sharps went off with a roar that near deafened everyone in the room. A man down below came off his feet as if someone had lifted him by the hair. His face disappeared in a fountain of red. Jordan hit one man in the neck, swept the Winchester to the right and fired again. The gunman cried out, dropped his weapon and grabbed his belly. Awah-Choop's man never made a sound; for a part of a second, he was amazed to find an arrow in his eye, and then he sank quietly to the ground. Patsy had hit someone with the Remington and sent them limping for the trees.

Three down, and two of those likely dead. Plus two more hurt and scared. Clay grinned at his crew. Not the nattiest looking army in the world, but they'd sure as hell do.

"They won't likely try that again," he said. "Awah-Choop, get back with Otapah, if you will. Patsy, go with her and take Jordan's Winchester with you. See if there's any of those shouters and hooters hanging around."

Patsy didn't smile, but there was a new glow in her eyes, and he knew what it was from. She'd earned herself some pride and felt good about herself.

"Jordan, that was good shooting, fine work. Not bad for a man stove up in a chair."

"I dance good, too," Jordan said.

"Uh-huh, I heard that you do."

They kept up the fire, a shot at the house now and then; Clay said it was to let them all know they were still out there. As if anyone inside had imagined that they'd gone. The diversion had backfired, and Scully's people had taken some losses they wouldn't forget. Now they'd be lying back and licking their wounds, thinking what they should've done and what they ought to do next; passing a bottle around and telling each other how they'd make those people pay when they hit the house again . . .

"I'm sorry," she said, "I've got no excuses for myself. I lost my nerve and there's nothing else for it. I heard that . . . yelling and shooting and I came on a coward. You and all the rest can pretend you didn't see it but you did."

Clay turned to face her. Meridel was framed in the doorway to the kitchen, hands down at her sides, her face, as ever, lost in the folds of her bonnet.

"Don't be too hard on yourself," he told her. "A bunch of howling rowdies coming at you shooting guns is enough to do anybody in."

"It wasn't anyone, Doctor. It was me."

"This time, yeah, it was you. What I'm saying—"

Meridel held up a hand to cut him off. She turned away and looked into the dark. "I want you to . . . listen to me, please. I owe you nothing; do not assume that I do. I wish to tell you this because I *want* to. Because it is something I want you to know.

"They used to come into my husband's store. They didn't want anything. Not when I was there alone. They wanted to . . . look at me. At my face, Doctor, and at my . . . at my physical form. I was supposed to be a handsome woman, you see. I have never dwelt on such prideful things. It is not a proper thing to do. Nevertheless, considering the female population of Fortymile, I suppose my . . . appearance was somewhat more presentable than many in the town.

"The looks they would give me, the things they would say, when they knew my husband was not around . . . I felt overcome with shame, with awful fear. I would take to my bed in terror and cry half the night. Mr. Huxley knew I was disturbed but I could not tell him what they said, the taunts I endured during the day."

Meridel paused. For a moment, Clay was afraid she would stop, that she could say no more.

"Perhaps you think I was foolish, but I knew if I said anything to my husband, he would feel bound to defend me, to face those men. He was a merchant, he was not young anymore, and he was certainly no match for those devils with a gun. They would have murdered him without blinking an eye. I knew this without a doubt. They were men like those outside my home now, men who fight others like dogs for the biggest piece of the kill. They have no morals, no feelings for any other except themselves. They want, and they take."

Meridel grasped her hands together; her breath came out in a ragged sigh. "I remember them all, every one. Every filthy word, every lewd smile. They live in my nightmares, and in my thoughts in the light of day. I— Forgive me. I have no right to waste your time with this. I was wrong to think I should ever speak of such things again."

"I think you have every right," Clay said. "And most especially with me, ma'am. You got to understand, it is . . . it's abhorrent to me to think of my father as anything less than the man I knew him to be. If he— God help me, if he's guilty of sins against anyone, against you—then I can only feel my own shame for that. I can't go back and undo what's been done. If I could, I assure you I wouldn't hesitate to do whatever a man could do . . ."

Meridel raised her hand, and for an instant, in the frail

light from the moonless night outside, Clay thought he could almost see her face, almost make out the features hidden in the shadow of her bonnet.

"Your father was never one of the men who fill my nightmares, Dr. Macon. All that happened back then . . . the time I've had to think on those things . . . I don't guess I can blame him too harshly for what he did. It's hard for me to say it, but I think he did what he . . . what he felt had to be done."

Clay stared. "What? Do you . . . do you seriously mean that?" He was stunned at her words, could scarcely believe his ears. From the first moment he'd met her, it was clear that Meridel Huxley was greatly affected by the horrors of her past, but now, now he wasn't sure that her mind hadn't strayed much farther than that.

"I hope you'll help me understand what you mean by this," he said, trying to choose his words with care, "if my father . . . if my father took another man's life, Lord forgive him, unless he was defending his own life, it was a terrible thing to do!"

"Maybe it was. And maybe I could live with that 'cause he felt that's what he had to do . . . but I can't forgive the other part, I cannot forgive him the rest . . ."

"You can't . . . can't what? You can't forgive what?"

Meridel didn't answer. A low cry started in her throat, then turned into a wail that sent a chill crawling up the back of Clay's spine. She fled into the kitchen, ran blindly into a table and sent a stack of china to the floor. Clay went after her, determined to know the rest, determined not to let her stop now. There were truths about Randal Macon locked in that woman's mind, and, more than that, very likely half-truths as well, things warped and colored by the dreams that had plagued Meridel across the years . . .

He was suddenly there, as if he'd simply appeared—

Otapah, his broad features empty of any emotion, his eyes dark as river stones.

"No talkin' to her now," he said. "No talkin' anymore."

Clay looked at him and nodded. "No, I won't," he said. "No talking to her, Otapah, I understand. Not now."

He turned away, angry, frustrated, sorry for the tortures of the mind Meridel must be going through, sorry he'd been responsible for bringing these things to light. And, damn it all, sorry for himself—

Patsy touched his shoulder. Clay jerked around, startled at the intrusion on his thoughts.

" 'Scuse me coming up like that," she said. "I thought I ought to tell you. I . . . saw him out there. Out in the trees. Just a minute ago."

"Who, you saw who, Patsy?" He asked, but he knew. He could see it clearly in her eyes.

"It was him, all right. I could see his ugly face plain as could be. He came out in the open for a second. Just stood there, lookin' up here." Patsy shuddered. "It fair gave me the creeps, it did. I thought that devil was smiling, an' I thought he was looking right at me."

Clay didn't answer. He looked out past her at the night.

It's time and past time; it needs to be done. Two of us greeting the morning is one too many, Scully Flatts . . .

THIRTY-THREE

HE WOKE UP startled, uncertain for a moment if the sound was real or had come up with his dreams.

"You all right, partner?"

"Yeah, I'm fine." Clay squinted at LeSec. He was a lesser shadow against the wall. A dim band of light striped his face.

"What time is it? I sleep very long?"

"It's late or too early, whichever you prefer. And you slept about a minute and half."

Clay moaned. "No wonder I don't feel rested real good." He leaned up and risked a glance outside. Everything looked the way it had before. Otapah sat cross-legged by the doorway to the stairs. The door was open a crack. Clay was certain the Koo-Chin hadn't moved half an inch all night.

Pulling himself erect, he stretched his legs and walked past Otapah to the kitchen. Meridel was sitting by the window. She turned to look at him but didn't speak. He checked on Patsy and Awah-Choop in the main room. He could see them clearly now, and decided it was less than an hour before the dawn. If they were coming, they'd have to come soon. It didn't make sense to show yourself in the light. And he couldn't think why they'd hole up and let another day go by. He knew now they weren't waiting for Scully Flatts. Patsy had seen the man, and Patsy ought to know.

I'd give a Morgan dollar to know what he's doing right now, Clay thought, *what's going on in that fat and ugly head of hi—*

The sudden roar of gunfire answered his thoughts. Lead whined through the room like a swarm of angry bees. Clay hit the floor. The acrid smell of powder filled the air.

Someone cried out. Patsy or Meridel, he couldn't tell which. A chair fell apart to his right and clattered to the floor. A bullet clipped his flesh and ripped at the fabric of his shirt.

"Clay—it's comin' in from everywhere!" Jordan shouted. "They're all over the place!"

Clay didn't answer. Jordan was dead right. The question that tugged at Clay's mind was *How? How in blazes did they get here?* One of his people might have slipped, let the shadows whisper by, drift in close to the house, but not *all* of them. No, that wasn't it; there was some other answer somewhere, something had happened out there he didn't know . . .

He crawled to the window and raised his eyes above the sill. A Winchester bellowed in the night, the shots so close together it sounded like a Gatling gun. He hugged the floor as bullets pounded the wall.

I don't like this business, I don't like it at all . . . He wiped the breech of the Sharps with his shirt, stood and risked another look. A man scrambled through the trees. Clay led him half a foot and fired. The man howled and ran for cover. Clay cursed silently to himself. He hadn't missed by more than an inch.

He glanced at Awah-Choop. She was kicking out shells and slamming new loads in the Remington. Patsy was braced against the side of the window, close, but out of the line of fire.

And Meridel was . . . where? Still in the kitchen, he guessed. He wanted to check but there wasn't any time. He drew another shell from his pocket. Two more in there, and maybe half a dozen in his pack. Everyone else was running short as well. Ammunition was heavy, and you didn't start out on a trek thinking that you'd run into a war.

Clay looked up, his fingers pressed against the stock of his weapon. The firing had stopped. The silence was almost oppressive. He heard Patsy draw a breath. A branch scraped against the roof. He bent down close to Jordan and motioned to Otapah to hold his position at the door.

"There isn't any way they could get this close," Jordan said, "no way at all."

"Yeah, but they did. And that isn't all. Awah-Choop made a pretty good count. She said, what—maybe seven or eight? We got a few first time they hit us, and hurt a couple bad."

Jordan nodded. "I know what you're saying. There's more of those devils than there ought to be."

"Scully held back. He didn't commit his whole force. He's got more shooters out there—"

"Doc-tuh!"

Clay turned in time to see the Koo-Chin move in a blur, twist to one side as a load of buckshot blew a ragged hole in the half-open door. The shotgun bellowed again; the door exploded and sent deadly splinters screeching about the room.

Clay shouted a warning, his voice all but lost in the deafening roar. Scully's men were suddenly there, right on top of them, howling and loosing a deadly volley as they bounded up the outside stairs. Clay went to his knees, swept the Big Fifty to his waist. An instant before he pulled the trigger he saw the face of the bearded man he'd fought at the spring. The man looked Clay in the eyes and then his head disappeared.

A gunman leaped over his dead companion and came at Clay, a Schofield .44 blazing in each hand. He fired one and then the other as fast as he could. Clay felt lead scorch his cheek. No time to reload—no time for anything at all. He gripped the long Sharps by the stock and swung the barrel in a wide and deadly arc. Bone cracked—the man grabbed his head, turned on his heels and went down.

A big man came at Otapah, slicing the air with a Bowie knife as long as his arm. Otapah ducked beneath the blow, grabbed the man around the waist and slammed him against the wall. The knife dropped from the killer's hand. Clay spotted it, gave it a kick and sent it clattering across the floor.

Bullets whined dangerously close to his ear. He glanced back and saw they'd come from Patsy Rabbitt on her belly, firing the Winchester at the door. *You want to drop me, girl,* he thought, *you can't come closer than that . . .*

"*Clay!*" Jordan yelled, and Clay saw his partner backed into a corner, pain twisting his features as he clutched his wounded side. A skinny man in overalls, the hair burned off his head, was clubbing Jordan with the back of a broken chair.

Clay started for his friend. A gunman got in his way. Clay punched him in the gut and put him down. Awah-Choop caught Clay's eye. Jordan's old Colt came spinning at him and he grasped it by the barrel, let the grip slide into his hand, squeezed the trigger and loosed two shots at the man beating Jordan on the head.

The man cried out, slapped at his face, took a step and went backward out the window without a sound. Clay looked at Jordan and saw his mouth drop open, saw his eyes go wide. He saw the white flash and felt the fire rip into his flesh. He yelled out, grabbed at his leg and went down, rolled to his side, tried to stand and fell again. A man grinned through broken teeth and leveled a long-barreled pistol at his head. The smile disappeared; buckshot bloodied his face and he turned on his heels and ran. Patsy and Awah-Choop stepped past Clay, standing side by side. The Remington coughed in Awah-Choop's hand. Patsy fired the Winchester, methodically levering one shell after another into the chamber.

A man shouted, covered his face and stumbled out of the withering fire. Clay leaned on one arm and snapped off a shot with the Colt. Men cursed and crowded for the stairs.

Suddenly the doorway was empty. There were two dead men on the floor. Another groaned and tried to crawl away. Otapah kicked him across the room and sent him sprawling out the door. He shrieked as he bounded down the stairs.

Clay sat up. "Everyone all right? Everybody here?"

"I'm . . . alive, I reckon," Patsy said, "and that's a fine surprise to me. How bad's the leg?"

"I'll make it," he quietly assured her, but he could still see the concern in her eyes.

"Otapah, see what you can see out there. I don't know how in tarnation they got to us, but I don't want it happening again."

Awah-Choop was on her knees, a short-bladed knife in her hands, cutting at Clay's trousers. She stanched the bleeding with a leather thong and wiped away the blood. The bullet had plowed through the inside of his leg, just above the knee. It was still in there, and it felt like a molten ball of fire. It had come as close to the femoral artery as it could and still miss. He tried to look at the wound with the dispassionate eye of a doctor, but it hurt too much for that.

"I'm open to ideas," Clay told the others. "They better be plenty good because we can't stand up to that again." He looked at Otapah and Awah-Choop. He didn't ask about Meridel. He knew where she was, and so did everyone else.

She had been in the kitchen when the gunmen broke in, and she hadn't come out.

"You two know the lay of the land here," he said. "How did that happen? How did they get in close like that without anyone seein' it happen? That just doesn't make sense to me."

The Koo-Chins looked at each other. They exchanged a few words, then Otapah shook his head.

"If you don't know, I don't guess anyone does. They pull that again, though, and we've had it. Everybody count your shells, see what you've got. Hand me that chair leg, Patsy, something I can use to lean on."

"Huh-unh, no." Patsy shook her head. "What you need to do is stay off your feet awhile."

"I ought to be having a fine steak dinner and a bottle of import wine at Charpiot's in Denver, but I'm not. Bring me that stick."

Patsy rolled her eyes and did as she was told. Clay grasped the chair leg but didn't try to get up.

"Otapah, Jordan—anything out there?"

"Nothing I can see," Jordan said. "But I didn't spot them the first time, either."

"Nobody did. That's what's bothering me . . . What is it, Awah-Choop, you hear something?"

"You be comin' . . . comin' back here an' look." She motioned him to the far corner of the room, where Meridel's bed was pushed flush against the wall. Clay followed with Patsy's help. Standing made him want to scream, but there was nothing to be done about that.

He watched as the big woman shoved the bed aside with no effort at all. She squatted down and pointed at the floor.

"Here . . . here bein' for the . . . for the warm-it-up, you unnerstan'?" She held her palms out flat, rubbed them together then held them flat again. "Warm-it-up, place here for doin' that."

"She means there was going to be a fireplace there. There's one started in the unfinished part downstairs. He was— There were plans to extend the fireplace up here as well, after the first floor was done."

Clay looked up with surprise at Meridel Huxley. Her voice was flat, with no feeling at all, and he knew she'd retreated into her shell again, that the terror of the gunmen in her house had thrust her into the darkness where she hid from other frights.

She stepped up beside Awah-Choop and spoke to her in the rapid Koo-Chin tongue. Awah-Choop answered, making broad gestures with her hands.

"Yes, I thought that was what she was trying to tell you," Meridel said. "I should have brought this to mind myself, but I did not."

She went to her knees and drew back the worn scrap of woolen rug. A section of the plank floor had been formed into a trapdoor. The door was hinged with leather straps, and the opening was close to two feet square.

Clay drew in a breath. Another entry and an exit, one that led to the unfinished rooms below—an entryway Scully Flatts could know nothing about. He looked at Jordan, and Jordan showed him a knowing grin.

Patsy glanced at them both, then frowned in alarm. "No, now, you can scarcely stand up as it is, so don't go thinking about what you're thinking now."

"Patsy . . ."

"I'm just saying what's true, an' there's no sense denying what's plain as day to anyone—"

"*Patsy!*" Clay turned on her and glared. "If that crowd out there comes storming up here again, how this . . . *leg* feels isn't going to mean a damn thing anymore. Nothing is, girl. I don't see why I have to tell you that!"

Patsy felt the color rise to her face. His words stung as if he'd reached out and struck her with his hands.

''I was . . . I just meant . . . I—'' She turned then and ran from the room.

Jordan let out a breath. ''You don't mind me saying, that was about as blunt as a stump, partner.''

A sharp pain ripped through Clay's leg and nearly brought him down. ''Fine,'' he said, ''you think of some nice way of telling her she's scarcely got a chance in hell of seeing another sun come up, you go ahead and do it, LeSec. If you don't, I'd be pleased if you didn't speak of it anymore.''

Jordan looked at his friend, saw the anger in his eyes, saw the sorrow and the pain, and knew there was little he could say to make anything different than it was.

THIRTY-FOUR

HE LAY ON his belly in the deep wet grass, taking deep breaths, letting the pain subside. It wasn't bad now. Not as bad as it was before—nothing could come close to that.

He had nearly passed out, going down the rope Otapah and Awah-Choop had fashioned from every sheet and blanket in Meridel's house. He had to use the strength in his hands; one leg was little help at all. And when he reached the bottom, and Otapah grasped his waist and helped him to the floor . . .

Clay peered up into the night. Clouds had scudded over the stars again, and he was thankful for that. It wasn't any secret anymore how Scully's men had gotten so close to the house. The storm had cut rivulets through the grass, washing away the soil and leaving dozens of twisting gullies in its path. The water-worn trenches were shallow for the most part, less than a foot deep—but that was enough to hide a man from sight while he bellied up under cover of the grasses and the night.

Now Clay and the two Koo-Chins were using the network of gullies to their own advantage. Crawling unseen from the shadow of the unfinished story of the house, they had taken up positions some fifteen yards apart around the outside stairs. Clay was nearly dead certain Scully Flatts would try the same tactics again. He had lost a few men, but he didn't much care about that. Storming the stairs was the smart thing to do. He had nearly overwhelmed the small force holed up in there before, and he knew they had to be short of ammunition now. One more rush would do it. He'd give his men a little whiskey, promise them extra pay. Maybe he'd promise them the women as well, if any of them came through alive . . .

Clay was counting on Flatts to do exactly that. He prayed they'd carry out the attack the same way they had before. Stopping them from the inside again was next to hopeless. Certain death for everyone. Catching them from the *outside,* though, rushing across the clearing, bunching up on the stairs . . .

He had taken the Colt and left the Big Fifty with Jordan. The Sharps was an awesome weapon, but next to useless to a man crawling about on the ground. Patsy had the Winchester, and the 10-gauge Remington when she ran out of .44 shells. And Meridel . . . Meridel was left with the scattergun and some birdshot shells. It was there, and she could use it if she would.

Come on, come on . . . !

In spite of the clouds, it was getting perceptibly lighter in the east. If Scully Flatts waited, if the gunmen caught them out there in the light . . .

No, too late, too late, too late!

He heard the morning wind in the trees, the first sound of waking birds; both things he'd greatly enjoyed all his life. Now, though, they only meant that it was likely all for nothing, that Scully Flatts had tricked him once more, that he'd won simply by doing nothing at all.

He wondered if he could get to the Koo-Chins somehow, let them know they should get back to cover if they could, try to reach the house before the fast-approaching dawn caught them lying out there.

Clay slid his elbows under his chest and started inching to his left, where Otapah ought to be. The pain cut through him, swallowed him whole. He gritted his teeth and closed his eyes. Opened them again to see the high Ring Ridge, the first hint of lighter shades slicing the purple shafts of stone.

Too late, too late, too late!

Clay froze. Something moved, something breathed close by. Without turning his head, he moved his eyes to the right. There, not two feet away was a dark head, just above the grass. A head and then a shoulder. One man, then another. And another after that, sliding by in silence. He could smell them, now—whiskey and fear and sweat. Hear the scrape of cloth, the creak of leather against the earth. Now, on the other side of him as well, closer than death.

Clay held his breath. They must be right on top of Awah-Choop—they'd run right into her, they had to spot her now! No, nothing, the killers passed her by. Clay shook his head. The Koo-Chin must have made herself vanish, melt into the earth. He believed in Indian magic; there were things the white man didn't know.

Two, no, three single columns, trailed swiftly through the gullies on their hands and knees, merged out of early morning shadow, came together now. Clay tried to count them—five in one group, four in another, the third too far away. No less than a dozen, then, maybe as many as fourteen.

Clay's heart slammed against his chest. He held his breath against the pain, came up on his good knee. They swarmed out of the gullies now, moving without a sound, no howling or firing off their weapons for a lark. This was the killing time, time to get the business done, the bloody business of death that had brought them out here.

He waited . . . waited until they were a single dark mass, making their way across the open, climbing up the stairs . . . Then he leveled the Colt, squeezed the trigger and felt the comfortable jolt as the weapon recoiled against his palm. He fired again, taking his time, picking his victims with the cold and deadly precision of a man at a target range.

The instant Clay Macon fired, two arrows whined through the air and, just as quickly, two men died. Flame blossomed from the top of the stairs, the Big Fifty's roar; then the sharp crack of the Winchester as Patsy joined in the fray.

The gunmen on the stairs bunched up, trapped in a terrible crossfire with nowhere to go. Men screamed in pain as bullets and arrows found their marks. They fired their weapons wildly into the dark, fought to get past their comrades and back off the stairs.

A tall scarecrow of a man slumped off the side of the stairs and fell limply to the ground. Another yelled like a panther, an arrow through his throat. The gunmen knew who was killing them now, and they poured lead into the grass. Clay flinched as bullets sang about his head. The first moment of surprise had taken its toll, but now Scully's men were leaping back to cover, firing at the house and into the grass, mad as hornets. This wasn't the way it was supposed to be; the slaughter was supposed to take place inside, not out on the stairs . . .

Not enough, not enough . . . Four, maybe five out of action, but plenty left to take us down . . .

Lead thunked into the soft earth and spattered Clay with mud. He rolled over twice, biting back the pain, and reloaded the Colt, fingering the shells in his pocket for a count—six, seven, no more than that.

They were regrouping now, off to the left, bunching up together. He could see them against the dull gray curtain of dawn. What were they up to? he wondered. Hadn't they learned that lesson on the stairs? Huddling up that way marked them as easy targets for anyone with a gun—worse still, they were no challenge at all for the Koo-Chins, who seldom missed a rabbit on the run, much less a man standing in a crowd. Otapah and—

Something cold clinched up in his belly. Otapah! Otapah wasn't firing anymore; nothing was coming from his position at all. And if the Koo-Chin wasn't using his deadly bow, then he was down over there—hurt bad or dead. Clay clenched his fists in frustration. There was no way he could get to the man, no way he could help. Even minus a bad leg, he'd never make it without getting hit a dozen times. Still, he couldn't just lie there, couldn't give the man up without a try—

Clay stopped as motion caught his eye. Something moved where the Koo-Chin ought to be. The grasses stirred, then a short, broad figure broke cover, running for the distant trees. Dark hair, bowlegged gait—he looked slow and clumsy but he ran like a deer.

The gunmen saw him, too, and opened fire. Lead sawed the grass. Otapah went down, got up and ran again. Clay cursed beneath his breath. The Koo-Chin was hit; Clay had seen the slug tug at his shirt, seen the puff of dust fly. Otapah didn't stop. Gunfire followed him through the forest behind the house, and then he disappeared.

Clay couldn't believe his eyes. Otapah wouldn't run, not in a thousand years. He was fiercely loyal to Awah-Choop, and he worshipped Meridel. There wasn't a trace of the coward in the man. He wouldn't run. He wouldn't but he did, and Clay couldn't for the life of him fathom that.

''Mistuh—you comin' . . . comin' now . . .''

Clay jerked around as Awah-Choop suddenly appeared.

''Where?'' he said. ''Awah-Choop, there's nowhere to go!''

''You comin' . . . comin' now.''

Clay didn't try to understand what she was saying. It

didn't much matter if he did. They weren't going anywhere, not out of this mess, not in one piece anyhow.

The Koo-Chin placed her arm under Clay's shoulder and helped him into a crouch. The pain of movement nearly put him under. She began dragging him through the wet gully toward the house, keeping as low as she could. Her face remained wooden, impassive. She had to know her husband had run off into the woods, was maybe dead in there; if this bothered her at all it didn't show.

He lived on pain now, thrived on it; pain kept him alive. Awah-Choop pulled him along; he imagined she hummed beneath her breath. Lead whined through the grass. The Koo-Chin didn't stop. Through his agony, Clay could see the blurred outline of the house. Ten yards, maybe . . . maybe a hundred miles . . .

A gunman spotted them and shouted to his friends. A volley of fire ripped overhead. Jordan answered with the Big Fifty, tearing off part of a tree and sending raiders running for cover. Clay gripped Awah-Choop's arm, pulled himself up and stood on his own, dragging his bad leg through the grass, snapping off shots as he stumbled toward the house. A lance of flame from above told him Patsy was still on the job.

Awah-Choop was ahead of him, ready to pull him into the shadow of struts and beams. Bullets spanged off wood, screamed into the clear morning air. Crouching there, Clay felt naked as a jaybird. The unfinished story offered little in the way of good cover—a few empty barrels, a framework of beams and studs.

He stretched out flat, found a target in the trees and squeezed off a shot. The snap of the hammer made a terrible sound. Empty! He groped in his pocket. Four shells, nothing more.

"Look, comin' on, you see? You seein', mistuh?"

Awah-Choop pointed. Clay felt his throat constrict. Men

walked out of the trees to join their friends. New men—six, seven and more! With the others, the gunmen who'd retreated from the stairs, close to a dozen now. Where in blazes were they coming from? he wondered. Did Scully Flatts have an *army* back there?

Not an army, maybe, but close enough. Clay grudgingly admired the man's skill. He might be a killer, but he was acting like a general now, sending his squads out one at a time, holding back his reserves until the moment when they'd count.

Clay watched them, saw them walk out of the woods toward the house, keeping roughly in a line but well apart, a dozen men coming out of the trees, crossing open ground, confident, deadly calm, scorning cover now, every man armed, every man blazing away at the house, their fire so heavy they were lost in a dirty cloud of smoke.

Clay loaded the last of his shells in the Colt, ready to fire, waiting for that one last moment when they'd take him, when he'd take one or two with him as well. He glanced at Awah-Choop. She had placed two arrows neatly by her side. Next to them lay a long and ugly blade with a worn hilt of caribou horn.

Where in blazes are you, Otapah? Why did you do it, friend? You need to be here by her side; this is where you ought to be . . .

Awah-Choop touched his shoulder. Clay looked back. Jordan LeSec was coming at him, braving the gunfire, clutching his side and waddling like an ape.

"What are you doing here?" Clay said. "You're supposed to be up there."

"You're not the only wounded acrobat in town." Jordan showed him a shaky grin. "I can fall down a rope as well as any man. Here." He shoved the Sharps rifle at Clay. "You've got three shells in that monster. I've got five in the Winchester. I think Patsy's got two in the shotgun. Lord help us, Clay, I've seen better armed men gigging frogs out in the swamp. Where's Otapah?'' He looked at Clay. ''He's not hurt, is he?''

''Might be,'' Clay said. ''He might've got hurt real bad.''

Jordan gave him a curious look. Clay squinted at the gunmen and Jordan left it there.

One raider shouted to another. His friend yelled back and fired a volley at the house. The others laughed and joined in. Clay aimed the Sharps, took a breath and let it out. Lead chipped wood at his chin and sent a shower of splinters to his face. He wiped at his eyes, took aim again. The weapon went off with a roar. A gun that could drop a buffalo as far as a man could see it made an ugly mess of a man just a few yards away. Clay's target didn't cry out. The Big Fifty's lead plowed through him without slowing down. Jordan added his two cents with the Winchester. Awah-Choop laughed . . .

. . . and Clay thought that was a peculiar thing to do, and then he understood that the Koo-Chin knew, was aware the very instant that it changed, that it all came apart, knew to the cold and deadly second when the end had begun, when it was over and done . . . As if by some silent signal, the gunmen came together and broke into a run, eating up the last few yards of open ground, guns spouting fire and death in their eyes . . .

Clay exchanged a quick look with LeSec. LeSec grinned back. Clay thought about his father and his mother, both of them gone, and he wondered if he'd see them somewhere soon. Is that what happened, you met those folks who'd gone before? He had a quick vision of Adele when she was fifteen. He wished he and Patsy had found time to talk, wished he hadn't snapped at her right before he'd gone . . .

He heard it, then the hollow roll of thunder, the deep percussion of sky and earth, a sound that seemed to shake the very mountains themselves. Clay threw back his head and laughed. "Too late, too late!" he shouted at the sky, "I've no right to complain, Lord, but you needed to drown those devils about five minutes ago. I reckon it's a little late now!"

THIRTY-FIVE

"CLAY, *CLAY!*"

Jordan shook him, but Clay couldn't hear. He was fumbling with a shell, trying to force it into the chamber of the Sharps. His fingers wouldn't work; the shell slipped away every time. Everything was a haze now, a misty red fog. He slapped at his face to wipe the veil away. His fingers came away red. Funny, he thought, he must've been hit somewhere, splinters . . . cut on his cheek . . . sweat or something darker stinging his eyes . . .

"Clay!"

Jordan's strong grip brought him back. He saw he'd been firing the Sharps again and again, pulling the trigger, trying to force an empty shell into the chamber, pulling the trigger, loading a shell again . . .

They were on him, now, a horde of howling demons with twisted features and murder in their eyes. Jordan fired the Winchester point-blank, fired until it was empty, then gripped the barrel and brandished the weapon like a club.

Clay held onto a thick beam, bit back the pain and pulled himself to his feet. He stared at the Sharps, wondered a moment what the thing was for.

The thunder was deafening now, drumming through the earth, up into his boots. A man suddenly appeared in Clay's face, pointing a pistol at him. Awah-Choop's arrow struck him in the jaw. The gunman's eyes opened wide, startled to find a feathered shaft protruding from his mouth.

"Take 'em," Jordan shouted, his voice hoarse with dust. "Take 'em and drag 'em down, Clay!"

"What . . . the . . . hell . . . am I supposed to be draggin' them *with*?" Clay shouted back.

The sound drowned his words. It stormed down the valley, roared into sight behind the house, cracking through the trees, driving a choking cloud of dust in its path. Clay stared, trying to bring reason to what his eyes could see. The thunder was a visible terror now, a monster of mottled browns and blacks, of sweating hide and drumming hooves and wide and frightened eyes. It filled the narrow draw between the forest and the house, trampled the grasses flat . . .

. . . And Scully Flatts's gunmen, caught there in the killing thunder's path, had a moment to look and see the horror that swept down to devour them, had an awful instant to know that there was no time at all, that there was nowhere to go . . .

Clay heard the beginning of their screams, then saw them vanish under the killing hooves. Twenty, maybe thirty mounts in all, but it seemed as if a thousand wild horses had bolted through that narrow draw. Thirty frightened horses and—

Clay stared, and Jordan LeSec, his face dark with gunpowder and dirt, cheered at his side as Otapah appeared out of the dust, riding at the rear of the herd, his bandy legs wrapped tight about a white-eyed pinto, a terrible apparition, his chest blood-red, his life running out and streaming down his side, the smell driving the mount mad. He shook his bow in a circle about his head and gave a warrior's chilling yell. His face was streaked with red clay, five harsh swipes of his fingers from his broad nose to his dark and matted hair.

Awah-Choop made a strangled sound beside Clay, broke from the shelter of the house and ran toward him. Otapah saw her, jerked his mount in a circle and galloped down the draw. A bloodied gunman sat up and shook his head, tried to come to his knees. Otapah relentlessly rode him down, then pulled his mount roughly to the right, searching for other prey.

The trampled ground in the draw was a horror. Many of Scully's men had died at once under the hooves of their own mounts. Others tried to drag ruined bodies to cover, stumbled a few agonizing paces and fell. Those who escaped stood about, stunned, frightened and grateful to be alive, drained of the will to fight.

Otapah raced toward his wife, slapping the mount with the flat of his hand. Awah-Choop stopped and lifted her arms. Otapah started to speak; his mouth dropped open and his eyes went blank. He rode another few paces, then slid off his mount and lay still.

"Got to get down there," Clay said, "got to help him, Jordan."

"He doesn't need it, partner. Leave him alone, he's doing fine right now."

Clay stared at his friend. It was over now, and no one had to get hurt, no one had to die . . .

Something brought his gaze around, some sense he couldn't name. He wiped the sweat and blood from his eyes and saw him coming out of the trees. He was unmistakable—the brutal bald head, the scraggly mustache, the ruined and pitted face. He even wore the same greasy sealskin coat Clay remembered from the second-story room above O'Toole's. He stalked across the draw, his buckshot eyes nearly shut, his face red with a mix of anger and joy.

Scully Flatts saw that Clay was hurt and grinned. "Hey,

Cheechako! You shot up pretty bad, huh? You want to rest awhile, Loosy-Anna boy? I cut you up some, you can lie down for good!''

Scully stomped toward Clay. He reached beneath his coat and drew a long knife from his belt. Everything about Flatts was dirty and soiled, everything but the shiny clean blade.

Clay drew in a breath. He looked at the ground, grasped the wooden beam, and leaned down on his good leg. He picked up Awah-Choop's knife. The weapon wasn't as long as Scully Flatts's, but the rough hilt of caribou horn felt good in his grasp.

''Clay, you can't do this, you can't even stand up, man.''

Clay didn't answer. He nodded and gently pushed his friend away. Scully was standing there, four feet from the house. He gripped the knife in his stubby fingers and smiled at Clay.

''You still smell bad,'' Clay said, ''and you're twice as ugly as I remember. Stickin' you's going to start my day off fine.''

Scully's smile vanished. He walked toward Clay, stopped, spat in his face, and swung his blade in a killing arc. Clay jumped back, felt the pain sweep like lightning up his leg.

Scully didn't wait. He whipped his knife at Clay again. The point razored through Clay's jacket and his shirt. He staggered back, a thin line of red across his chest.

''Hah! You are too easy, *Doctor*. You die too quick, it ain't any fun for Scully Flatts.''

''You better check my pulse,'' Clay told him. ''I don't figure I'm dead.''

Scully cursed, then bent in a crouch, circling Clay like an animal with his cornered prey. Clay stood his ground. Scully feinted, backed off, then came in fast as a snake, his blade whipping by Clay's eyes in a blur. Scully slashed left and then right, marking a deadly X in the air. Clay faked a strike chest high, then brought his blade down and came up fast between Scully's hands. The blade sliced Scully's cheek open wide. Scully yelled and his face turned white. He staggered back, stunned by Clay's attack, awed by the swiftness of a man who ought to be dead on the floor.

The big man let the blood flow down his cheek into his mouth. He spat on the ground and came at Clay again. Clay backed off, trying to keep the killing weight off his leg. The pain nearly brought him down. The wound in his head was pounding, too, and that didn't help at all. Everything was starting to swim before his eyes and he knew he'd just spent his best shot. One more good strike and the man would have him; his leg would give out and Scully would gut him like a fish.

Scully could smell his weakness, knew he was going down. He showed Clay an ugly grin, tossed his knife from hand to hand, teasing his victim now, taking his time.

Now, now, now, or it's over and done—

He groaned, took a dizzy step back and clutched at his chest. He was close enough to going down; the charade for Scully wasn't all that hard to pull off.

Scully gave a yell of triumph and came in fast. Clay let the man's blade thrust straight for his heart, then swept his own down in a butcher's blow with everything he had.

The blade struck home, slicing Scully's wrist to the bone, jerking the knife from Clay's hand. Scully dropped his own knife and howled. He gaped at the red blood pulsing out his life, grabbed his wrist and stumbled back.

Clay was on him at once, throwing his body like a weapon, driving the big man to the ground. Scully bellowed out his anger, kicked out to drive Clay away. Clay pounded blindly at the man's dark face. Scully roared, raised his bearlike arms and crushed Clay to his chest. Clay gasped for breath. The man's life was flowing out of his veins, but his massive strength could still squeeze a man to death.

Clay pounded at Scully, both fists tearing at the man's ruined cheek. Scully's nose snapped; his face went slick with blood. Scully yelled in pain and anger, and tightened his grip on Clay. Pain screamed in every muscle and tendon of Clay's body. Searing lights whirled in his head.

He can't last forever; he's got to die, he's got to quit and die . . .

Clay shook his head to clear the cobwebs out. If he passed out now, just let it all go . . .

"No! Damn it all, *no!"*

Everything was gone, nothing was left at all. He sucked in a breath, fought to free his arms from Scully's grasp. Scully held him in a vise, arms as strong as iron. Clay struggled, slid one arm free and inched it up his chest. He could feel Scully's hot and fetid breath. The lights in his head began to fade, fall into shadow, into the comforting dark.

He inched his hand loose, squeezed his knuckles tight, forced his hand up Scully's chest, screamed out his pain and thrust the sharp edge of his fist into the mass of flesh and cartilage under Scully Flatts's jaw.

Clay heard it all shatter and break, heard it all give way. A strangled cry escaped Scully's lips. His whole body stiffened, the thick arms loosened and collapsed.

Clay didn't move. He drew in a ragged breath. Jordan lifted him free, leaned him against a sturdy column of wood.

"Clay, you look like something my old dog dragged in. You all right, friend?"

Clay moaned and closed his eyes. "You've asked a . . . a whole lot of dumb questions in your day, Jordan. That . . . that about tops 'em every one . . ."

He glanced at the horror by his side. Scully Flatts stared up with open eyes at nothing. His face was death-white; his life had drained away through the cut that had sliced his wrist down to the bone.

Patsy was suddenly there by Clay's side, with a rag of

cool water for his face. She was talking to him, telling him something, but Clay couldn't hear. Her words were drowned in a terrible wail, a high and keening sound. Awah-Choop was kneeling in the clearing, bending over Otapah's still form. Her body moved rapidly up and down, her hands tore at her face.

You never stopped, friend, you kept on going, you fought until it was done . . .

"Clay, Clay, well, I'll be—look there!"

Jordan stared past Clay, and Clay turned from Patsy to the bloody draw. A man was walking toward him across the clearing. Two men were with him; they stayed in the trees and watched.

Ash. Fullerton Ash! Clay could hardly believe his eyes. He'd shed his town clothes for once and was dressed in denim, a buckskin jacket and knee-high boots. He paused at the scene of carnage, shook his head, and stopped a few feet from Clay. He glanced at Patsy and Jordan, then let his eyes rest on Scully Flatts.

"I've never wished a man's death, even a man like that. But I can't say I'm sorry to see this devil on his back."

"I have to say I'm surprised to see you, Mr. Ash. What in all the—"

"I wish I could have been here sooner, sir, and with adequate help." Ash spread his hands. "I am afraid the good people of Skagway are more talk than anything else. I tried, Dr. Macon, but there is too much fear in those folks—and greed as well, I'm sorry to say."

"You followed Scully Flatts up here? All by yourself, with nothing to back you up?"

Ash looked embarrassed. "Not . . . entirely by myself, no. I brought two men for the packhorses. They were with me earlier, in that encounter where I was fortunate enough to be of some service to you and your people."

"Wait, I've got to understand this," Clay said, brushing

Ash's words aside. "You just . . . walked right in here the minute everything was all over, just like that. That's amazing is what it is. It's damned hard to believe, Mr. Ash."

Ash sighed and nearly closed his eyes. "Yes, I rather thought it would be, Dr. Macon—"

It was almost too quick to see. In a single blur of motion, Ash's hand moved slightly, the little silver derringer slipped into his palm and he brought it up fast, the twin barrels aimed at Clay's chest. Clay had the small part of a second to see the cold light in Ash's eyes, see the muscle tighten at the corner of his mouth, see the start of a terrible smile as the flesh and bone and tendon disappeared and left a bloody mask of red . . .

Ash slumped to the ground. Clay jerked around, and saw Meridel Huxley with the shotgun still at her shoulder. She lowered it slowly, then dropped it to the ground.

"It's been some time," she said, "but it's hard to forget a man who shows up in your nightmares every time you close your eyes."

She turned to Clay. "I told you about 'em. The ones that came looking and taunting me all the time. That one called himself Henry somethin' in Fortymile. Him and his friend there was the worst of the bunch." She looked down at Scully Flatts. "I don't recall this one's name. He wasn't all that fat at the time, but that's him."

She turned away then and looked out over the valley. "There's things I've tried to put aside, but it seems like the memories that are good are the ones you forget. The others just keep hanging on."

She faced Clay again. "I tried to say this to you once before. I think I ought to do it again. Your father was wrong in what he did to me, and I can't forgive him for that. But . . . putting that gun to my husband's head and taking me out of Fortymile, in my heart I know that's the finest thing he ever did . . ."

THIRTY-SIX

THEY HELD A Koo-Chin funeral for Otapah two days after
the battle at the house. The ceremony took place in the lush
green hollow at the head of the slope, the first spot Clay,
Jordan and Patsy had seen when they came out of the rocky
canyon into the valley.

There were seven Koo-Chins on hand by then. They'd
simply arrived, or Awah-Choop had somehow conjured
them in, though Clay Macon couldn't imagine how. Most
of them were older, men or women who were victims of
the harsh realities of tribal life, which declared that those
who could no longer pull their weight must be left behind.
Most of those who were vanquished died, but some—like
Otapah and Awah-Choop and the others gathered here—
survived that first terrible winter on their own, or moved
to the edges of the white men's towns.

"They walked in here three years ago," Meridel told
Clay. "I don't know who was happier to see another human
face, me or them."

She gazed off to the north, to the thick stand of fir, then
abruptly turned away. Past those trees were the graves of
Scully Flatts, Fullerton Ash, and the men who'd died in the
gunfights around the house, and under the fury of Otapah's
stampede. Clay was grateful that Awah-Choop's friends

had come along when they did. Neither Clay nor Jordan LeSec had the strength to carry the dead away and bury them, and even in the relatively mild climate of a Yukon spring, dead bodies very quickly became a nuisance to have around.

There were still a few gunmen roaming about the wilderness, but none of them were drawing Scully's pay anymore, and none had the urge to pick a fight. Awah-Choop had taken Meridel aside and solemnly informed her that many things could happen to a white man alone in the mountains, and that it would surely be a wonder if any of those poor souls survived. Meridel nodded, and told the Koo-Chin she was certain this was so.

They were walking past the back of the house, where Meridel's greenhouses lay in ruin. Everyone insisted that Clay stay on his back, but he would have none of that. The crutch he'd fashioned served him just fine, he said, and though this wasn't quite true, it was clear no one was going to keep him down.

"When I first saw what they'd done, I didn't think I'd ever be able to look at them again," Meridel said. "But I don't feel that way now. I feel *angry* is what I feel, just plain mad."

"I think that's good," Clay said. "I think getting mad's the best thing we can do sometimes."

"It'll take a while, but I want to build them back, Dr. Macon. Maybe do more than I did before, but we'll have to see about that."

She walked away then and looked down at her hands. "You have been very patient. I have seen your bewilderment, but you have not sought the answers that I know you long to hear. Believe me, I am grateful for that. This is most painful to me, and— You have a right to hear this, Dr. Macon. You have as much right as I do to know what happened here."

"There are things I wish I didn't have to know," Clay said, "but I can't let all this stuff keep tearin' at my head. You said— You said my father murdered your husband, and I've got to live with that. It's something that can't be undone, no matter how much I wish it could. What I don't know is *why*. No matter what, I can't see my own father as a killer. And more than that, begging your pardon if I say it, I can't for the life of me forget what you said after you— after Fullerton Ash died. That murdering your *husband* was the finest thing my father ever— Lord help me, you can't mean that!"

"Please, Dr. Macon!" Meridel raised a hand to cut him off. "You used the word 'murder.' I never said that, never in my life. Your father was *not* a murderer. I cannot imagine him committing such an act!"

Clay stared. "Yes, but you said—"

"I said he put a gun to my husband's head, and he did. He killed him, Dr. Macon. There is no question of that. I— It took me a long time to forget that act, to put that terrible image out of my mind. This—all that has happened here— has helped chase a lot of the demons out of my head. I have forgiven your father for what he did a long time ago, but I can never forget the horrifying act itself."

Meridel hesitated. "Your father came to Fortymile after he and his partner had prospected along the Stewart River and, as many men did, failed to find the gold he sought. He—Jack Foster—became terribly depressed. He argued with his partner, who went off on his own seeking gold, leaving your father behind. My husband, Toby Huxley, and I became his friends. We took him in, and I believe our companionship helped to bring him around to his natural self again. Still, he remained somewhat moody, ashamed of his failure . . ."

"And took to drink," Clay finished. "Though he'd seldom had more than a social glass in his life."

"Who told you that?" Meridel shook her head. "I never once saw your father touch the bottle. That is simply not true."

Ash . . . more of your betrayal, more of your lies . . .

"When your father's partner returned from the gold fields, we staked them both to another try. This time they were successful, though the man with your father died before he could return. It was a terrible winter that year, and he was not the only miner who never came back from the wilds. In spite of his sorrow, your father was elated by his find, and paid back my husband and I handsomely for what we had invested. Your father was eager to go back again, for he had brought back only a rich sample of his discovery.

"Word of such strikes is too soon common knowledge, Dr. Macon, as you can well imagine. Everyone in town knew your father had found a rich field somewhere. And I'm afraid both he and my husband did little to hide what they should have kept to themselves. Toby even displayed a great nugget in his store!

"The night they came—and I know, of course, two of them were the men who died here—those two and the others came to force your father to tell them the location of his strike. Your father was out. He had taken some barrels to the blacksmith shop for Toby. I was at the house of a friend. Toby was home by himself . . ."

Meridel paused and brought a hand nervously to her throat. "They were angry at not finding your father there, and they took out their frustrations on my husband. I expect they were all quite drunk at the time, they usually were. They may have thought Toby knew where your father had found his gold, since we had staked his venture. He *didn't* know, but that didn't matter to them. They . . . they tortured him horribly. Did things—unspeakable things I won't describe. I arrived home and found him. Your father returned shortly after that. He found me hysterical, of course, screaming over my husband's body. I yelled at your father, cursed him, demanded he get Toby a doctor. He was still alive, you see, and in my grief I— I thought he would be all right, that— I know, now, that the things they did to him, what they left of him . . .

"Your father took me bodily into another room and locked me there. I . . . heard the shot, and I knew what he had done. You have to understand how I felt, how I saw it all then. Though my husband was suffering beyond belief, I called Jack Foster a murderer, too. I could not understand that he had done the most merciful thing a man could do.

"I lost my senses then. I screamed and tore at your father's face until he struck me and the darkness closed in. He knew the men would be back when they discovered their mistake. He knew, too, though I had never spoken of it, that those men wanted me as well—"

"Wait." Clay cut her off. "Your brother, Baxter McKay. I know he lived with you and your husband until shortly before the tragedy. Was he still in Fortymile at the time? Could he have been around your home and seen something when all this occurred? I ask, because I have to tell you the man saw my resemblance to my father. He attacked me in Skagway, and tried to kill me on the way to White Pass. I'm sorry, but a policeman had to—"

Meridel shook her head. "I do not *have* a brother, Dr. Macon. My maiden name is McKay, but . . . I don't understand this. Toby had a man named Baxter who worked for him now and then. He was . . . somewhat feebleminded, but he did his work well. Where did you hear all this?"

"From Fullerton Ash," Clay said. "Another of his tales. I'm sure he thought it would enhance his story if he said the man was your brother."

"What these people have done . . . the cruel things they have brought about. I cannot say where that poor man was that night. I can scarcely stand to recall all that happened myself.''

She sighed and looked away. ''After . . . after I came to my senses somewhat, your father gathered together what he could, saddled two horses and hastily loaded a pack mule and took us away from Fortymile for good. He brought me here. He treated me kindly, and always with respect. I didn't try to get away. I had nowhere to go. The living was hard for a while. Your father brooded and kept to himself most of the time. I was lost in my own grief and horror, and there was little I could do about his.

''When he got the inspiration for this house, he changed—there was joy in him then, and he lost himself in his work. He built what you see here, and the green-houses as well. He talked about a life up here, what a fine place it could be. And, in time, I saw the valley as he saw it, and fell in love with the land . . .''

Meridel stopped abruptly. It was as if she had come to a solid barrier of some kind and could go no farther. Finally, she rubbed her hands across her shoulders and gave a great sigh.

''I told you, once, that while I could forgive him one thing, there was another that I could not. I could not forgive him, any more than I could forgive myself. I committed a great sin here, Doctor. I had loved my husband dearly, but after a time here, I came to love your father as well. The sin, I will tell you, was only in my heart. It never went further than that. I never let him know, never let him see my feelings. I told myself that I was certain, given time, he would come to love me as well.

''Then, one evening—he told me things. Things we had never talked about before. He told me about his wife, you, his family in New Orleans. I knew he was married, of course, that I had no right to love him, but— New Orleans was another world, a place so far away from here.

"He said . . . he said that he had built the house for *her,* that he would return to her soon and bring her here. He told me that he had come to see that he had proven himself; he had found the gold that would restore his pride, and he could return to his family with honor, now."

Meridel paused. "And then—he told me that the house he had built here was *the same house he had built for her in New Orleans . . .*"

Meridel's voice became harsh, brittle with sorrow and anger. "*My* house, you see? Only it wasn't my house, he had built it for her! I was simply the poor grieving widow he'd rescued and brought to the wilderness! How could I tell him, then, what my feelings were? I could not. I had betrayed my dead husband and made a fool of myself. I had nothing, nothing at all.

"I left that night. I did not speak to him; I simply disappeared. I rode to a small town south of here which doesn't even exist anymore. I worked in a store there. After all, it was a trade I knew well. I stayed for a year. When I rode back to the valley, he was gone. I told myself when he came back with her, he could explain my presence here. In my bitterness, I thought a great deal about that day. It never came, of course. I didn't know he was dead—that she was dead as well—until you appeared."

Meridel looked at him a long moment. "I believe that the way men saw me, Dr. Macon, the appearance they take for beauty, caused my husband to die. I know they would have managed to take me somehow, even if that tragic night had not occurred. Yet this so-called *beauty* could not bring me the love of another man. He never saw beauty in me. His only feeling for me was pity; he had taken me from tragedy and now he was . . . stuck with this burden, this woman he never saw as a woman at all."

Meridel brought a hand to her throat and loosed the tight strings beneath her chin. "The years have treated me harshly, Doctor. There is no longer beauty here . . . There is nothing in this face now that can bring me despair, nothing of the young girl who ruined her own life, and the life of another as well. Look at me, Dr. Macon. Look at the way I am now!''

She grasped the bonnet in her fingers and swept it from her head. Clay drew in a breath, and a cold chill touched the back of his neck. He saw a woman who was nearly forty now but looked all of twenty years. Her skin was ivory touched with gold. China-blue eyes, a royal, sculptured nose, a full and lovely mouth. Her hair fell down across her shoulders, thick and raven-black. Standing against the great stone heights of the valley, in the fading evening light, she was clearly one of the most breathtaking women Clay Macon had ever seen in his life . . .

When Meridel Huxley turned away and walked back into her house, Clay never saw her again. She spoke with Awah-Choop, and once invited Patsy Rabbitt in for a noonday meal. Patsy never spoke about her visit, and Clay didn't ask. He did learn that during Patsy's stay Meridel had worn her bonnet again.

He believed now that Randal Macon had done what he felt was right and proper to do. Right or wrong, he had always been his own man, and the decisions he made were his and his alone. He wondered if his father—if any man in his senses—could truly be blind to the beauty of a woman like Meridel. Surely he had seen how lovely she was. And if indeed he had, only the rigid, stubborn code of a Randal Macon could have kept him from straying from the path.

Clay felt it was better that Meridel did not know all that had happened as a result of that one terrible night in Fortymile. That ''Black Jack Foster'' was branded as a madman, that awful crimes had been committed in his name by

the men who later called themselves Scully Flatts and Fullerton Ash.

It irked Clay no end that Ash had taken him in from the
beginning, that he and Scully had worked hand in hand all
along—even "rescuing" Clay and his friends to put them
at ease, so they'd no longer look over their shoulders for
Scully's men.

Scully's men . . . He had no sympathy for hired killers,
but to shoot down your own people like that in cold blood
. . . Well, what could you expect from a man who cheated
at cards and smelled worse than a bear?

Jordan's wound was healing, but he still spent a great
deal of time in a rocker in the sun. He said if he had a
decent doctor, he'd likely be well in no time. Clay said
he'd hit him with a crutch if he didn't shut up. Patsy said
they were both acting like a pair of cranky Confederates
who couldn't find their way back home.

"I'm trying to think where that might be," Clay told
her. "I'm not real certain anymore. This is fine country,
and there's plenty more to see, but I keep thinking about
hot Louisiana days . . ."

". . . and New Orleans nights," Jordan added, "with the
smell of flowers so sweet in the air you could slice the
aroma and sell it like cake."

"Ah, go on now," Patsy said, "it's the Irish who are
supposed to tell stories like that, not you lazy Southern
boys."

"A man isn't lazy, just because he's sitting in a chair,
with a mortal wound throbbing in his side, without hope
of a cup of coffee or a good cigar."

"A mortal wound's one you die from," Clay reminded
him. "Take it from your physician, you're likely to survive."

"Fine. My physician's a man hobbling about on one leg.
I'll be lucky to make it through the day."

"If you do," Clay told him, "that cup of coffee might appear, but I doubt you'll get the cigar."

"What?" Jordan stared at his partner. "What coffee? What are you talking about?"

"Keep your seat, friend. Those mortal wounds can be tricky sometimes."

"Are you going back then, you think?" Patsy said. "The way you were talking, I felt that's what you had in mind."

They were walking under the trees by the three bubbling springs. It was as far as Clay had gone since the fight, since he'd taken a bullet in his thigh nearly two weeks before. He was as proud as if he'd walked a mile.

"I think so. There's lots for a man to see. I stay in one place too long, I get the feeling something's going on somewhere and I'm the only one who's not there."

"That's a man for you," Patsy said and sighed. "Never in the right place, never satisfied."

"You know all about men, do you?"

"Well, sure I do. I *was* one for some time, you'll recall."

Clay grinned. "I know you'll be wanting to get back to Skagway and setting your sister free, Patsy. I wanted to tell you, Jordan and I will be going through there to get the boat to Seattle, of course. There might be some of Scully's men still raising hell there. Jordan and I, we'll make sure that bunch doesn't cause any trouble for you, or anyone."

"I'm greatly obliged," Patsy said.

"Well, I'm pleased to help any way I can ..." He looked at her then, caught her looking right at him, saw what was in her eyes. She flushed, and quickly turned away.

"Patsy ... there's things you and I haven't gotten off our minds ..."

"Hush, now, all right?" She touched a finger to his lips. "There's more things that shouldn't be said than should. And if there's ever a time to say 'em, it isn't now. I care for you, Clay Macon. I know you don't have that kind of feelings for me and I'm not blaming you for that." She grinned and tossed red hair off her face. "I'm telling you one thing, though. I'm not finished with you. You can run off to the Lord knows where, but I'll find you out sometime."

"I'll look forward to that," Clay told her, brushing a strand of hair from her cheek, "I truly will."

Patsy reached up and touched the necklace of stones he had gotten from the Koo-Chins on the trail. She laughed, and the color rose to her face again.

"What's so funny? That's a very fine piece. Cost me a lot of good bear meat."

"Oh, it's real nice," she said. "Awah-Choop told me what it means, and I guess congratulations are in order."

Clay looked blank. "For what, then?"

"That's a real special necklace. The only person who ever wears it, though, is a Koo-Chin woman expecting her first child. Why, Clay Macon, I didn't even know . . ."

He had tried to keep the thought of gold off his mind. He knew he wasn't the first man to come away with empty pockets from this land. Still, his father *had* found the stuff up here, brought it out pure and fine. Where, though? Where had all those riches come from? If he hadn't found it here, when the route he'd given Clay had led him to this very place—then where?

He knew, now, there were reasons Randal Macon had come home with only a few chamois bags of yellow gold. He wasn't planning on staying; he was planning on going back. He was going to take his wife to the home he had built, and there was no reason to bring a great fortune back to New Orleans. The safest place to leave it was in the ground. Once he got back, he could funnel the gold back to banks in the states, a little at a time. Clay, and everyone named Macon in Louisiana, would never have to want for a thing.

But his wife, Clay's mother, was dead when Randal Macon came home. His heart was broken, and he would never return to the Yukon again . . .

There was another reason for secrecy as well, Clay knew. While Meridel had never imagined the legend of Black Jack Foster was spreading across the Yukon, Randal Macon had known he'd be blamed for Toby Huxley's death. He certainly couldn't help but know later, when he'd traveled up-river to trading posts to buy the materials for his house.

. . . And he had to have gold for that; he had to get it somewhere . . . Randal Macon's gold was there . . . but where?

Clay's answer came three days later, in the form of a message delivered by Awah-Choop. She guided the three to the cellar beneath the house, where Meridel had locked up Clay and Jordan when they'd arrived in the valley.

As ever, the place was cool and pleasant with the smell of salted meats and dried fruit.

"Here," Awah-Choop said. She handed Clay a shovel from the corner and gave a clawbar to Jordan.

Clay looked at the Koo-Chin. "Fine, what are we supposed to do now?"

"You be diggin'," she said, pointing a finger at the floor. "Be diggin' *here*."

"What for?"

"Diggin' here," she told him again.

Clay dug. Jordan didn't have the strength for the clawbar, and Patsy took the job of wrenching nails from the wooden floor until a circle of earth was revealed. Clay and LeSec spelled each other with the shovel. When they both gave out, Patsy took over.

Two and a half feet down, the shovel hit something hard

that went *chunk!* Clay and Jordan looked at each other a long moment, then forgot their wounds and clamored into the shallow hole.

Jordan found it first. A gold hump protruding from the earth. Gold pure and fine. It was that rarest of all strikes, a prospector's dream—Randal Macon's "dragon spine" was solid gold, gold flakes, and gold crystals, veritable boulders of gold bound together in a web of white quartz. The more dirt they scraped away, the more gold they found. Randal Macon had chipped off a mere handful of nuggets; the hump Clay and Jordan had exposed was four feet wide and six feet long.

Clay was staggered by the size of the thing. How big was it? There was no telling how far the spine burrowed into the ground. It was clear his father had not even attempted to find out. There was enough solid gold right before his eyes to make a man rich a hundred times over. What if it went down ten feet—twenty, forty feet? There was no way of knowing, no way to tell.

"Here," Awah-Choop said. "You be readin' this. Readin' right now." She handed Clay a folded note. Clay opened it and read the neat, spidery script:

Dr. Macon:

Take all of this you wish. As you can see, there is plenty here for anyone's needs. I ask only one favor— that I be left in peace, that you and your friends do not reveal where you have been. In trust,

Meridel Huxley

"We might look like a bunch of tramps," Clay said, "but we're rich as railroad men, friends. I expect I'll be getting a new shirt. One that smells good and doesn't have gunpowder all down the front."

"I expect you can buy two or three—or a hundred if you like," Patsy said.

"What I'm thankful for," Clay said, "is you won't have to smoke those cheap cigars anymore, Jordan. And I won't have to smell them."

Jordan bounced a nugget the size of an apple in his hand. "There's one thing wrong with that," he said. "I know it's a shameful thing, but that's the only kind I like, Clay. I've tried the good kind, and they don't satisfy. A cheap cigar's still the best friend a man ever had . . ."

EPILOGUE

IT SEEMED AS if nothing had changed at all. The long line of prospectors still struggled up the slopes of White Pass. Even in the spring, a cold wind sliced down off the rugged heights.

Clay leaned back in the saddle and squinted to the south. Skagway was there down the trail. He and Jordan and Patsy had an extra mount each, all from the plentiful herd Scully's men had little use for anymore. They also had three sturdy mules packed with gold, more of the precious yellow stuff than those poor prospectors climbing the pass would likely ever see. If anyone knew what they were carrying under smelly bear hides . . .

He glanced north and west then and thought about Meridel. Meridel, and the house that looked much like his own. She'd likely never finish it, but it looked just fine to him the way it was.

He felt she'd make it now. The greenhouses would flourish, he was certain of that. The country was growing fast, and there was a need for more than cold beans, wild onions and caribou meat. There were all kinds of riches in the ground up here—yellow gold that hardened the hearts of men, and green gold as well, like the giant-sized fruits and vegetables that grew beneath Meridel's houses of glass.

It was something she could live for, he felt, nourishing growth in the earth. And maybe growth would heal her sorrow; perhaps not all of it, but some. And there might be a day, Clay hoped, when she could look in a mirror and know she was beautiful again . . .

Jordan LeSec let his horse stop for grass. He had found a prospector with half a dozen of the worse cigars known to man, and a pall of gray smoke now circled about his head. They didn't smell all that bad, Clay decided, but he'd never lower himself to ask. Jordan would give him one, but he'd never let him forget.

Patsy rode up beside him, her extra mount and mule trailing behind.

"I'm glad we're coming out, instead of going in," she said, shaking her head at the pass. "I'm thinking I've had all the rocks and climbin' I need for a while."

"We'll be camping in an hour," Clay told her. "We could go on into Skagway, but I don't see any reason to wear ourselves out."

"That's . . . kind of what I wanted to talk about." Patsy looked up at the sky, as if there was something of interest there. "I'm thinking there's people I don't want to see in that town. And people I don't want to see me. I feel I'd like to ride past the place, and catch a boat from there."

Clay shook his head. "That doesn't sound like a good idea to me. I told you Jordan and I would handle any trouble you ran into in Skagway. And besides, the boat doesn't stop anywhere else."

Patsy grinned. "I'll bet it does. I bet they'll stop most anywhere for a rich lady like me. Why, I bet I could get one to take me the whole way to New Orleans someday."

Clay looked at her. A thought suddenly struck him and he pulled back on his reins. "What are you thinking about, Patsy? You're not leaving Fiona in Skagway, I know that. What are you—"

"This is *real* embarrassing to me, you know what?"
Patsy rolled her eyes and sighed. "I mean, seeing as how
I gave up lying back in the woods somewhere, when I gave
up being a boy. The thing is, that was a kind of exagger-
ation, you might say, when I was still bandying the truth
about. I don't *have* a sister, you see. There isn't any Fiona,
I'm afraid, there's just me."

Clay stared. "Patsy, how could you tell me such a—".

Patsy slapped the reins of her mount. The horse kicked
up dirt and trotted down the trail.

"Listen, you come back here," Clay said, "come back
here right now!"

Patsy twisted in the saddle. "I'll come back, Clay Macon, I promised you that. Don't even *think* you can get
away from me . . ."

He thought about going after her, and knew better than
to try. He watched her disappear down the slope. He
watched her lean form and watched her fiery hair blowing
in the wind. Patsy Rabbitt was a woman, there was no
mistaking that. He wondered how he could ever have imagined she was anything else . . .

GREAT
STORIES
═══ OF THE ═══
AMERICAN
WEST II

Eighteen short stories from Western giants including:
Louis L'Amour ● John Jakes ● Evan Hunter
● Jack London ● Erle Stanley Gardner
● Loren D. Estleman ● Chad Oliver
and eleven more!
Edited by Martin H. Greenberg
__0-425-15936-1/$6.99

Also available:
GREAT STORIES OF THE AMERICAN WEST
Edited by Martin H. Greenberg
__0-515-11840-0/$6.99